I0562029

LOVE AT THE PENTAGON: A NICK & GIA STORY

BY

Kimberly A. Biggerstaff

Love at the Pentagon: A Nick & Gia Story.

Copyright © 2024

This novel is a work of fiction. Names, characters, businesses, organizations, places, events, and incidents other than those clearly in the public domain are either the product of the author's imagination or, if real, used in a fictitious manner. Where real-life historical persons appear, the situations, incidents, and dialogues concerning those persons are entirely fictional and are not intended to depict actual events or to change the entirely fictional nature of the work. In all other respects, any resemblance to persons living or dead is entirely coincidental.

Cover design by Kimberly Biggerstaff using www.canva.com

Cover model information

ID86128425

© Andrey Kiselev|Dreamstime.com

Novels by Kimberly A. Biggerstaff

A Rogov Romance

Lex's Story

Lex's Story Part II: Life Unguarded

Love at the Pentagon: A Nick & Gia Story

Other novellas and novels by Alex A. Jameson (Kimberly A. Biggerstaff)

The Sam Barrett Ops

Operation: Running Brook

Operation: Russian Roulette

Operation: Returning Home

Operation: Rising Son

Operation: Payback (coming soon 2024)

DEDICATION

To all my American Legion friends who encouraged me through this journey, thank you.

Contents

Kimberly A. Biggerstaff © 2024

CHAPTER 1 - NICK

Nick sat staring at the photo he kept in his wallet. The tear fell and interrupted his thoughts. He closed his eyes, and his thoughts drifted back.

Nicholas Foster was a marine's marine. It wouldn't surprise anyone if he bled red, gold and grey. The colors of the Marine Corps flag.

"Uncle Nick!" Barb yelled as she ran to him. She jumped up into his arms and he hugged her.

"Hi, Pumpkin. What's new?"

"The fleet came in, and Mommy and Daddy and I went to see the ships."

"Did you see any marines?" Nick asked her.

"Yes sir."

"What did you say to them?"

"Semper Fi!" Barb yelled.

"That's my girl," Nick said, hugging her tight.

"Welcome home, Nick," Jason said, shaking his hand. "How are you doing?"

"Fine," he said.

"Uncle Nick, you have a string."

"Where?"

Barb pointed to the small string protruding from a button on Nick's Oxford button-down shirt.

Kimberly A. Biggerstaff © 2024

"Good eyes, Pumpkin. I'll get it in a minute."

"Uncle Nick." Barb looked at him.

"Okay, let's find the scissors," he said, setting her down and asking Jason for some scissors.

"Nick, how are you doing? Seeing anyone?" Deborah asked him.

"Sis, I'm fine. You ask me that every time I come home."

"It's been five years. I worry about you." Deb worried a lot about her younger brother. Not just because Nick had gone to the Naval Academy and was a marine. Five years ago, Nick's wife had died. She was the love of his life. She got pregnant when they were stationed in Okinawa, Japan. But during one of her checkups, they told her she had cancer. She and Nick talked about it, but Kaya refused treatment. He met her at a Japanese language class he was taking. She was the teacher. They dated for a year and got married. She got pregnant a few months later, and then they found the cancer. It was aggressive and they both died.

Nick was devastated. He poured himself into his work. He became one of the best officers in the Corps. He tried to date every once in a while, but no one made him feel the way Kaya did. He was a good-looking young man and had no trouble getting a plus-one for any official functions.

But he always took the woman home and went back home alone.

He wore his wedding ring for two years. Nick was with a group of other officers playing poker one night when a new guy asked him where his family was.

"My sister and her family live in New Rochelle, New York," Nick answered.

"No, I mean your wife. You wear a ring."

Nick tossed his cards on the table and stood up. "I'm . . . out. See you guys later." He took his money and left.

"Ow. What was that for?" the new guy asked.

"Don't ever ask him about his wife. She passed away and he hasn't gotten over it."

* * * *

Nick did something he never thought he'd do. He took the ring off and placed it in the ornate wooden box Kaya had given him as a wedding gift. He made himself a drink and downed it. Then he took a cab downtown and found himself a hooker.

He felt terrible the next day. He had a hangover and felt guilty. The new guy sought him out and apologized.

"Sorry, Foster. I didn't know."

"Forget it. Don't bring it up again," Nick told him.

He didn't and without the ring, no one ever asked.

Chapter 2

"Uncle Nick, I'm ready for inspection," Barb told him, standing proud and at attention.

Nick walked into her bedroom and looked around. It was perfect. The bed was made without a wrinkle, and every toy was in its place. He went to the closet and was surprised by what he saw. The shoes were lined up on the floor of the closet. The clothes on hangers were neatly hung up. The hangers were evenly spaced, one inch apart.

"Barb, did you do this?" Nick asked her.

"Yes. I have this step ladder, and Daddy watched me to make sure I didn't fall. Is it okay?" she asked.

"It's . . . better than any marine's closet I've seen. You pass with flying colors," he told her.

"Thank you, sir." She gave him a salute, which he returned.

Nick went back out to find his sister. "Deb, how's Barb doing?" He was concerned about his niece.

Deb looked at him. "Did she show you her room and closet?"

"Yes. Is that normal for a five-year-old?"

"The doctor says not to worry unless it starts interfering with her life," Deb told him. "You know how she likes to make you proud of her."

"Yeah."

Jason came into the kitchen and stole a piece of carrot Deb was cutting up.

"Jason, how's med school?" Nick asked.

"Tiring." Jason admitted.

"What's your specialty?"

"I'm going to be a hand surgeon. That way, I can integrate my practice with Deb's business," Jason said. The business made and sold braces of all types for hands, arms, knees, or whatever was needed.

"Smart," Nick commented.

"Uncle Nick, look." Barb was holding an aircraft carrier made of building blocks. "I built this all by myself."

"Barb, that's amazing. You really built that without any help?" Nick was impressed.

"Yes. It's the Intrepid. We went and visited it."

"Oh, well, I guess you won't want what I brought you then," he teased her.

"Yes, I do. Please. I aced my inspection," Barb practically begged him.

"So you did. Okay." He went to his room and Barb followed him.

Nick handed her a large package. She opened it and looked at it. "It's a clock," she said.

"It's a cuckoo clock from the Black Forest in Germany. See, whenever the big hand lands on the twelve, a bird will come out of that door and cuckoo the number of times that little hand is on."

Barb smiled and gave him a hug. He always brought her a present from wherever he was stationed.

Chapter 3

As the years passed, Nick rose in the ranks of the Corps. He continued to come visit Barb and the family when he could.

"Ready for inspection, Uncle Nick."

"Barb, aren't you a little old to keep this up? You're in high school."

Barb just stared at him. She didn't move. She wasn't sure what to do. "No. You have to come inspect."

"Maybe later, honey," he said, hoping she'd forget about it.

"No. You come home, say hello and inspect my room and closet. You have to do that. You have to."

"Nick, please go and do it," Deb said. Something in her eyes told Nick it was necessary.

"All right." He went to her room and looked around. As usual, her room was perfect. But her bed was different. Same bed, but she had made it with hospital corners. It was tight, just like at recruit training. He was very impressed. He walked over to her closet and opened it. Her shoes were lined up straight in two rows. He saw that her dress shoes were shined to a glassy finish. Her shirts were pressed and starched along with her pants. He was speechless.

"Did I pass, sir?" She held the salute.

"Yes, you passed." He returned the salute. "There's a package on my bed. You can go get it."

"Thank you, Uncle Nick." She walked off.

Nick stood there thinking. Jason came in behind him. "She has obsessive-compulsive disorder (OCD)," Jason told him.

"How bad?"

"It seems to be getting worse," Jason said. "She worries about you. A fear that you'll be hurt. So she does all these other things to make herself feel better. But it's a temporary fix."

"Are there therapies or medicine?" Nick asked.

"She won't take any medicine, and we don't want to force her. She's trying different therapies."

"I know you may not want to hear this, but the military might be good for her. The discipline, the structure. Maybe it will help."

"I've thought about that and I agree. We just need to talk to Deb about it."

"How are her grades?" Nick asked.

"Straight As. A 4.0 GPA. She'll probably take some Advanced Placement classes next year."

"Has she said anything about what she wants to do?" Nick asked.

"Join the Corps. It's all she talks about. She wants to go into Intelligence."

"What?" Nick had no idea she wanted that.

"She's been researching online, and she even spoke to a JROTC instructor at one of the high schools that has a Marine Unit."

"What do you think about the Naval Academy? It'll keep her in that structured environment."

"I think she wants to follow you," Jason told him.

"That's not why I suggested it. I just want to help her. You know how much I love her," Nick said.

"I know. We'll talk to Deb tonight and then Barb," Jason said.

Chapter 4

Jason and Nick spoke to Deb, and in the end, Deb said she'd consider it. Barb was a sophomore, so they still had a little bit of time before they needed to start any applications. A few days later, Nick went to dinner with Jason and Deb.

"Nicky, don't be mad," Deb said.

"You only call me Nicky when—what did you—"

"Steph. So glad you could make it," Deb said as Jason and Nick stood up. "Nick, this is Steph. She's one of our distributors. This is my brother, Nick."

"Pleased to meet you," Nick said.

"You too, Nick," she said, sitting down. She was a very pretty woman, and Nick noticed, but he still wasn't happy about this set-up.

They spoke and ate their meal. Nick was polite and a gentleman. He even walked her to her car.

"They didn't tell you I was coming, did they?" Steph asked.

"No. I . . . uh . . . "

"It's okay. Look, I had a nice time, and if you'd like to go out again, call me. But I understand if you don't want to. It was nice to have met you, Nick Foster." She handed him her business card and smiled. "Thank you, again."

Kimberly A. Biggerstaff © 2024

After she drove off, Nick walked back to Jason's SUV. "Don't talk to me, Deb," Nick said.

Deb knew he'd be mad, but it was worth it just to give him a push. She didn't like to see him alone.

* * * *

Nick spent the next two days thinking about Barb. Occasionally, Steph popped into his head. He finally gave in to his thoughts and called her. He was in his room getting ready when Barb finally spoke.

"Where are you going?" Barb asked.

"Out to dinner," Nick said.

"With whom?" she asked.

"A friend. Why?" he said, putting his wallet in his jacket pocket.

"Just gathering intel," Barb said.

"I'll see you later, Pumpkin." He kissed her on the forehead.

Nick picked Steph up and took her to a restaurant that Jason recommended. He was still upset with Deb, but he was talking to her.

The date went well, and Nick was enjoying himself. He drove Steph home, and she invited him inside for a drink. He hesitated, then agreed.

Kimberly A. Biggerstaff © 2024

They sat and talked some more. Nick finished his drink, and as he set it down, Steph kissed him. He pulled away.

"I'm sorry," Steph said.

"No, I . . ." He suddenly kissed her back, and then things started to heat up. Steph began unbuttoning his shirt, and he inched his hands under her dress. But as suddenly as it started, it stopped. Nick stopped and pulled away. He stood up and buttoned his shirt.

"I'm sorry, I just can't." He reached for his jacket and went to the door.

"Nick, it's okay."

"No, it's not. I don't want to waste your time. I'm sorry." He walked out. Nick couldn't get Kaya out of his head. He pulled into a parking lot and took her photo out of his wallet. "Marines don't cry, but you make me cry, Kaya. I miss you so much." He sat there for twenty minutes and cried. Then he drove to a hotel bar and had a couple of drinks.

"You look lonely, friend," a woman said. She was nicely dressed, but Nick was pretty sure she was a high-priced call girl.

"I'm not in the mood to talk," he said.

"What are you in the mood for?" she said seductively.

Nick closed his eyes, took a breath, and opened them. "Do you have a room here? Because I don't."

Kimberly A. Biggerstaff © 2024

"I can take care of that," she said.

Nick followed her to the elevator, keeping an eye out in case she was setting him up for a mugging. They arrived at the room and she knocked. A man answered. Probably her pimp. Again, Nick was on high alert. He didn't drink anything the woman offered. The man left, and Nick did a check of the room, the closet and the bathroom.

"What are you doing?" she asked, watching him.

"Making sure there's no one in here to jump me."

"You can trust me."

"No offense, but I don't trust anyone." He pushed a chair in front of the door. "I don't want to talk. Let's just get this over with and don't kiss me on the lips," he said.

* * * *

The next morning, Deb smiled and said, "You got in late. Did it go well?"

"No, it did not. I ended up at a hotel bar and had sex with a hooker. I hope you're happy," he said, taking his coffee and going back to his room.

Deb gave him some time and then went up to apologize. She knocked on the door and opened it a little. "Nick, may I come in?"

"Yes."

"I'm sorry. I shouldn't have set you up without at least discussing it with you." She sat beside him on the bed.

Kimberly A. Biggerstaff © 2024

"I know you mean well, Deb. The date was fine until we went back to her place. I just can't get Kaya out of my mind."

"You tried. I was surprised you called her for a date. You aren't ready. I didn't realize how much you still love her." Deb grabbed his hand.

"I would have traded places with her if it was possible. I still think about her. Deb . . . I never told you she was pregnant."

"Oh, Nick. Why didn't you tell us?"

"I was going to surprise you when we came home, but she got too sick to travel. There just didn't seem to be any point after that," he said, trying to hold it together.

Deb put her arms around him and hugged him. "You're my brother. You can tell me anything. I know there's an age gap between us, but I want us to be able to talk to each other."

"Our age gap is nothing compared to you and Jason. You practically robbed the cradle with him," Nick teased her.

Deb smiled. His teasing didn't bother her. "Did you really go to a hooker last night?"

"Sometimes a guy has to—"

"Never mind. Too much information," Deb said. "Are we okay?"

"Yeah, just don't set me up anymore."

Kimberly A. Biggerstaff © 2024

"I won't," she promised.

Chapter 5

Nick came up from Camp Lejeune, North Carolina, to see Barb off at the Naval Academy. Her parents were there as well.

"Thank you, sir," Barb said. Nick was in uniform, and Barb wanted to properly address him.

"Are you nervous?" Nick asked her.

"A little, but I think you've prepared me. I just worry about the other thing." Barb had done her best to control her OCD. She was trying aversion therapy. She had a rubber band on her wrist and would snap it when she became anxious or had unwanted thoughts. But this summer, she'd probably have to take it off. She'd have to figure something else out.

"You can call me anytime that you're able, plebe (freshman at the Naval Academy)." Nick smiled at her. "You'll do fine. I'm proud of you, Barb."

When it was time for her to leave, she hugged her parents and Nick. As he watched her march off, he couldn't help but think about his child. He always hoped to send his own to the Academy.

"Nick? Are you all right?" Deb asked him.

"Yes. I feel closer to her now than ever before. She's going to do fine."

"You'll check in on her, won't you?" Deb asked him.

"Not directly. It's better for her if I'm not seen doing that. She'll be fine, Deb. I'll be Uncle Nick when she needs me. She knows that. Try not to worry."

* * * *

Nick was available to Barb whenever she needed him. He always took her calls or got back to her as soon as he was able to. He visited only once a year to check in and physically see how she was doing. She had a couple of minor hiccups during her plebe year but was able to overcome them and worked even harder the next two years.

She called him to tell him her news.

"Brigade Executive Officer (XO). That's wonderful, Pumpkin!" Nick said, smiling.

"Sir, please."

"Sorry, Midshipman. I'm so proud of you."

"I was hoping for Brigade Commander," she told him.

He could hear the disappointment in her voice. "Hey, they only pick one. Brigade XO is nothing to sneeze at. In some ways, it's more important. You have to be ready to take over for the Brigade Commander, and you have your own duties." He would have been proud, no matter what.

"How's Miami, General?" she asked him, changing the subject.

"The weather is nice," Nick said. "I'll bring you a palm tree when I see you," he said, laughing.

Kimberly A. Biggerstaff © 2024

* * * *

Nick had moved to the Pentagon and was working as a senior military assistant to the Secretary of Defense when he heard about the helicopter that went down. He didn't think much of it until he received a call.

"Jason. What can I do for you?" Nick asked.

"Tell me that Barb's okay," he said with fear in his voice.

"What do you mean?"

"We received a call. She's missing, along with two others. A helicopter went down. Don't you know? For God's sake, you're at the Pentagon!" Jason was angry.

"Calm down, Jason. Yes, I know about the chopper, but I . . . Don't worry. She's a fighter. I'll get back to you." He hung up. He had been so busy that he barely scanned the report and the names. He found it and re-read it. *Missing were . . . and Captain Barbara Harris, USMC.* "Shit." He took a deep breath. "All right, Marine. Let's see what you got. Stay strong. Use your survival skills. You will make it. You have to make it." Nick went to find out what he could.

* * * *

"Captain! Are you with me?" A voice called.

"Yes, sir!" Barb answered.

"We've . . . only . . . got . . ." He struggled to speak.

Kimberly A. Biggerstaff © 2024

Barb looked around and grabbed the survival gear. "I've got the raft, sir. Let's go." But the pilot had lost consciousness. Barb went to him and tried to undo his seat belt but couldn't. She grabbed a knife from the pocket of her flight suit and cut the pilot out. She had thrown the door open and tossed the raft out as it inflated, holding onto the rope so it wouldn't get away from them. The helicopter shifted and threw her against the side.

"Aghh!" she yelled as she hit something. "Major! Get in the raft!" she yelled at him. She struggled with him as he was in and out of consciousness, but they managed to get out, and she helped him in the raft.

He came to and yelled, "Where's Jenkins?" But then he saw Barb dive down under the water. "Captain! Captain, no!" He tried to stay conscious. He started to lose hope, but then Barb popped up with Jenkins and swam to the raft. Major Norton helped get him into the raft and then helped Barb. "He's not breathing." She started CPR, and he spit out the water and coughed.

"Good job, Captain," Norton said, grimacing in pain.

"Hang in there, Major. They'll find us," Barb said. She assessed his wounds and then checked Jenkins. Barb took inventory of their rations and supplies.

Murphy's Law: Anything that could go wrong will go wrong.

Barb gave Jenkins and Norton part of her rations when they started to get low. The weather had been bad off and on, making them drift farther from where they went down. The emergency beacon was intermittent. At night, it was cold.

"You need to stay strong, Captain. Stop giving us your water," Norton told her.

"You guys are hurt. I'm okay." But Barb was hurt. When she was knocked against the side of the craft, she landed on something and had a very bad bruise forming on her back. She had a bruised kidney.

"Don't lie to me, Captain," Norton said.

"You guys are worse off than me. How's that for accuracy, Major?" She kept messing around with the beacon, trying to get it working.

"Do you know what you're doing with that?" Norton asked.

"I took an electronics class once. I don't think I can make it worse," she said, smiling at him.

* * * *

"Barb? Sweetheart?" Deb said.

"Mom?" Barb opened her eyes and saw her parents standing beside the hospital bed. "Dad? Where am I?"

"The Naval Medical Center, San Diego," Nick said from behind them.

Kimberly A. Biggerstaff © 2024

"Jenkins and Norton?" Barb asked, concerned about her fellow marines.

"They're fine, thanks to you, Marine," Nick told her. "You did great, Pumpkin," he whispered. Then he stepped outside so she could talk to her parents.

He let out a sigh of relief and said a silent thank you as he closed his eyes.

Chapter 6

Months later, Barb stood at attention as the citation was read. Nick pinned the medal on her, shook her hand, and Barb saluted him. Nick returned the salute. "Congratulations, Major."

"Thank you, sir."

"I think your CO (Commanding Officer) is pissed because he didn't get to pin that medal on you," Nick told her.

"I don't care. I wanted you to do it." She smiled at him. "Where are you going next?"

"Quantico," he said.

"Sir, can we have dinner? There's something I want to tell you."

"I'd love to have dinner with you. Tonight?"

"That would be fine. Thanks," she said.

Nick could see she seemed nervous about something as she snapped the band against her wrist.

* * * *

Nick met Barb at the restaurant she had chosen. He arrived early and was waiting.

"Nick." Barb smiled at him.

"Sweetie," he said. Then he asked, "Is it okay to call you that?"

Kimberly A. Biggerstaff © 2024

"Yes. I like Pumpkin, but it makes me feel like I'm five years old again." She snapped the band against her wrist.

They were shown to their table, and they ordered drinks.

"Are you nervous?" Nick asked her.

"A little, yes."

"Relax, you know you can tell me anything," he told her.

She drew in a deep breath and said, "I'm seeing someone. A . . . woman."

"Dating is good," he said without missing a beat.

"Nick. Did you hear me?" She was surprised by his attitude.

"I heard you, and I don't care as long as you're happy."

She stared at him. "Mom and Dad gave you a heads up, didn't they?"

"Yes. But don't be mad at them. They wanted to know if it could affect your career."

"What did you say?" she asked.

"I told them you were an outstanding marine, and in today's Corps, it shouldn't matter."

"You know me, Nick. I'm not going to flaunt it or anything. Especially not in uniform. I'm a Marine Corps officer first and foremost."

"Semper Fi. You should still be careful. May I ask you something?" Nick looked at her.

"Yes."

"Have you given men a chance? Or did one piss you off so bad there's no going back?" He was curious if something had happened.

Barb smiled. "I still like men. It's just . . ."

"You don't have to explain to me. I just want you to be happy." He looked at the menu. "So, I think I'm getting steak and lobster to celebrate your medal. How about you?"

Barb smiled and went back to her menu.

No matter what she told him, Nick still worried about her. Many older officers wouldn't approve of that lifestyle. He just hoped she wouldn't run into any of them.

* * * *

A few years later, Barb found herself at the Pentagon. Nick was there too.

"Settled in, Major?" Nick asked over the phone.

"Yes, sir," she said.

"Good."

"Are you enjoying being assistant commandant?" She wanted to know.

"Yes."

"You're being nominated for commandant, aren't you?" she asked.

Kimberly A. Biggerstaff © 2024

"Yes."

"That's great," Barb said proudly.

"How's what's-his-name?" Nick said, changing the subject.

"Bruce. I know you don't like him."

"He just strikes me as someone who is only thinking of himself. I'm afraid he's using you." Nick was honest with her about this marine she was seeing. She was right. He didn't like him.

"Not many people know you're my uncle. I like it that way. He may suspect, but I'm not telling him," she assured him.

"Just be careful," Nick told her.

"Yes, sir," she said. They said goodbye, and Barb thought about what he said. She was planning on breaking up with Bruce anyway.

* * * *

Nick was confirmed as commandant of the Marine Corps. He sat at his new desk and pulled out the photo from his wallet. "I wish you were here to see this, Kaya. You're the only thing missing from making this perfect."

"Sir? You have a briefing," his aide told him over the intercom.

"On my way."

Kimberly A. Biggerstaff © 2024

Chapter 7 - SAM

After she broke up with Bruce, Barb was in the mood for something different. It had been a few months, so she went to a lesbian bar. She was talking to a woman but couldn't keep from glancing at another one sitting at the bar. The woman smiled at her.

"It was nice talking to you. Would you excuse me?" Barb said. She went over to the woman, sat on the stool next to her and took a sip of her wine. She glanced at the service dog at the woman's side.

"Hello. Would you like another drink?" the woman asked her.

"Yes, thank you," Barb said. The woman ordered another glass of wine for Barb and a shot of whisky and a beer for herself.

"This place doesn't seem to be your kind of place," the woman said.

"I came with a friend. She wanted to go someplace new," Barb said. "Have you been here before?"

"No." The woman smiled and set her hand on Barb's thigh. "I'm Sam."

"Call me Barb, Colonel." She smiled.

"Dammit, you know me?" Sam removed her hand.

"I met you at Lex's promotion ceremony," she said.

Kimberly A. Biggerstaff © 2024

"God dammit. Go back to your friend," Sam said angrily.

"Why? Maybe I enjoy talking to you."

"I didn't come here to talk," Sam told her, looking around.

"Yes, I got that impression." She smiled at her and set her hand on Sam's thigh.

Sam leaned over and whispered in her ear, "You better make sure this is what you want. I'm not in the mood to play games." She kissed Barb gently on the ear lobe.

"What happened to the General and the . . . others?" Barb said.

"The General did something stupid. The others are at home." Sam ran a hand up Barb's thigh and kissed her neck. Sam took her hand and led her to the bathroom. She took her to a stall and kissed her, moving her hands up under her blouse. Sam sensed some hesitation from Barb and stopped. "I told you, I'm not in the mood for games. Maybe you should go back to your friend."

Barb looked at her and kissed her hard. They continued and after Sam had satisfied her, Barb went to reciprocate.

"No. I don't need that," Sam said, zipping her pants.

"Are you sure?" Barb asked.

"Yes." Sam left and went back to the bar. She popped a pain pill on the way and sat back down. She ordered another beer and drank half of it.

"In the mood to talk now?" Barb asked, sitting next to her.

"No," she said. "But you can sit there," she said. Barb sat next to her, drinking her wine. Sam didn't talk. A few women came up to Barb and asked her to dance or if they could buy her a drink. Barb politely turned them down. Sam just sat and sipped her beer.

A woman dressed in biker gear came up to Barb and asked if she could buy her a drink. Barb again politely declined. The woman put her hand on Barb's thigh and said, "Come on, sweethcart. Be my bitch tonight." The woman was drunk.

"No thanks."

But the woman wouldn't take no for an answer and tried to kiss Barb. Sam started to move, but Barb grabbed the woman's two fingers on her right hand and bent them back, taking her to her knees. The woman was almost crying. "I said no. Now go away, understand?" The woman nodded. Barb let go of her, and the woman wandered off, holding her hand.

Sam smiled and took a sip of her beer. "What's your last name?" Sam asked after ten more minutes.

"Major Barbara Harris, ma'am."

"I think we're past the ma'am, part. Call me Sam." She smiled at her. "Do you work at the Pentagon?"

"Yes, but I don't work for the Major or the General. I'm in a different department."

"Being coy?"

"Semper Fi," she said, raising her glass.

"Oh, crap. You're a fricking jarhead," Sam said.

Barb smiled. "I hear you've got one coming down the pipe."

"Yeah, my son. About to graduate and be an aviator," Sam said.

"Congratulations." Barb raised her glass. She looked at her watch. "Well, I have to work in the morning, so I better go. Can I call you a ride?"

"No, I have a regular guy I use. Dog friendly," she said, looking at her service dog.

"May I wait with you?" Barb asked.

"Sure. Are you babysitting me?"

"I just want to make sure you get your ride," she said. "I'm sure you can take care of yourself."

"As can you. That was a nice move," Sam said, paying her and Barb's tab. They walked outside and waited. Sam's ride came first, and she went to get in the car.

Kimberly A. Biggerstaff © 2024

"I meant to ask, what did you do to your foot?" She noticed Sam was wearing a boot (walking cast) on one foot.

"I kicked my boyfriend's prosthetic leg." She smiled and Barb laughed. Sam gave Barb a quick, unexpected kiss. She got in the car and went home to her house.

Barb watched the car as it drove off. "Wow. So that's Samantha Barrett." Barb went to her car and drove home. She couldn't stop thinking about her. But they didn't exchange numbers, so unless she went looking for her, she probably wouldn't see her again. Maybe she'd get lucky and run into her at the Pentagon.

When Barb arrived home, she went to her bookcase, pulled the book off a shelf, and looked at it. *The Samantha Barrett Ops: Her Life in the U.S. Air Force and Central Intelligence Agency.* The book was written by her daughter, Quinn. Barb tried to read the book a few years ago but never got past the first chapter. It was a best-selling book, but something always came up and interrupted her reading.

Sam Barrett had started off in the security police career field in the U.S. Air Force. She then became an agent for the Office of Special Investigations (OSI), where she spent the rest of her career until she was forced to retire after a head injury resulted in seizures. She now had a seizure-alert dog that went everywhere with her. The book covered her personal and professional life. She sometimes did work for the CIA as well.

Barb only knew a few personal things about her. She knew Sam had a son, Jonathan, at the Naval Academy. His father was Air Force General John Burke, who was also at the Pentagon. She had a stepson, Lex Rogov, who was at the Pentagon as well. Barb had attended a few briefings with Lex, who was an air force intelligence officer.

Sam was an interesting woman. She was older than Barb, but that didn't bother her. She was an attractive woman, and Barb would have liked getting to know her. She started to read the book but was tired and fell asleep.

* * * *

Sam came to the Pentagon to take Barb to lunch. She had come up before and found her office, and they had lunch a week or two previously. Barb enjoyed Sam's company.

"We need to make a stop before we leave," Barb told her.

"We?"

"Yes. That's a nice suit. It's perfect."

"Perfect for what?" Sam was curious.

"You'll see." She led her to another office. A large office with a sign outside that said, "Commandant of the Marine Corps."

"Wait. Are you taking me to meet . . ." Sam asked.

"Yes. He wants to meet you," Barb told her.

"Why?"

"He wants to meet the wingnut who reamed his marine. His words, not mine."

"Wingnut?" Sam got serious.

"Remember, he's a four star," Barb said.

"Wingnut?" Sam repeated. There was always some rivalry between the different branches of service. Nicknames were sometimes used. Wingnut, zoomie, grunt, jarhead, and squid were some of the common ones.

"Colonel Barrett?" a marine colonel said.

"Yes, ma'am," Sam said.

"I'm Colonel Nelson. I believe you've met Major Nichols."

Sam looked at Bruce. She had a run-in with him the first time she came to take Barb to lunch. He walked away and mumbled something derogatory. Sam put him in his place.

She had a reputation around the Pentagon and at Quantico. She was known as "Barrett the Beast". Sometimes her temper got the better of her. Much of that was due to multiple concussions over the course of her career. John Burke took the brunt of most of her anger, but they still loved each other and had a sexual relationship.

Kimberly A. Biggerstaff © 2024

"Ma'am. I sincerely apologize for what I said the other day and for my attitude," Bruce said, extending his hand.

"A good officer will apologize and move on. A better officer will apologize and make sure no one else makes the same mistake. Learn from it." She shook his hand.

"Understood, ma'am."

"Dismissed, Major Nichols," Colonel Nelson said. "Colonel Barrett, this way, please." She led them into another office.

"Thank you, gentlemen," the General said as the men who were in his office stood up and left.

"General Foster, this is Colonel Samantha Barrett," the Colonel said, introducing them.

He shook her hand. "So, you're the wingnut who reamed my marine?"

"And you're the jarhead who made him apologize. Thank you, sir."

Barb and Colonel Nelson were shocked that she called him a jarhead. He smiled and then laughed. "Anyone else and I'd have you thrown out on your ass. Of course I wouldn't call just anyone a wingnut. How is Mr. Trask?" Nick asked her.

Now Sam understood. He knew her father. Of course he did. Mr. Trask was an alias for Sam's father. But only a few people knew that. The world knew her father, James Watson, as a CIA officer who died in the line of duty. But that's another story . . .

"He's well, sir. Thank you."

"Good. Would you care for a drink? I understand you favor scotch.

"Yes, sir."

"I brought this back with me after a trip. An eighteen-year-old Macallan." He handed her a glass. "Colonel, Major, help yourself," Nick said to Barb and Colonel Nelson. He looked at Sam and raised his glass. "To teaching the young ones." He tapped her glass and took a sip. "What do you think?"

"It's good, very good. Ever tried Redbreast? It's Irish."

"No, I haven't."

"I'll send you a bottle," Sam told him.

Nick looked at Colonel Nelson, and she set her glass down and left with Barb. It did not go unnoticed by Sam.

"You have something to say, General?"

"There have been some inquiries into a certain Chinese national."

Sam smiled and took a sip of the whisky. "Are you warning me off, General?"

"On the contrary. You may do as you wish." He reached into his pocket and handed her a flash drive and a note. "I wish you luck. But you may want to tell the others to back off. General Burke is being looked at for Chief of Staff, Air Force. He needs to back off. And someone over at Fort Meade should, as well. It's better that way." He nodded, indicating she should read the note. It read:

"Major Harris will take you to a SCIF (Sensitive Compartmented Information Facility). This information can't leave the building. Return the drive to Colonel Nelson today. Eyes only."

She gave the General the note back after she read it. He took a lighter, burned it, and dropped it in the trash can. "You're welcome to come back for a drink anytime, Colonel. I'll be looking for that bottle."

"Sir, did you send Major Harris . . ." Sam then wondered about the night they met.

"Absolutely not. I've been looking for an opportunity to meet you. Major Nichols presented that opportunity," Nick said quietly, "I never did like him." Then, in a normal tone, he said, "Colonel, I try to stay out of my niece's personal and professional life. She earned her way on her own."

"Niece?" Sam confirmed.

"My sister's kid. Not many know. I'm sure you understand her need to make her own way. Your son, Major Rogov, tries, but it can be difficult."

"Yes. He once told me that even with a different last name, others knew."

"He's a good officer. Got back on track. I'm glad you took Hammer to help get him when he was in trouble. Hammer was a good SEAL. He's very impressed with you."

"You know a lot, General," Sam said, remembering when she hired Hammer and others to help her rescue Lex when he was captured overseas (Lex's Story).

"Yes. I know General Burke is a good man. Major Rogov seems to be doing well, and I hear we'll be adding a certain midshipman Burke to the Corps. I'll probably see you at graduation."

"Yes, sir. It was a pleasure meeting you, General."

They shook hands and Sam left.

"Hmm. Interesting woman," Nick said to himself.

Chapter 8 - GIA

Gia graduated from high school at seventeen. Her grandmother signed the papers so she could enlist in the Marine Corps. Gia's mother had been killed overseas while working in a missionary camp, and she never knew her father. Her grandmother told her he was a doctor her mother met while helping him in the missionary camp they visited every summer. Gia was sent to Italy to live with her grandmother after her mother died. They lived in Naples, and Gia saw the Navy personnel around town because it was home to the U.S. Naval Support Activity. She loved their uniforms and still had a sense of American pride, having been born in America. Her grandmother told her she should be proud to be an Italian American. If her mother hadn't died, she'd still be in America. Sometimes Gia would try to talk to the sailors and marines.

When Gia was in high school, she told her grandmother she wanted to join the United States Navy. Gia was smart and got good grades, but her grandmother knew she wasn't ready to go off to college. The U.S. military would give her a chance to grow, travel, and figure out what she wanted to do.

But Gia became fascinated with the Marines, and when the time came, she joined the United States Marine

Corps. Gia was the best marine she could be. She became an intelligence analyst and excelled, making rank fast.

Then she met Frank Lorenzo. They dated and eventually married. They waited a couple of years before deciding to have a child. Kevin was Frank's pride and joy. He loved his son more than anything.

One day, when Kevin was two, he kissed him and Gia goodbye, as he always did.

"Dada," Kevin said.

"See you later. We've got a training flight."

"All right. Be safe. I love you," Gia told him automatically.

Later that day, she was visited by two U.S. Marines. It was the worst day of her life, next to her mother's death. The aircraft went down, and there were no survivors. The investigation revealed it was a mechanical failure. Pilot and maintenance errors had been ruled out.

Gia was about to be promoted to gunnery sergeant. She put in for an assignment at the Pentagon, hoping the change would do her and Kevin good. There were too many memories in California. Eventually, they moved to the Washington, D.C., area and settled in.

Even though he was young, Kevin knew Daddy wasn't there. He was sad and had become quiet. Gia tried to explain to him where Daddy was, but he didn't understand.

Kimberly A. Biggerstaff © 2024

Gia still wore her wedding ring. But after a year, she felt it was time to put it away. She looked at it, but then changed her mind. She wasn't ready.

Chapter 9

AUTHOR'S NOTE

The Joint Chiefs of Staff for all branches of the U.S. Military would have a car, driver, and security. (Nick is Commandant of the Marine Corps, also a member of the Joint Chiefs of Staff) What occurs between Nick and Gia would be highly unlikely in real life.

Gia was ready to go to work. "Kevin, let's go." But Kevin didn't answer. Gia went to his room and saw Kevin looking at George. "Kevin, we need to go."

"George needs more food," he said, looking at the lizard.

"Okay, we'll get some after I pick you up this afternoon."

He walked over to her and hugged her. "I miss Daddy."

"I know, I do too. It's going to be okay, Kevin. Daddy would want you to make friends and be happy. Don't you like the kids at daycare?"

He shrugged his shoulders.

"You need to try, honey. Please try for me. Daddy is watching you from heaven."

"Can't you go get him and bring him home?"

Kimberly A. Biggerstaff © 2024

"No, Kevin. You can't come back from heaven. But we'll go visit a special place someday. And we'll see your Nanna and Gramps. Okay?"

"Okay." He let her go, and she drove him to the childcare center at Ft. Myer-Henderson. Gia had spoken to the director when she enrolled Kevin and explained the situation.

"Is he talking or playing with the other kids?" Gia asked one of the ladies.

"A little bit. It may take more time."

"Let me know if there are any changes. Thank you," Gia said, leaving.

* * * *

Nick had gotten to know Sam a little better since Barb had been dating her. But Sam had issues. One of which was all the concussions. She was at Barb's one day and was getting something from the top shelf of a closet when a portable fan fell on her head. Sam blacked out for a moment and couldn't remember anything from recent memories. She thought she was back in Officer Training School. That was before she knew John, Barb and everyone else in her life. John tried to help Sam, and when Barb began to distance herself, he went to her to convince her not to quit on Sam.

But things turned very emotional, and John and Barb ended up sleeping together. They continued to see each other

Kimberly A. Biggerstaff © 2024

even after they found out Sam knew what happened. It had been a difficult time for everyone. Eventually, they all made up. Although John still loved Sam, she always refused his marriage proposals. Sam had been married twice. Her husband was killed in Afghanistan, and her wife died saving her life just a few years earlier. Sam had no interest in marrying again, not even to John. But John fell in love with and married Barb. They had two baby boys.

"Hello . . . Nick," Sam said.

"Sam. I'd ask how you are, but it looks like you've gone a few rounds," he said, noticing the bandage on her head.

"Yeah, you should see the other guy. So . . . winding down as commandant?"

"About nine months left. Since you came to see me, I guess this means you and Barb made up?" he said.

"Yes. We're all good."

"That's good. Care for a drink?"

"Yes. But I can't. Not yet. I had a brain aneurysm. The squirrel decided to chew on a vessel or whatever," she told him.

"Why doesn't that surprise me? I'm glad you stopped by. Might as well say it now since you brought it up."

"Brought what up?" Sam asked.

"My retirement. I won't be here to look out for her."

Kimberly A. Biggerstaff © 2024

"John's here. At least until he retires. And who knows, maybe one of you will get tapped as Secretary of Defense."

"God help us," Nick said.

"Do you plan on moving?"

"No. I just . . . " Nick began.

"Worry about her. She'll be fine. May I ask you a personal question?" Sam asked him.

"I suppose."

"Do you date?" Sam had wondered.

"Are you asking?" he joked, smiling.

"My life is complicated enough," Sam said.

Nick paused and thought about how much to divulge. "I was . . . married once. She . . . passed away. Cancer."

"Sorry. So did my mom. I was four," Sam told him.

"Thank you. And sorry about your mother."

"Thanks. Dad never dated either. Well, not that I know of. I don't know what he did after I left home. But . . . Mr. Trask is married now, and he has a son."

"Really?" Nick was surprised that she told him that.

"Yes. He's very happy. Anyway, on another note, I wanted to know if John came by to see you today."

"No. Why?"

"We met a little boy today when we were dropping the twins off at daycare. John is supposed to give you a message. He wants you to make sure his father is okay . . . in heaven," she added.

Nick didn't say anything. Then he cleared his throat. "What happened?"

"An Osprey went down in California about a year ago."

"Yes, I remember." After Barb's accident, Nick was more conscious and aware of all accidents concerning his marines. It wasn't that he didn't care back then; he just let work get in the way. Now, as commandant, he personally called or visited any relatives of marines killed or injured. When that Osprey went down, he was traveling overseas and wasn't able to make a personal visit. He had probably spoken with the boy's mother on the phone.

"This is Kevin's mother." Sam had copied her name from the article she had found online. "Check with her before you go see him. She works here, somewhere. Oh yeah, be sure to give him one of your coins. John did."

"Sam . . ."

"Just do this, please. I'll get you another bottle of Redbreast."

"That's not what I . . . of course I will. The other stuff . . . my wife. That stays between us."

"Yes. I understand," Sam said.

After Sam left, Nick asked his aide to track down Kevin's mother and have her come to his office.

It didn't take long, and Gunnery Sergeant Lorenzo was in the outer office. "Sir, Gunnery Sergeant Lorenzo."

"Yes, come in, Gunny." Nick was looking at some papers.

"General. It's a pleasure to meet you," she said.

She took Nick by surprise. He didn't expect her to be as striking as she was. He had no expectations at all. She was tall—at least five nine or ten. She was wearing a skirt and heels, which emphasized her long legs and svelte body. Her dark hair was pulled up in a bun. Not a hair out of place. Smokey, dark eyes. She looked too young to be a gunnery sergeant already.

"Sir?" she said.

"Yes, uhm, my . . . uh, General Burke and his wife met your son this morning. They were dropping their twins off, and . . . Kevin, is it?"

"Yes, sir."

"Kevin asked General Burke to tell me to make sure his father is okay in heaven. I'm very sorry for your loss, Gunny."

"Thank you, sir. You called me after it happened. I appreciated that. General Burke? Isn't he the Air Force Chief of Staff?"

"Yes, he married my niece, Major Harris."

"I see. I'm sorry Kevin bothered General Burke with this. He still misses his father."

"I wanted permission to talk to him. Just reassure him his father is okay."

"Sir, you don't have to do that. I'm sure you have more important things to do."

"The Corps is a family, Gunny. Once a marine . . . ," Nick began.

"Always a marine. Semper Fi, sir." She smiled and agreed to let Nick speak to her son. She would meet him there at the childcare center after work. "Thank you, sir."

"You're welcome. Dismissed, Gunnery Sergeant." He walked her to the door and opened it. Nick closed the door behind her and sat down at his desk. He stared at the door. Then he snapped out of it. "What's the matter with you, Foster? Wake up." He got back to work.

That afternoon, he went to the childcare center and met Gia. Nick spoke to Kevin and assured him his father was okay and then gave him his coin. The boy smiled and Gia saw a slight change in his attitude.

"Thank you, General. That's the first time he's seemed happy in a long time."

"No problem, Gunny. Well, maybe I'll . . . ," Nick started to say.

Kimberly A. Biggerstaff © 2024

"Hello, General. Come to see your great nephews?" Barb asked.

"Well, since I'm here. Uh, this is Gunnery Sergeant Lorenzo. Kevin's mother. This is Major Harris, my niece."

"Nice to meet you, Gunnery Sergeant. Hello, Kevin. Remember me? I was here this morning."

"Where's the pirate lady with the brains falling out?" Kevin asked Barb. That's how he described Sam.

Barb smiled. "Colonel Barrett went home."

"Oh, she's funny," Kevin said. "I like her."

"Well, I'll be sure to tell her," Barb said.

"We better go. Nice meeting you, Major. Thank you again, sir," Gia said.

Nick watched as they left. Barb got the twins, and Nick helped her put them in the SUV.

* * * *

A few days later, Nick was at his desk and finally said to himself, "The hell with it." He stood and went to his aide. "Where's Gunnery Sergeant Lorenzo's office?"

"Sir?"

"A few days ago, I had you get her to come to my office. Where is her office?"

The aide told Nick where she worked. "I'm going to follow up on something," he said, leaving. He walked to her office. He hesitated before going in. "Get a grip," he told himself and walked in.

"ROOM TEN HUT!" a marine yelled, seeing Nick.

"Carry on," Nick said to everyone. "Gunnery Sergeant Lorenzo, I wanted to follow up and make sure your son was doing okay."

"Yes, sir. He's fine. He really likes the coins you and General Burke gave him. Thank you again," Gia told him.

Nick didn't say anything and then realized he was staring at her. "Good. Fine. Well, carry on." He turned and left to go back to his office. Nick shook his head as he walked. "What is wrong with you?" he mumbled down the hallway.

"Sir?" a navy officer asked him.

"What is it, Commander?" Nick said.

"Sorry, sir, I thought you said something to me."

"No, carry on," Nick said.

"Aye, aye, sir." The Commander continued walking.

Nick was silent as he made his way back to his office.

"Sir, your plane leaves in three hours," his aide told him. Nick had to go visit his troops. He was flying out to Arizona first and then California. He'd return in about five days. But he couldn't get the gunny out of his head. The entire flight, she was all he thought about. He finished his visit in Arizona and began thinking about Gia again. When he arrived at Miramar, he asked to speak to the Commander of Marine Aircraft Group 16.

"Commandant, what can I do for you?" the Colonel asked.

"Colonel, were you here when the Osprey went down over a year ago?"

"Yes, sir. It was a mechanical failure, sir."

"Yes, I read the report. I'm interested in talking to anyone who knew Staff Sergeant (SSgt.) Frank Lorenzo. Preferably those who knew him and his family personally."

"I'll see what I can find out, sir. Is this a priority, sir?"

"Yes. You have three hours," Nick ordered. "I'll be on base until then," Nick said. "Now, give me a tour, Colonel."

The Colonel got another officer to show him around. When he finished his tour, Nick went back to the Colonel.

"Colonel? Did you complete your mission?"

"Yes, sir. This way, sir." He showed him to the conference room.

"ROOM TEN HUT!"

"At ease," Nick said, looking around the room. There were about ten marines in the room. "All of these marines knew SSgt. Lorenzo?"

"Yes, sir. He was a popular man. SSgt. Wilcox probably knew him best."

"Wilcox," Nick called.

"Sir." The marine snapped to attention.

"How did you know Lorenzo?"

"We were battle buddies, sir. Best friends. Our wives had our kids about the same time. We played cards together, sir."

"Walk with me," Nick said. "Keep everyone here," Nick told the Colonel. As they walked, Nick asked what kind of man Frank was.

"He was a stand-up guy. Friendly. Fun to be around. He had your back if you got into trouble."

"What about his family?"

"He loved his wife and son, sir. He took her out to dinner whenever he could. He took his son to the park and played with him all the time. He was the best dad and husband. And friend."

Nick listened to all of them. It was more of the same. He was a great guy. A great husband and father. And an outstanding marine.

"Sir?" Wilcox said as Nick was getting ready to leave.

"Yes."

"His wife is at the Pentagon now, right?"

"Yes, Gunnery Sergeant Lorenzo."

"This is our squadron flag. It was signed by all of us back when SSgt. Lorenzo was . . . before the accident. Could you see that his son gets it, sir?" He handed it to Nick. "We

Kimberly A. Biggerstaff © 2024

want him to have it. And sir?" He pulled an envelope out of his flight suit and looked at it. It said GIA on it. "We had a deal, sir. If anything ever happened . . . I was supposed to give this to her, but . . . it was difficult at first, and then time just . . . It's from him." He teared up and cleared his throat.

"Yes. I'll make sure she gets it." Nick knew the pain he felt. He'd not only lost his wife but friends in combat as well. Nick gave them all his coin and took a photo if they wanted. Then he had someone take him to the Marine Corps Exchange (store). He found a toy Osprey plane and bought it. He completed his tour and eventually returned to Washington.

It was a week later, and Nick was sitting in on a briefing. His mind began to wander. He was thinking about the gunny. Gia. What a beautiful name. He needed to give her the things he received in California.

When the briefing was over, he just sat there. "Nick? Nick?" John said.

"Hmm? Yes?"

"Are you all right?" John asked him. "You looked miles away."

"Fine, thanks." He got up and left. Without realizing it, he was outside Gia's office. He started to leave when she appeared behind him. She had taken some papers to another office.

"General?"

"Oh, uh, hello, Gunny."

"Was there something you needed, sir?" she asked.

"Um, do you have a few minutes? I was going to get a grab-n-go meal. Walk with me?"

"Yes, sir. Let me tell the Sergeant," she said.

Nick waited for her. They walked to the food court. Nick didn't say much. He was stalling and he was a bit nervous. "How's your son?" he asked.

She smiled at Nick. "He's doing fine, sir. Thank you. Sir, is it normal for a high-ranking general like yourself to wander the Pentagon alone?"

Nick found a table and they sat down. "I told them I don't want that. I try to do as much as I can by myself, and I don't need an entourage following my every move." Nick wanted to talk about her. "Was the move difficult? To Washington?"

"A little. Kevin was born in California and didn't really understand why we had to move."

Nick tried to come up with questions to keep her there a little longer.

"General. How are you today?" Sam asked.

"Colonel Barrett. I'm fine. How are you?" Nick said, standing.

"Good," Sam said, glancing at Gia.

Kimberly A. Biggerstaff © 2024

"Having lunch with the Major?" Nick asked her.

"Yes, but she's busy, so we're eating in the office." Sam looked at Gia. "Hi, I'm Colonel Samantha Barrett. Retired."

"Sorry, this is Gunnery Sergeant Lorenzo," Nick said, introducing them.

Then Sam spoke to her in Italian. "Do you speak Italian?"

"Yes. It was almost all my grandparents spoke," Gia responded in Italian.

"You're Kevin's mother. I met him that day at the childcare center.

"Yes, ma'am, he referred to you as the pirate lady with the brains coming out."

"Not the worst thing I've been called." Sam smiled. "Did the General speak to Kevin?"

"Yes."

Nick gave Sam a look that said go away. "Well, I better go. Nice meeting you, Gunny," she said in English.

"I better get back to work. I have a corps to run," Nick said.

"Yes, sir," she said, quickly standing as he walked off.

Nick walked to John's office. He didn't wait and went straight to John's desk. "Tell your girlfriend to stop flirting with my marines!" He didn't wait for a response. He turned and strode back to his office with purpose.

John was stunned. "What?" He sighed and called Barb's office. "Is Sam there?"

"Yes."

"Let me speak to her, please," John said.

"Hello," Sam said.

"What did you do?"

"What are you talking about? Nothing," Sam said.

"Nick came in here and told me to tell you to stop flirting with his marines."

"I didn't—oh, I wasn't flirting. I spoke to her in Italian and she spoke back."

"Sam. You have a way of . . . being charming without trying," John told her.

"Well, I can't help that. I didn't do it on purpose. I was being polite. But you know . . . she is a very beautiful woman. Tall, long dark hair, dark eyes, great legs . . . hmm."

Barb looked at her over the desk.

"You have enough people in your life, don't you think?" John reminded her.

"I know. I'm not interested in her, but I think the General might be."

"Stay away from her." John hung up.

* * * *

Another week passed. Nick was at home and was trying to read a book. But he couldn't concentrate. He stood and went to his office and found the phone number. She's probably seeing someone. A man would have to be dead or gay not to be attracted to her. He set the number down and went back to his book. Then he got up again and got the number and dialed.

"Hello?"

"Oh, hello. This is General Foster. Um . . . Nick Foster."

"Yes, sir, what can I do for you?"

"This is an informal call and we're off duty. Please call me Nick."

"Nick, I'm Gia."

"That's a beautiful name," Nick told her.

"Thank you. It was my grandmother's."

Nick didn't know what to say. "I . . . uh . . ."

"Did you want to talk to Kevin?" she asked.

"No, I wanted to ask you . . ." He stopped as he struggled to get the words out.

"Ask what, Nick?"

"Uh, I haven't done this in a very long time. I'm sorry. Maybe this was a mistake. I'm sorry to have bothered you at home."

"Wait. Please. Go ahead and ask me." She tried to encourage him.

He took a deep breath. "Would you like to have dinner with me?"

"Yes, I would," Gia said.

Nick smiled, but he was surprised she said yes. "Do you have a babysitter, or would you rather bring him along?"

"I have a neighbor. Kevin plays with her son."

"Are you free on Saturday night at seven? Is that okay?" Nick asked.

"Saturday at seven will be great."

"Okay, see you then," Nick said.

"Nick?"

"Yes?"

"Do you have my address?" she asked him.

"I can get it, but why don't you tell me?" he said, feeling more comfortable.

She gave him her address and they hung up. Gia looked at her hand and took the ring off. She went to her bedroom and placed it in her jewelry box.

Nick smiled and fixed himself a drink. "Crap. Reservations." He had no idea where to take her. He looked online but didn't find anything he liked.

"I'm never going to hear the end of this." He dialed the number.

"Nick? John gave me your message. I won't bother you," Sam promised.

He took a breath and said, "I need a recommendation for dinner and some discretion, Sam."

"Good for you. You asked her out."

"Dinner for Saturday. I haven't been on a date in . . . forever. I don't have a clue where to take her," Nick confided.

"Give me a minute to think," Sam said.

"I'll call you back. I need to check something." He hung up and called Gia back. "Do you have any allergies or any foods you don't like?"

"No. Is this formal, dressy, or casual?" Gia asked.

"I'll have to get back to you on that," Nick said. He called Sam back. "Anything is fine. No allergies. What about Italian?"

"No. Not for a first date. She's Italian and nothing will beat Grandma's cooking."

"Oh." Nick felt like a boy going on his first date.

"I know a place. How about Hell's Kitchen?"

"They're probably booked for weeks."

"I'll call you back." She hung up.

Nick shook his head and looked again online. Ten minutes later, Sam called back.

"Okay, you are all set for Saturday. But reservations are at eight. Is that okay?"

Kimberly A. Biggerstaff © 2024

"Yeah, I was looking at the menu. It looks good. How did you get reservations?" he asked.

"I know people."

"Thank you, Sam. I owe you."

"Yes, you do. Wear your best suit. Or buy a new one."

"I can dress myself," Nick said.

"Really? When was the last time you wore a suit to dinner? Not your uniform."

He sighed.

"Tomorrow after work, we'll go find something. I like buying suits for men," Sam said. "See you at sixteen thirty (4:30 p.m.), your office." She hung up.

Sam arrived promptly, and she gave him directions to one of the finest menswear shops in DC.

"We need three suits. Two-tailored and one for Saturday," Sam told the man.

"I only need one—"

"If things go well, are you going to see her again?"

He stared at her.

"Yeah, three suits," Sam said.

Nick was fitted and they picked out shirts and ties as well.

"This is too much."

"No, it's not. You can mix and match. It's perfect. Try these shoes."

"I have—fine." He was tired of arguing with her.

When he went to pay, the man said, "It's already been taken care of, sir." Nick went over to Sam.

"You are not buying my clothes."

"I picked the best place in DC. You will look the best you have ever looked, and she will love it. You want to pay this?" She held up the receipt.

"Oh my God, I need a drink."

"Champagne, sir?" A man appeared.

"Yes, thank you," Nick said, taking the glass and a sip. "Is this what it's like to be wealthy? Or to be you?"

"I think you know I don't live the lifestyle of the rich and famous. But when I travel or decide to take someone on a special date, then I tend to go all out."

"John told me about the time you took him to Vegas."

"What did he tell you? I thought what happens in Vegas stays in Vegas."

"Don't worry, he didn't say much. Mostly told me about the suite and playing poker. Is there anything else I need?" Nick asked her.

"No. I think that's it. Unless you need etiquette lessons," she teased him.

"Well, I guess the least I can do is take you home. If there's room in my vehicle."

"No, I can get a ride," she said.

"No, I'll take you," Nick insisted.

* * * *

Saturday morning, Nick received a call from Gia.

"Nick, I'm sorry, but we may have to postpone. My neighbor's son is sick, and she doesn't want Kevin to get sick. I'm really sorry."

"Oh, well, that's okay. These things happen. Kids get sick. Another time," he said disappointedly.

"I'd still like to go out. I just don't have anyone to watch him."

"It's okay. I'll talk to you later," he said and hung up. Then he called Sam.

"Calling for last-minute advice?" she teased him.

"Her babysitter's son is sick. Know anyone who'd be willing to watch a three-year-old?"

Sam sighed. "Only because those reservations cost me a lot. Okay, he can come here, and we'll watch him."

"Which we?" he asked. It could have been Michael or Andrew. He didn't approve of Sam's lifestyle. Three men and a woman, his niece. And all her kids. But he gave her credit for raising good kids. The older ones were successful, and the little ones all loved her. She inherited a lot of money after her father's "death." But the kids were never spoiled. Sam loved her family and would do anything for them and for her friends. The few friends she had.

Kimberly A. Biggerstaff © 2024

"It's Andrew tonight. I'm at Luke's swim meet, but we should be home by six."

"Great, thank you," Nick said.

"You owe me."

"I was thinking about that. Don't I get credit for giving you that information about a certain scientist?"

"I lost my eye chasing down that SOB," Sam said angrily. Then she took a breath. "But he paid for it all. Yeah, I guess you get partial credit."

"I'll call you tonight." He called Gia back. "I hope you don't mind, but I may have a babysitter for you. Colonel Barrett agreed. She and her . . . friend Andrew. They have a girl and a boy. I would trust her with my life."

"Are you sure it's okay?"

"Yes, and this way we can still be discreet, if you know what I mean," he said. But he knew they were taking a chance. She was enlisted, and he was an officer. Fraternization. It could destroy both of their careers.

"Yes. I was wondering about that."

"It's just dinner," he said.

"So, what time do we need to be ready? Kevin likes the pirate lady, so he'll be fine."

"With traffic, uh . . . six?"

"Where does she live?"

"Stafford."

"That's a lot of driving. Are you sure? She's welcome to come here. She can even bring her kids."

"No, I think this is best for now. She'll have help if she needs it," he said.

"Okay. We'll be ready at six. By the way, may I ask what happened to her eye? Do you know? Kevin was asking."

"She went to find the man who poisoned her wife. She was captured by him, and he . . . put something in her eye. She lost it. I think she enjoys the patch."

"I'll figure something out to tell Kevin. Did she get justice?"

"Yes, Major Harris and her team took care of it."

"I see. Thank you for telling me."

"Gia, I don't know how much you know about Colonel Barrett, but . . . she's the person you'd want to be next to you in battle. But don't tell her I said that."

Gia smiled. "I understand. If you trust her, I do too. We will be ready for you at six."

"Looking forward to it."

* * * *

Sam told Nick which shirt and tie to wear with his new suit. So he wore it. He wasn't used to having someone, other than the Corps, tell him what to wear. But since he hadn't been on a date in years, he listened. He tried to date over the years after his wife passed, but no one captured his interest or heart

. . . until now. If he needed a plus one to a military event or Embassy party, he usually took Barb.

Nick looked at one of his security men. He sighed and walked over to him. "This is a bit sensitive. I mean I need some discretion, it's just dinner."

"Sir, we're here to protect you. Nothing else. Please don't worry."

When Gia opened the door, he almost fell over. She was the most beautiful woman he had ever seen. She was wearing a black cocktail dress. "You look wonderful. I didn't know your hair was so long."

"Thank you. I love your suit. That tie is perfect."

"Thanks. Um, are you ready?"

"Hi, General." Kevin saluted him. "What's in the bag?"

"Carry on, Marine." Nick saluted him back.

"Oh, yeah. Um . . . I was visiting the troops at Miramar, and . . . uh . . . Staff Sergeant Wilcox asked me to give this to you, Kevin. This is your father's squadron flag. They all signed it a long time ago."

"Wow!" he yelled.

"Those are the names of the marines your father flew and worked with," Gia told him, looking at it. Then she saw his name. Nick could see her face change. "That one . . . here.

This is your daddy's signature. His name." She swallowed the lump.

"Um, I also picked this up for you. That's his aircraft. MV-22 Osprey." He handed him the toy.

"Wow! Thank you! Can I take it with me?"

"Let's put the flag in your room. We can hang it up later. Maybe get it framed. But you can take the toy with you," Gia told him.

"Okay." He ran to his room and laid the flag neatly on his bed. He came back out and said, "Mommy says the pirate lady is going to watch me."

"Yes, she is. She has triplets your age. And a boy and a girl older than you."

"Triplets?" Gia said.

"Yes. They live next door. It's complicated. But I trust her. Does he have a booster seat or something?"

"Yes."

"We better get going. Traffic." Nick took the car seat and put it in the SUV.

"Kevin, do you have your backpack?"

"Yes, Mommy. I'm good to go. Squared away."

Gia smiled at his military jargon, and so did Nick. "Is your entourage following us?"

"Yes. Sorry, but it comes with the job. Just ignore them," Nick told her.

"I understand."

Andrew answered the door when they arrived. "Hi, Nick."

"Andrew, this is Gia and Kevin."

"A pleasure to meet you both," Gia said.

Finn ran up and looked at the boy. "I'm Finn."

"Oh, this is one of Sam's triplets, Finn," Nick said.

"Sam thought it would be nice if he had someone close to his own age. Luke and Jess are here, too. Please come in," Andrew said.

"Where's the pirate lady?" Kevin asked.

"Right here. How are you, Kevin?" Sam asked him.

"Good."

"You can call me Sam."

"She's my mommy," Finn said.

"You better get going to make that reservation, Nick. Nice suit. And Gia . . . wow! If I had more room in my life for another—"

"All right. We're going," Nick said, interrupting her.

"Thank you, Colonel." Gia bent down to Kevin. "I want you to be on your best behavior, okay. Play nice, share and be courteous. Please, thank you, sir and ma'am. Clear?"

"Yes, ma'am." He saluted her.

"I'm not an officer. You don't salute me," she reminded him.

"Oh, yeah. Got it, Gunny," Kevin said.

"What's a gunny?" Finn asked.

"I'll explain later, Finn. Have fun," Sam said to Nick and Gia. "And I'm a retired officer, Kevin. A Colonel. So if you want to salute me, it's fine."

"Yes, ma'am," Kevin said, saluting her. She returned it.

"Thanks, Andrew, Sam," Nick said.

Andrew closed the door. "Wow. She is . . . really hot. Way out of his—"

"She's out of everyone's league," Sam said, smiling.

* * * *

Nick drove to Gordon Ramsay's Hell's Kitchen. They arrived fifteen minutes early. Nick opened all the doors for her. A few men turned and looked at Gia as they walked by. Nick noticed and stood taller.

They ordered dinner, and the manager came by and asked if everything was okay. Nick said it was perfect. He brought them a bottle of their best wine. "Compliments of Colonel Barrett."

"Thank you," Nick said. "I have to be honest, Gia. Sam made the reservations, and she picked out this suit."

Gia smiled. "You look very handsome, and I would have been happy anywhere. You know, this is my first date since my husband."

"Really? I would have thought men would be beating your door down."

"No. I was still wearing my ring until you called me. And I think men are . . ."

"Intimidated. That's what they are. You are a very beautiful woman, and that can be intimidating to some men."

"Not you?"

"Yes. Me too," Nick admitted.

"Well, I'm glad you asked me," she said.

"So am I." He smiled at her.

"You went by his squadron?"

"Yes, I wanted to know what kind of man he was. They all said the same thing. He was a great friend, husband, and father. I hope you aren't mad."

"No. I'm glad they gave you the flag. And that was nice of you to get the toy for Kevin."

"He should have those things."

Nick asked a lot of questions about her life. They found out they had been stationed at a base at the same time. And served on the same ship, but at different times. After dinner, they drove back and picked up a sleeping Kevin. Nick carried him inside Gia's place and put him in his bed.

"I remember doing this a few times when Barb was little."

"Would you like a drink? Maybe coffee? I have some decaf or regular," Gia said.

"Um, I should . . . well, coffee sounds fine."

They closed Kevin's door and went out to the living room. Gia went to the kitchen and made them coffee. Nick looked around the living room of the apartment. She had a family photo of Kevin, Frank, and herself. And a photo of herself with an older woman.

"Is this you and your grandmother?" he called.

"Yes," she called back.

A framed American flag was on the mantle. Frank's funeral flag, he assumed.

"Here we are," Gia said, handing him a cup. "I had an old friend send me this from Italy. I hope you like it." She smiled. "Nick, thank you for dinner. I had a great time, and the food was wonderful."

"You're welcome. I enjoyed it too." Without thinking, he took a big sip of the coffee. "Mmm." He spilled a little on his shirt. "Oh, no. I guess you can dress me up but can't take me out." He was embarrassed.

Gia kissed him. It was unexpected, but he enjoyed it. When she pulled away, he smiled.

"Now that the kiss is out of the way, give me your shirt."

"What?"

Kimberly A. Biggerstaff © 2024

"I don't want that to stain. I'll take care of it," she said.

"Oh, it's okay," he tried to tell her.

"No, it's new isn't. Give it to me." She pushed his jacket off.

"I can . . . okay." He removed his tie, then his shirt, and gave it to her. He was wearing a white undershirt and was glad that he was. It was too early to show any skin. He was in shape and had nothing to be ashamed of, but it was the first date.

"I'll be right back," she said, going to the laundry room. He picked up the coffee and blew on it and took a small sip. Better, but he had burned his lip. He sat down on the couch. "Idiot," he said quietly to himself.

A few minutes later, Gia came back. Nick stood up. "I should go. It's late."

"What did you think of the coffee?" she asked, trying to get him to stay. She enjoyed talking to him.

"It's very good. Gia, I had a wonderful time. May I take you out again?"

"Yes, please do."

He picked up his jacket and tie and walked to the door. "Good night." He leaned in for a kiss. Just a sweet goodnight kiss. Then he remembered the letter. "Oh, I almost forgot. Wilcox asked that I give this to you. He apologizes for holding on to it for so long." Nick smiled and left.

Chapter 10

Nick was in an extremely good mood for the next few days. And people noticed. On Wednesday, Sam came by after her lunch with Barb.

"So, I didn't get a chance to ask how it went?" she asked him.

"It was great. Right up until I spilled coffee at her apartment."

"You got coffee on your new suit?" Sam whined.

"Just the shirt. A drop, and she took care of it."

"What do you mean?"

"She took it and soaked it or whatever."

"You sly dog. You took your shirt off." Sam grinned at him.

"I had an undershirt on underneath."

"Oh. Old-fashioned. But that's good."

"I have to admit, the suit, the restaurant, everything was great. Thank you for your help and for the last-minute babysitting."

"You're welcome. Glad it went well. There was one thing I wanted to mention."

"What's that?"

"Protection. Carry two," Sam said, smiling.

"Get out!" he yelled at her. That was the last thing he wanted to discuss with her or anyone.

"You don't want any accidents, young man. Never trust the woman to take care of it. Be safe," she said on her way to the door.

"Out!"

After she left, he chuckled. John came by later that day.

"What's going on with you?" he asked.

"What are you talking about?"

"You seem different. Happy. I mean a different kind of happy." John couldn't explain what he meant.

"Is that bad?" Nick asked.

"No, just . . . it's . . . watercooler talk."

"What are they saying?"

"Some think it's just 'short-itus' (the time shortly before you get ready to retire, move to a new duty station, or get out). Others think you have a girlfriend or boyfriend."

"Boyfriend? You better quash that rumor right away!" Nick yelled at him.

"Nick. You're not married. No one has seen you go on a date."

"I am seeing someone. A woman. But keep that to yourself."

John smiled. "Good for you. It's about time."

Nick took a breath. "John, I was married. Long ago. She had cancer and passed away. No one else has ever interested me until now."

"Barb never told me that," he said.

"Barb was a baby. We were overseas when we found out, and she refused treatment."

"Why?"

"Because of the baby. But it was an aggressive cancer, and I lost them both."

"Nick, I'm so sorry." He looked down. "Sam lost one of ours," he told him. "We didn't even know she was pregnant until she miscarried. It was early, but . . ."

"It still hurts," Nick said. "Sam knows I was married, but I didn't tell her about the baby."

"I won't say anything," John said. "I'm glad this woman makes you happy." He had a feeling he knew who it was.

"It was just one date." Nick smiled.

"Well, if you need anything, let me know."

"John. It's a little complicated. I need discretion."

"I understand. Lex had his own . . . issue . . . before his wife went to OTS."

"She was enlisted?" Nick asked.

"Yes. And she used to work for Sam at Quantico."

"I'll bet that didn't go well at first."

"No. But she's a great daughter-in-law, mother, and wife. So, don't worry about us. This will be difficult for you because of your position and rank. Anyone else know?" John asked.

"Just Sam. I needed some recommendations. It's been a long time. Oh, and Andrew. They agreed to babysit at the last minute."

"What? She's always refusing to babysit for us, but— oh, never mind. Good luck, Nick."

* * * *

That evening at home, Nick called Gia. "Hi. How are you?"

"Good. How was work?"

"Work is fine," Nick said. He wasn't really one to make small talk on the phone. He usually stated his business and moved on, but he wanted to hear her voice.

"I was going to call you. Kevin was wondering if you'd like to go to the zoo with us on Saturday."

"The zoo? Yes. I'll go with you to the zoo," Nick said.

"Good."

"Oh, let me know if you hear any rumors."

"Oh no. Did someone see us?"

"No, I was told I seemed . . . happy. In a different way. Anyway, it seems others have noticed."

Gia smiled. "Is that a bad thing?"

Nick chuckled. "That's what I asked. No, I don't think it is."

"I'll let you know if I hear anything." She paused. "Nick?"

"Yes?"

"Thank you for bringing the flag for Kevin. He also loves the toy airplane. And, Nick, thank you for the letter. It really meant a lot to me."

* * * *

Nick picked Gia and Kevin up on Saturday morning, and they went to the Smithsonian National Zoo. He knew he probably shouldn't, but at times Nick held Gia's hand as they walked. He glanced at his security every once in a while. He asked them to try and be inconspicuous. They did their best. He was probably more recognizable than she was. But in civilian clothes, he looked different and he wore a baseball cap. More than one man did a double take when they saw Gia. Their wives or girlfriends gave them a smack if they were caught looking. Nick smiled to himself. Whenever he thought he recognized someone, he let go of her hand.

"If you're worried, you don't have to hold my hand," Gia told him.

"I want to hold your hand. But we need to be careful."

"Nick, pick me up, please," Kevin asked.

Nick picked him up and put him on his shoulders. "Where to next, Kevin?"

"Umm, pandas and then lizards!"

"Good choice."

* * * *

When they returned to Gia's apartment, Kevin had fallen asleep. Nick once again carried him inside, and Gia got him ready for bed.

"Kevin had a great day. He's worn out."

"Me too," Nick said.

"How about a glass of wine?"

"Sure."

She went to the kitchen and poured two glasses of wine. When she came out, Nick was asleep on the couch. He was sitting up, but his head had fallen back. Gia smiled. She placed the wine on the table and covered him with a blanket.

When Nick woke up, he saw something staring at him from the coffee table. "What is that?"

"That is George the gecko," Gia said.

"Where did he come from?"

"Kevin's room. Didn't you see the aquarium?"

"I guess not."

"Have something against dogs?"

"He belonged to my husband."

"Oh. Sorry I fell asleep." Nick suddenly felt old.

"That's okay. It was a long day, and we did a lot of walking. Let me put George back. He's been out long enough." Nick noticed she had taken off her shoes and socks. He watched as she picked up the gecko and took him back to Kevin's room. After washing her hands, she came back out and sat in the chair next to the couch.

"Are you reading Sam's book?" Nick asked.

"Yes. It's very interesting. She's led quite the life."

"Hmm."

Gia put the bookmark back and closed the book. She set it on the coffee table, sat next to Nick and handed him his glass of wine. Nick took a sip.

"What did you like best about today?" Gia asked him.

"Holding your hand." He smiled.

"What was your favorite animal?" she asked.

"Were there animals?" Nick teased. He leaned closer and kissed her. He took her glass and his and set them on the table. Then he kissed her again. This time, it was a long kiss. Gia moved a hand and set it on his thigh. But then Nick slowly pulled away.

"I should go."

"Nick, is something holding you back?"

"I guess maybe I'm still old-fashioned. We've only had two dates," Nick said.

Gia smiled. "I just wanted to make sure it wasn't me."

"No. Definitely not." He smiled and touched her cheek. "I'll call you." He kissed her and went to the door and left.

Thirty seconds later, her phone rang. She smiled and opened the door.

"How about another date? Right now?" he asked. She let him in, and he kissed her more passionately this time. They stood there for a while, just kissing. Then Gia took his hand and led him to her bedroom.

* * * *

They both were quiet as Nick held Gia in his arms.

"Are you all right?" Gia finally asked him.

"Yes. You?"

"Yes. You're just . . . quiet."

"Did you want to talk about something?" Nick asked her.

Gia smiled. "No. I mean, not unless you want to."

"I think we're making this weird by trying not to make it weird."

"The first time is always a little uncomfortable," she said. "From what I remember."

"Maybe we should rectify that . . . in a little bit."

"Whenever you're ready." Gia smiled.

* * * *

Kimberly A. Biggerstaff © 2024

Nick had meant to leave and not stay the entire night. At one point he told his security (who had been hanging around outside the apartment) to wait in the SUV. They took shifts with one staying near the apartment and the other going to the vehicle to rest. He told them he wasn't sure how long he'd be. Nick loved holding Gia and having someone next to him. He woke and nudged her. "I should go before—"

"Mommy!" Kevin knocked on the door.

"Too late," Gia said, opening her eyes.

"Uh, I don't know what to do in this situation," Nick told her.

"And you think I do?"

"No, I mean . . . it's so soon."

"Mommy," Kevin said again.

"Coming," Gia called to him. She kissed Nick and got up and put on a silk robe. Nick couldn't take his eyes off her. "I've died and gone to heaven," he thought silently.

Gia barely opened the door. "Are you okay?"

"My pullup leaked," he told her sadly.

"That's okay. It happens sometimes. Go to the bathroom and get undressed. I'll be there in a minute."

"Okay." He turned and went to the bathroom.

"I'm going to have to help him," Gia whispered to Nick.

"That's fine. It'll give me a chance to sneak out."

"Nick. I don't want you to have to sneak out."

"What do you want me to do?" he asked her.

"Take a shower, get dressed and join us for breakfast."

He just looked at her. "You don't think this is too fast?" Then his phone buzzed. He texted his security that he was fine.

"He knows you and likes you. As long as he doesn't see us in bed, I think he'll be okay. And if he has questions, I'll answer them. It's been over a year since I had a man spend the night. And that was my husband."

"Any women?"

"What? No."

"Just asking. Nowadays, you never know. And after knowing the Colonel and her tribe . . . I don't know what to think."

"I must not be far enough in the book to understand that."

"Has she met Katrina yet?" he asked, referring to Sam's book.

"No."

"Yeah, you're not that far."

"Mommy!" Kevin yelled.

"Take a shower and come out when you're ready." She left to go help Kevin.

Kimberly A. Biggerstaff © 2024

Nick took a shower in the bathroom in Gia's bedroom. He dressed and went to the door. Opening it, he looked out and nodded to one of the security men. He asked if they wanted any coffee or anything but they declined. Their relief would be arriving any minute. Nick closed the door and went to the kitchen.

Gia was still helping Kevin. She helped him get a bath and picked out his clothes. He dressed himself and helped Gia take his sheets off the bed so she could wash them.

"Kevin. We have company for breakfast. Nick is here," Gia told him.

"Goody!" He grabbed the stuffed panda Nick bought him and ran out to the kitchen. "Good morning, Nick."

"Uh, hello."

"Look, I still have my panda."

"I see. That's great." Nick was making coffee. "Did you have fun yesterday at the zoo?"

"The best. Will you take me somewhere today?" Kevin asked.

"Um, I'm not sure. Your mom may have things she needs to do."

"Oh." Kevin was obviously disappointed.

"But maybe next week," Nick told him.

"Okay."

Kimberly A. Biggerstaff © 2024

"Hey, are you ready for breakfast?" Gia asked, coming back.

"Yeah," Kevin said sadly.

"What's the matter?" Gia could see something was wrong.

"I want Nick to take me somewhere today."

"Nick might have things to do. We have laundry and errands to run. Maybe another time, okay?"

"Okay." He was still disappointed.

Gia made chocolate chip pancakes for them. That cheered Kevin up a little bit. Just before they finished their pancakes, Nick said he needed to pick up some items at the hardware store.

"Would it be okay if Kevin went with me? I need some help picking out some things."

"Just the two of you?" Gia asked him.

"If that's okay. We can run to my house and then go to the store." Nick wanted to go home and put on fresh clothes. He really did have something he needed to fix at his house. He had put it off, but this would give him a chance to fix it.

"Don't you live in the Commandant's House at the Marine Barracks?" Gia asked.

"Yes, but I bought a house years ago as an investment. I rent it out when I'm not using it. But I need to get it ready for myself since I'm going to retire soon."

"Kevin? Would you like to go help Nick?"

"Yeah! I mean, yes ma'am." He smiled.

"Good manners and best behavior, right?"

"Right," Kevin promised.

"Okay. When you finish, go brush your teeth."

Kevin smiled the biggest smile, finished his pancakes and ran off.

"I hope that's okay. I probably should have asked you privately first. This is all new to me," Nick said.

"I trust you with him. And I know where you work," she said.

"We'll go to my house first so I can get fresh clothes and double check what I need. Then we'll get the things I need, and he can come back and help me. Is a fast-food burger or nuggets okay for lunch?"

"Yes. Not all the time, but yes," Gia said.

"I'm ready, Nick," Kevin said.

"Oh, I found a spare toothbrush and used it," he told her quietly.

Gia gave him a smile and a quick kiss when Kevin wasn't looking. "He doesn't wear pullups during the day. But

Kimberly A. Biggerstaff © 2024

take him as soon as possible if he says he needs to go. There's spare clothes and stuff in his backpack."

"Okay. Call if you want me to bring him back," Nick told her.

"Are you kidding? A Sunday morning to myself for a few hours. Have fun," she said.

"Load up, Marine." Nick looked at Kevin.

"Yes, sir." He grabbed his backpack, and Nick took the car seat he had brought up the previous night.

"Nick. Thank you for yesterday," Gia said.

"Can I take my panda?" Kevin asked.

"Sure," Nick said. "I mean, if it's okay with your mom."

"Yes."

* * * *

They drove to Nick's house in Arlington.

"Nick, why do those men follow you?" Kevin asked.

"They're my security. Bodyguards. Since I'm the Commandant of the Marine Corps I need protection."

"I wish someone had protected my Daddy." Kevin said sadly.

"I do too, Kevin. I'm really sorry about your father and all the Marines that die under my Command."

"But Daddy is safe and watching over me right?"

"Yes, he is."

Kimberly A. Biggerstaff © 2024

"Wow. This is your house?" Kevin asked when they arrived.

"Yes. It's really too big for me. Why don't you sit here and look at your book? I'll be right back. Are you thirsty, or do you have to go to the bathroom?"

"Can I have some milk?"

"Yeah. Sit there." Nick pulled out the milk and checked the date. Then he smelled it. "This has gone bad. Uhm. How about some water for now?" He found a plastic cup and gave it to him.

"Thank you."

"I'll be right back." Nick ran upstairs to his bedroom and changed into fresh clothes. In his free time, which wasn't often, he was working at the house to get back in shape. He came back downstairs and asked Kevin if he wanted to help him.

"Yes."

"Okay, come on." He led him to the garage. "I want to add a shelf here above this work bench. What do you think we need?"

"Uh." Kevin looked around. "Like that one?"

"Yeah, but here."

"You need a piece of wood and those two things holding it," Kevin said.

"Right. A board and two brackets to hold it. How do the brackets stay in the wall?"

Kevin walked to the other shelf, but he was too small to see that high. Nick came over and picked him up.

"See that? Screws. How many do we need?" Nick asked him.

"One, two, three, four. Four screws," Kevin said.

"Right, but always buy extras. Or a pack with more than you need." He set Kevin down and looked for a tape measure. Nick let Kevin help him measure, and they made a list of what they needed.

"I think that's it. Let's go to the store."

* * * *

A few hours later, Kevin knocked at the door to the apartment. He was wearing a kid-sized Home Depot work apron, some protective goggles, a tool belt and tools. "Look, Mommy. I made a bird feeder."

"That is awesome, honey," Gia said.

"And I helped Nick put a shelf up in his garage. I'm going to show George." He ran off to his room.

"Is the shelf straight?"

"He did great. He listened and followed directions."

"Thank you. I haven't seen him this happy since before his dad passed," she said. "What did you eat for lunch?"

"We ate at my house. PBJ sandwiches, grapes, and apple juice."

"You had that at home?" Gia didn't think he'd have any of that since he probably spent most of his time on base at the Commandant's House.

"We made a stop," Nick admitted.

Gia kissed him. She quickly backed away when Kevin came back.

"Mommy, can we put the bird feeder on the balcony?" Kevin asked, admiring his work on the birdfeeder.

"We'll have to ask the manager. Then we'll have to figure out how to hang it."

"If the manager says no, you can keep it at my house, Kevin," Nick told him.

"Okay. Thank you for the zoo and panda and today and all this stuff." Kevin went over to him and hugged him.

"You're welcome. Thank you for helping me with my shelf. I'll see you later."

"Are you going home?" Kevin asked.

"Yes."

"Will you come back?"

"As long as your mom lets me. Maybe I'll take you to see the Silent Drill Team or a parade. Or meet Chesty."

"Chesty?" Kevin was confused.

Kimberly A. Biggerstaff © 2024

"Ask your mom about him." He walked to the door and looked at Gia. "I'll call you."

Chapter 11

Once again, Sam showed up at Nick's office.

"You know, if you keep coming here, they're going to think you and I are involved," Nick told her.

"I already started that rumor. A distraction. You're welcome," Sam said.

"Sometimes I don't know if you're kidding or not," Nick mumbled.

"Did you go out again?" she asked.

"Yes. Kevin wanted to go to the zoo, so we spent Saturday at the zoo."

Sam looked at him as he spoke. He wasn't looking at her. She smiled. "You got lucky."

"I'm not discussing that with you," Nick told her.

"Fine. Where are you going next?

"I don't know," Nick said.

"Do I have to make reservations again?"

"No."

"Taking her to dinner?"

"Probably."

Sam rattled off the questions quickly on purpose. "What did you have for breakfast?"

"Chocolate chip pancakes," he said before he realized.

"I knew it. You slept with her."

"Get out! Is that how you interrogated suspects?"

"Sometimes. I'm happy for you."

"Different cast?" he asked, changing the subject. Sam had hit a guy and broken her hand. It wasn't the first time.

"Yeah, Jason came down and checked it. It's a Terminator hand now. I have little metal plates and screws in there."

"You can be violent," Nick said.

"Only when I need to be. Or I flip out."

"How are the twins?" Nick asked her, knowing she probably saw his great-nephews more than he did.

"They're great. I have another reason for coming. I wanted to invite you, your girlfriend, and her son to a barbecue at my house next Saturday. Not this Saturday. The next one."

"Who's going to be there?"

"Just my family. That means John and Barb."

"John knows. Lex?"

"Lex has been in your position. He knows enough to keep his mouth shut. Besides, no one will know she's . . . you know. Is this placed bugged?" Sam asked.

"It's not supposed to be, but you can never be too careful." He told her.

"Barb will know. She met her when I went to talk to Kevin that day at the center," Nick said.

"Just come. Kevin can play with the kids. I'm getting a bounce house for them."

"Is there an occasion for this?" Nick wondered.

"Lex and the family will be PCSing (Permanent Change of Station) to SHAPE (Supreme Headquarters Allied Powers Europe), Belgium, soon. I just want to get everyone together before they leave," Sam said. She was still sad about it but knew it would be good for his career. Lex and his wife Laura were extremely lucky to have been in Washington for as long as they had been.

"Can I let you know?" Nick asked.

"Yeah . . . just bring them," Sam said, exasperated. "See you next Wednesday."

"Don't you have anything better to do than check on me?" Nick watched her walking to the door.

"No," she said, opening the door. "Love you, General," she said loudly before closing the door.

"GET OUT!" he yelled. "That woman is"—he sighed—"something else."

Chapter 12

Out front, Nick pulled up and parked in the driveway.

"Ready?" he said to Gia.

"Yeah! Deploy!" Kevin yelled.

"Kevin. Best behavior and good manners," Gia told him. "Where did you learn that word, deploy?"

"From Finn. Mommy?"

"Yes?"

"Are you and Nick friends?" Kevin asked.

"Yes. Good friends."

"Should I step outside?" Nick asked.

"Give me a minute, please."

Nick got out of the SUV. Ashley was shooting hoops. Nick walked over to her. "Hi, you're Ashley, right?"

"Yes. And you're Barb's uncle, Nick."

"Right."

"Are they okay?" Ashley asked him.

"Yeah, she just needs to talk to him for a minute. The Colonel said you were moving to Belgium."

"Yes. I guess it'll be okay," Ashley said. She didn't seem too excited about it.

"You're the soccer player, right?"

"Yes, sir." Ashley passed him the ball. He took a shot and it bounced off the rim.

"That's a great place to get better," Nick told her.

"That's what the Commander said. The Colonel."

"You know, I have an old college buddy who coaches soccer in Europe. He did his time in the Marines and then played for Bayern Munich for a few years before he got hurt. I could ask him for tickets if you ever want to go to a game or need advice," Nick offered.

"Wow, that would be great! Thanks." She passed him the ball again. He shot and made it this time. "I think they're ready," Ashley said.

He walked over to Gia. "Everything okay?"

"I think so. I had to explain the hand holding at the zoo and that he might see us kiss."

"Now? You told him that now?"

"He's fine. He knows I'll always love his daddy. But he's not coming back, and he would be happy if we're happy. He said he likes you. He said that Daddy will be happy because you make us happy."

"He understood that?" Nick asked.

"For now. Are you going to introduce us?" Gia asked.

"Uh, yeah." He helped Kevin get out, and Kevin pulled him down by the hand and looked him in the eyes.

"Nick. Daddy's happy because we're happy. Thanks." He held out his hand to shake it. Nick shook it and then picked him up and hugged him.

"Thanks, Kevin. You and your mom make me happy too." He set him down and walked over to Ashley. "Ashley, this is Gia and Kevin. This is Lex's oldest, Ashley."

"Nice to meet you," Ashley said. "Kevin, do you want to kick a soccer ball with me?"

"Yeah."

"Come on. We'll go into the backyard. I have a portable goal. You can try and score on me. The Commander got a bouncy castle, too."

"Who's the Commander?" Kevin asked.

"Sam, the pirate lady," Nick told him, following them and taking Gia's hand as they walked.

"Hey, about time you guys got here. There's coolers on the deck labeled with what's in them. Juice boxes are in with the water. Wine is in the kitchen. If you want a specialty drink, I have a machine downstairs. Fuzzy navel, Tom Collins, Martini's, whatever. Andrew and Michael are cooking the burgers and dogs."

"Why aren't I cooking?" John asked.

"You don't live here anymore, so the boys got promoted. This is John, Gia."

"Welcome to the crazy house, Gia," John said.

"Sir."

"No rank here. Call him John or asshat." Sam smiled.

"Swear jar, Commander." Alek appeared.

"Why do you always appear when I swear?" Sam reached into her pocket and gave him a five.

"Only five?" Alek commented.

"Inflation. Besides, I've given you enough money over the years to send you to Julliard for ten years."

"Yeah, you have." Alek smiled.

"This is Alek. Lex's second," Nick said.

"Nice to meet you, Alek," Gia said.

"Wow, she's really pretty," Alek said in Italian. "She's out of Nick's league."

"Thank you, Alek. Too bad you're not older," Gia replied in Italian.

Alek got red in the face, suddenly embarrassed.

"Gia Lorenzo. She's Italian. Should have gone with Russian," Sam told him.

Alek blushed. "Your eyes are like the night sky waiting for the moon to come out," he said in Italian.

"Where did you learn that?" Sam asked him.

"Pop Pop."

"Is he flirting with her? What did he say?" Nick asked with jealousy.

"Alek, go outside," Laura said. "Sorry about that. He likes a girl at school and is trying to get her attention. I'm Laura. Lex's wife."

"Gia, nice to meet you." Gia shook her hand.

Kimberly A. Biggerstaff © 2024

"Gia, wine or something else?" Sam asked.

"Wine is fine. Thank you."

"This is from my vineyard in Tuscany. Let me know what you think," Sam said.

"You have a vineyard? In Italy?"

"Yes, and one in Napa. Would you prefer a California wine?"

"No. This is fine." She took a sip. "Very nice."

"She has a villa near Aviano Air Base, too." John told her.

"When I was ten, I moved to Naples and lived with my grandmother."

"I heard my son was flirting with—" Lex stopped and stared. Laura backhanded him in the stomach. "I love my wife," he said quickly. "Hello. I'm Lex," he said in Italian, taking her hand and kissing the back of it.

"Like father like son," Laura said.

"I've seen you somewhere," Lex said. "Oh. Oh." Then, in English, he told Nick, "If you need any advice on subterfuge . . ."

"I'm a marine. Do you think I'd take advice from the air force?" Nick told him firmly.

"Sorry, sir," Lex apologized.

"Just messing with you kid." Nick smiled. "Now get me a beer."

"Yeah, right." Lex laughed.

"No, really, may I have a beer?" Nick said.

"Yes sir, follow me," Lex told him.

"Don't listen to anything she says," Nick told Gia, referring to Sam.

"Let's see. That's Barb over there. And Michael and Andrew are at the grill."

John was now throwing the football to Alek. Ashley ran over and intercepted the ball in front of Alek.

"Ash," Alek whined.

"Nice interception," John told her. "You're the best player in the family."

"Surprised you aren't afraid of hurting those delicate fingers," Ashley told Alek.

"You're a—"

"Alek. Ashley, don't be mean," John said.

"Give me the ball," Alek said.

"Tackle me, little brother," Ashley said, running from him. "Come on, Pop Pop. Let's play a game."

"See how many will play," he told her. "Throw me the ball."

Nick was sitting with Barb and the twins. "They're getting so big," he said. "Oh, uh, Barb, you met Gia a few weeks ago."

"Yes. Hello. Uh, Kevin seems to be getting along with the other kids," Barb said.

"Yes. He met Finn a couple of weeks ago. They got along," Gia told her.

"How did he meet Finn?" Barb asked.

"My babysitter cancelled at the last minute, and Sam offered to babysit."

"She did what?" Barb said a little angrily. "Excuse me. Would you watch the boys, Nick?"

"Yeah."

"Did I say something wrong?"

"I don't know," he said, smiling at Eddy. "You're going to be a marine, aren't you? You are too." He looked at Eric.

"No, air force," John said, appearing.

Michael nudged Andrew and said, "Maybe they'll join the army."

"Or the CIA," Andrew said, putting his two cents in.

"Go back to school. Oxford boy. Boo. The CIA, no way." They all teased him. He was the only one not military.

"Uh oh, are they fighting?" Michael asked while watching Sam listen to Barb, who seemed to be scolding her.

"Twenty bucks says Sam kisses Barb and they leave the room," John said as they watched.

"You're on," Lex said.

Kimberly A. Biggerstaff © 2024

"John's right," Andrew said.

"Yeah, she'll turn on the charm. Apologize for whatever and kiss her. Oh, and move a hand under her shirt," Michael said.

They watched and it was just as they said. "Now she'll take her hand, and they'll go to the bedroom," Andrew said.

Andrew was right.

"Twenty bucks, Lex," John said.

"Wait, she and . . . the two of them . . . I thought it was you three guys," Gia said.

"It is. And Barb."

"Separately, of course," Andrew said. "Except for John and Barb."

"Hey, do you mind not discussing my s-e-x life? That's none of your business. Delivery boy."

"Old man," Andrew said.

"I can still take you," John said.

"Let's go, Pop Pop, or is it Gramps?" Andrew said, turning to him.

"Would the two of you stop," Michael said.

"You're still the low man in our squad," John said to Michael.

"No, Barb is," Michael said. "She was after me."

"No, it's still you, big guy," Andrew said.

"So Sam is . . .?" Gia asked Nick.

"You need to keep reading that book," Nick told her.

"She likes whoever," John said.

"You all get along? No jealousy?" Gia asked.

"We make appointments. Schedule time."

"Hey John, aren't you going to join them?" Andrew teased.

"Why? You want to watch?" John said.

"You know that's my mom," Lex said.

"You and five others here."

"Stop scaring the guest," Laura said. "Gia, I've got a story for you. I think it was Thanksgiving. She and Michael were in the guesthouse. It was the first time she brought him over, and all the women—Emily, me, Bae, Quinn—oh, and Caleb watched as she took him inside the guesthouse. Quinn made a bet with Emily about trying to get him to take his shirt off. But Sam knew we were watching and lured him outside without his shirt."

"I remember that. John got my shirt back for me. I added some ink since then."

He lifted his shirt and showed them.

"Show-off," Andrew said.

"Cut it out," John said.

"What are you doing?" Sam asked Michael.

"Showing them my ink. Laura was telling Gia about the time you took my shirt after the . . . guesthouse. You know, the Thanksgiving you invited me, Duke and the boys."

"Oh, yeah," Sam said, remembering and smiling.

"Where's my wife?" John asked.

"Right here," Barb said. "What are you talking about?"

"Lex finally lost a bet," John told Sam. "And Gia will never come back again."

"Andrew and John were going at it," Michael said.

"No, I'll stop. I wouldn't want to give him a heart attack. Oh, wait, that's Barb," Andrew said.

John looked at him.

"Uh oh. Too far?" Andrew asked.

"You better run and run far." John stood and chased him off the deck.

"Come on, you really want to do this?" Andrew stopped, but John tackled him.

They wrestled. "Stop it, old man," Andrew said.

"I said I could take you," John replied.

"Aren't you going to stop them?" Nick asked Sam.

"Not yet. They do this every few years," Sam told him.

The kids stopped and watched. "Get him, John!" Finn yelled from the bounce house.

Kimberly A. Biggerstaff © 2024

"Come on, Dad!" Luke yelled.

"Go John!" Alan yelled.

John's security appeared and started to move in but Sam said they were okay.

"Okay boys! Go get them. Incoming!" Sam yelled, signaling to the kids to go join in." Luke, Alan, Samuel, and Finn ran over and piled on them. Kevin watched.

"All right. All right," John said. "That's enough." They started tickling each other. Kevin ran over and joined in.

"Nick," Gia said when she saw him.

"He'll be fine," Nick said, taking her hand. "Boys need to get it out sometimes."

Sam walked over to the pile. "Okay, break it up. Who wants a hot dog?"

"ME!" some of the boys yelled. They ran over, and Michael told them all to go wash their hands. The boys went inside.

Sam looked at Samuel, who was breathing hard, and walked back. She saw him take a puff on his nebulizer and kick the ground. She caught up to him. "You okay?"

"Yeah. It just makes me mad," he said.

"I know. But you're my miracle boy, right?"

"Yeah. You'll come visit us, right, Commander?" he asked.

"Of course I will," she said. "Go wash up." She walked back to John and Andrew. "You two have issues," Sam told them as they sat on the ground.

Andrew got up and held out his hand to help John up.

Then he said, "I don't know what you mean." He kissed Sam on the cheek.

"Yeah, no issue here." John smiled and also kissed her on the cheek. "Did we get you worked up?"

"No. Your wife took care of me."

"Too bad." John smiled.

Michael handed out burgers and dogs to the girls, and then the boys came back and got theirs.

"John, I don't know how you made general," Nick told him as John stepped back on the deck.

"Fighting with him keeps me young."

"John did you call Marie?" Sam asked him.

"Yes."

Sam called her. "Is everything okay? Are you coming over?"

"Yes. Pop was just a little tired. We're just down the street." She hung up.

"John, go help Marie. She'll be here in a minute. And she said Mike was tired. Make sure he's okay."

John went inside and washed his hands and went out front to wait.

Kimberly A. Biggerstaff © 2024

"Gia, I hope we haven't scared you off," Sam said.

She smiled. "No. Family dynamics are interesting. And yours is . . . very interesting."

The twins began to fuss, and Laura helped Barb take them inside to feed them. She still nursed when she could and pumped when the boys were at daycare. She sat down on the couch in the family room. Laura handed her Eric after she had Eddy set up.

"You've been quiet, Barb. What do you think of Nick and Gia?" Laura asked her.

"I love Nick. I guess I'm just surprised," Barb said.

"Surprised he's dating or dating her."

"I don't know. Maybe a little of both," Barb said.

"Is it the age difference or the fact that she's enlisted?"

"My father is twenty years younger than my mom, and John is older than me. No, that doesn't bother me. I guess I just don't want to see him get hurt."

"That's a part of life," Laura said.

"I know. I guess it's just strange to see him with a woman. Dating. He seems happy, though, doesn't he?" Barb said.

"Yes, he does. Hang in there. Need anything?" Laura asked her.

"No, we're good. Thanks."

Kimberly A. Biggerstaff © 2024

* * * *

John walked Mike in. "I'm fine," Mike said.

"I know," John said.

Marie and Jacob walked in and went outside. "Sorry we were running late."

"Pop was napping," Jacob said, hugging Sam. "Hi, Commander."

"Hi, Jacob. This is Kevin and his mom, Gia. This is my grandson, Jacob, and daughter, Marie, and John's with his father, Mike."

"Hello, Director," Gia said to Marie.

"Gunny. How are you?" Marie said, surprised to see her.

"Call me Gia, please."

"You two know each other? How?" Sam asked suspiciously.

"Work, Mom." Marie knew how she thought. "Ted and I are fine."

"I go back and forth to Fort Mead," Gia said.

"More secret squirrel stuff?" Sam asked.

"Yes."

"I never asked what you do, Gia," Sam asked.

"No, you didn't."

"You gave her a mission," Lex said. "Now she'll try and figure it out. You might as well tell her your MOS."

Kimberly A. Biggerstaff © 2024

"0239. Intelligence Analyst."

"But you never worked with Barb?"

"No," Gia said.

Nick got up and went to find Barb. "Hi, Pumpkin. We haven't had a chance to talk. How's everything going?"

"Fine," she said.

Nick sensed something in Barb's voice. He sat down in a chair next to her. "You still feed both of them at the same time?"

"Yes," Barb said.

"Pumpkin, what's wrong?" Nick asked.

"You could have told me you were seeing someone. And you could have told me who it was."

"It happened so fast and it's complicated."

"Don't get court-martialed before you retire," Barb told him.

"Barb. I'm . . . being careful. Aren't you happy for me?" Nick asked her.

"I don't know. I mean, I never thought of you with anyone," she admitted to him.

Nick sighed. It was time he told her. "Sweetie, when you were a baby, I was married. I loved her more than anything and would have done anything for her. But . . . she had an aggressive form of cancer and passed away when we were overseas." He swallowed. "She kept refusing to seek treatment because . . . of the baby. It took both of them. I never thought I'd find someone that made me feel the way I felt for Kaya. I tried to date every so often, but no one . . . made me feel the way she did. Not until now."

"Nick. I'd hug you, but the boys . . . Why didn't you ever tell me?" Barb asked him.

"It was too difficult, and then it didn't seem necessary."

"I'm so sorry." Barb felt terrible. "She makes you happy?"

"Yes. I know it's early, but I really like her and want to get to know her," Nick said.

"I've never seen this side of you. It may take some getting used to."

He stood up, leaned over and kissed her on the forehead. "You'll always be my Pumpkin."

"Uncle Nick, I'm glad you're happy and shared what you did."

Nick smiled and went outside. Gia was helping Kevin with his plate. "I'll help him. Go get a plate." He gave her a kiss and took the plate. Gia smiled and went off. "All right, Marine, you have a hot dog. What else do we need?"

"Beans and a drink," Kevin said.

"Baked beans are a good choice. Hear you go. Let's get a juice box, and you can eat at the table with the other kids. Are you having fun?"

"Yeah, lots. I like Finn. The other boys are nice too."

"Good." They went inside to the dining room table. Nick set the plate down for him.

"Thanks, Nick," Kevin said.

"You're welcome, bud." He rubbed the top of his head and went to fix his own plate and find Gia.

* * * *

Nick grabbed a backpack he had put in the back of his vehicle and put it on. Then he picked up Kevin and carried him to Gia's apartment.

As they walked, Gia asked, "What's in the backpack?"

"Call it an 'In Case of Emergency Pack'." He smiled.

"Uh huh." She smiled to herself, figuring he had spare clothes in it.

They tucked Kevin in and went back to the living room. "Did you enjoy yourself today?" Nick asked as she poured two glasses of wine.

"Yes, I did. Despite the small moments of drama, it was fun," Gia said.

"I'm glad we went. It's nice to socialize with others who understand," Nick told her.

Kimberly A. Biggerstaff © 2024

"What do you mean?" Gia asked.

"Evidently, Laura was enlisted when she and Lex started seeing each other. She ended up going to OTS."

"Oh. Does it bother you that I'm enlisted?"

"No. I just worry about what would happen if someone pressed it. I wouldn't want to ruin your career," Nick told her.

"No, I have Kevin to think of," she said.

Nick sensed she was starting to have doubts. He didn't want to start an uncomfortable discussion, so he set his glass down on the coffee table and stood up. "Yes, Kevin is your priority. I agree." He walked to the door, picking up his backpack.

"Nick."

But he just opened the door and left.

Gia tried to go over what had just happened. She was stunned and felt an emptiness.

* * * *

On Monday, Nick was irritable and short-tempered. He had a scowl on his face, and his aide was taking the brunt of his mood. After a briefing, John followed him to his office.

"What do you want, General?" Nick growled.

"General? What's the matter?" John asked him.

"None of your concern. You can go."

"Nick, something happened. You can talk to me. When you left on Saturday, everything seemed fine. What happened?"

"Leave me alone, John. I have a Corps to run."

"Okay. But try not to beat your aide up too much. He looks like you reamed the hell out of him," John said, leaving.

It was still early, but he fixed himself a drink. He drank it and went and sat down on the couch against the wall. He tried to convince himself that he did the right thing. But it only made him madder.

On Tuesday, Barb came and tried to talk to him. But he refused to talk about it, and he sent her away.

As usual, Sam showed up on Wednesday.

"Get out, Colonel. I'm not in the mood."

"You're an idiot. I'd call you an asshat, but that's reserved for John. Idiot will have to do."

"Get out of my office!" he yelled.

"I don't know what happened, and you don't have to tell me, but for the past month, you've been happy. Probably the happiest you've been since you were married. You finally met someone who gives you that feeling—the butterflies when you kiss, the feeling you get when she smiles at you. Her son lighting up when you help him with his hot dog. You're an idiot if you throw that away." She started to walk away but turned and came back, standing in front of his desk.

"I lost my husband in Afghanistan. I didn't think I'd find anyone after that. I didn't know what love was until I met Katrina. As much as I love John, Andrew, Michael, and Barb—and I love them with all my heart—it's nothing like what I felt for Katrina. When you find that person, you hold on to them, no matter what. Pull your head out, Marine!" She turned and left, slamming the door behind her.

"Dammit," he said, sitting down in his chair. "You screwed the pooch, Foster," he said to himself. "Why is she always right?"

* * * *

Gia was in a SCIF with some other marines, going over some intelligence. But she was distracted and couldn't concentrate.

"Gunny? Gunny!"

"Yes, Staff Sergeant?" Gia finally said.

"May I have a word?"

"Yes." They stepped away from the table.

"Are you all right, Gunny?"

"What do you mean?" Gia asked.

"We've worked together for a while now, and I've never seen you like this. Something is on your mind," she said. "Is it a man?"

"Why would you ask that?"

"I'm one of the few females around here. When a new female arrives, the men talk. You were the topic of a lot of conversations. The men stayed away from you mostly because they heard you lost your husband. Some just thought they wouldn't have a chance with you. But then they noticed you removed your ring."

Gia looked at her left hand.

"Some are trying to decide to pounce or not. But there's a rumor that you might already be seeing someone. You seemed happy until now. I'm sorry if this is too much. I just . . . wanted you to know that if you needed another female marine to talk to, you have one."

"Thank you, Sergeant. It's complicated, and I may have said something that pushed him away."

"So there is a man?"

"Like I said, it's complicated. Thank you for bringing this to my attention. I shouldn't let my personal life interfere with work. It never has before." Gia stood tall and they went back to work.

* * * *

Nick told his aide he needed to run an errand. He found the flower shop and looked around.

"May I help you, sir?" a woman asked him.

"I need something that says I'm sorry and I'm an idiot," Nick said.

"I can help with the 'I'm sorry' part." The woman smiled.

Kimberly A. Biggerstaff © 2024

"Yes, thank you."

She showed him a nice display of flowers. "Sometimes simple is better. "May I ask if it is for a relative, friend, or wife?"

"Uh, girlfriend," he said quietly.

She showed him a bouquet of red roses and calla lilies in a red vase. He liked it. "Can you deliver this today? To an office here in the Pentagon?"

"Yes, sir. We have cards over there."

"Just one of those small ones will do." He wrote on the card, "I'm sorry – N." He put it in the envelope and addressed it to her office. "Today, right?"

"Yes, sir. I promise." She smiled.

"Thank you," Nick said after paying. He walked back to the office. He had another briefing to go to.

* * * *

"Gunny, you have a secret admirer," the Sergeant said, looking at her desk.

She had just returned from Ft. Meade. She looked at her desk and saw the flowers. Not showing any emotion, she took out the card and read it. Then she smiled.

She wanted to call and thank him. But that wouldn't be smart. Then she had an idea. She shuffled some papers, and then on a blank piece of paper, she wrote a note. She placed it in an envelope, wrote something on the front and sealed it. Then she placed it in an inter-office large envelope.

"Sergeant, I need this paperwork delivered to Major Harris. Here's her office information."

"Yes, Gunny. Should I wait?"

"No. Just give it to her or someone in her office. Thank you."

He found the office and gave the envelope to Captain Jackson.

"Ma'am, this just came for you," Jackson told Barb.

Barb opened it and took out the envelope. "Please deliver to General Foster."

"Jackson, who gave you this?"

"A Sergeant. He said it was from Gunnery Sergeant Lorenzo."

"Thanks." She waited a few minutes, then came out and gave the envelope to Archer. "Take this to General Foster."

"The Commandant, ma'am?" Lieutenant Archer asked.

"Yes. Give it to his aide and come back. Is there a problem, Lieutenant?"

"No, ma'am. On my way, ma'am." Archer left and went to Nick's office. He gave the envelope to Nick's aide and left.

"Sir, this just came for you."

"Who is it from?" Nick asked.

"Lieutenant Archer said it came from the Major."

"Thank you." He opened the envelope and smiled. It read, "Thank you for the flowers. They're beautiful. But you forgot the chocolates. Dinner. My place, tonight, 1900 hrs. (7 p.m.). Bring your backpack."

* * * *

Nick picked up a nice box of chocolates on the way home. He showered and changed into nice slacks and one of the shirts Sam bought for him. He grabbed a sports coat, the chocolates and his backpack. Then he realized that the next day was Thursday. He needed his uniform if things went well. He placed everything in a garment bag and took it all to his SUV. One of his security men gave a slight smile when he saw him place the garment bag in his SUV.

"Is there a problem?" Nick asked.

"Not at all, sir."

"Just do your job," Nick ordered him.

"Yes sir."

Nick stood at her door and knocked. She opened it wearing a casual dress and low heels. "I remembered the chocolates," he said, handing them to her. She smiled and took them, stepping aside so he could enter. She placed the chocolates on the kitchen counter.

"You can hang that in that closet," she told him. He hung up his garment bag and went to the table in the dining area.

"Where's Kevin?" Nick asked.

"Next door. Nick, I need to know why you left," Gia said.

"I was . . . an idiot, as someone told me. I'm sorry. I thought you were having doubts, and I didn't want you to have to choose between me and your career. I don't like sneaking around, but I don't want to jeopardize your job or life. I didn't want to talk about it or get into an argument, so I made the decision for us. That was wrong and I'm sorry."

"Yes, if we're going to have a relationship, it needs to be a partnership. I know we moved fast and that's partly my fault. I let you into Kevin's life and mine. If there's a problem, you need to talk to me. I was having doubts, but that doesn't mean I wanted to stop seeing you," Gia told him.

"Do you still have doubts?"

"I worry about Kevin. You're the first man in his life since his father. If we don't work out, he'll be hurt. I should have taken it slower. But this is new to me just as it is to you. I suppose I saw how happy you made Kevin and just didn't think things through."

"We're both learning. We'll make mistakes. I have eight months left. I'd like to think we can try to make it until then. I'm willing to try if you are. Gia, you woke something inside me that I had pushed far down. I built a wall with concertina wire and grenades and . . . well, you get the idea. That first time I saw you was like a SEAL team came in and blew apart that wall. Thirty years of emotions came to the surface, and I'm . . . falling for you. I want to try and make this work." He moved in and kissed her.

"That's a . . . good start," she said quietly. "I made dinner. One of my grandmother's recipes."

"I'm looking forward to it." He smiled.

* * * *

"Oh my God, will you leave me alone?" Nick said to Sam.

"No. Tell me what happened," Sam said.

"Why?"

"Just tell me and I'll go. I have to go give Andrew a quickie in his office," Sam said.

"You are unbelievable. I sent her flowers, and she invited me over for dinner last night."

"And . . .?" Sam wanted more.

"That's classified." He smirked.

"Well done. See, that wasn't so hard. Now I can go and mess with Andrew. Bye." She left, smiling. "See you later, sweetheart," she called back.

"Oh my god. She's been hit on the head too many times," Nick said as she left. "I need a Barrett alert."

Kimberly A. Biggerstaff © 2024

* * * *

Nick was sitting on the couch with Gia. She was nervous and her hands were sweaty.

"I'm sorry, you're what?" Nick said. He swallowed. He heard her but needed her to say it again.

"I'm . . . pregnant," she said.

He didn't know what to say. "But I always . . . we used . . ." He swallowed and stood up. A thousand things began racing through his mind. They had been seeing each other for four months. He had five more months left. They had been careful and used protection. But, of course, nothing is foolproof.

"Nick." Gia watched him pace.

"Just . . . give me a minute please." Then he saw it. He went over to the table and opened the book and took out the bookmark. He dog-eared the page and undid the small ribbon attached to the bookmark. He walked back over to Gia and kneeled on one knee. Taking her left hand, he took the ribbon and tied it loosely around her ring finger. "I would have done this differently in the future, but, Gia, I love you. I love Kevin. And I will love our baby. Will you marry me?"

She looked at her finger. "That is the sweetest thing—"

"You're turning me down?" he suddenly said.

"What? Would you let me finish? That is the sweetest thing you could have done. Kevin and I love you too. I'd be proud to marry you." She smiled and they kissed.

"I'm going to be a father." He took a deep breath. "Pack a suitcase. For you and Kevin. Uh. A couple of days."

"What do you mean pack a suitcase?" she said.

"We're going to Vegas to get married. Right now," Nick announced.

"Nick. No. We can't just—"

"Why not?" Nick said. "You said yes. We don't have to tell anyone. Well, I need to tell the White House, the SECDEF (Secretary of Defense), and my Deputy I'll be out of pocket for a few days, but no one else needs to know why. Everything can be the same here. Once I retire, it won't matter. Please. I want Kevin to be my best man. Do you feel okay? I don't want my baby born out of—I want it to have my name. That's why you've been sick?" he rambled.

"How did you get to be Commandant of the Corps? You're a wreck," Gia said.

"We can go?"

"Yes, I'll start packing." She relented. "I'm glad it's Friday night," she said.

"I'm going to make a call to see about getting us there faster." He pressed the number.

"Hello?" Sam said.

Kimberly A. Biggerstaff © 2024

"I need a favor."

"You are knee-deep in favors," Sam told him.

"I wouldn't ask if it weren't important. You have a plane, right? Is it available right now?"

"Why do you need my plane and where are you going?" Sam was suspicious.

He knew he could trust her but still hesitated.

"Nick. My pilot needs to file a flight plan, and he'll tell me."

"Las Vegas," he said.

"Vegas. Seems sudden. Friday afternoon. Unexpected trip to Vegas for the weekend. Either you're being spontaneous, which I doubt, or . . . you knocked her up. Now you're pulling a Lex and running off to marry her. You knocked her up, didn't you?"

Nick sighed. "Yes."

"I told you to use protection, young man," she teased.

"We did. You should know that shit happens."

"Got some strong swimmers, Marine. Congratulations. Or were you using the same condoms from high school?" She teased him. "Yes, you can use my plane. I'll call Frank, my pilot."

"Um, hold on," Nick said.

Sam could hear them talking in the background.

"Gia wants to ask you something," Nick said.

Kimberly A. Biggerstaff © 2024

"Sam, come with us and be my maid of honor."

"What? No," Sam said.

"You can fly now, right?" Gia was concerned because of the operation Sam had a while ago.

"Yes, but you don't want me. . . ," Sam began.

"Sam. Nick told me how you kicked him in the ass when he tried to break up with me. Please. I'd like you to stand beside me."

"Okay. Tell Nick I'll take care of everything. But he owes me. I'm charging him for the fuel." She smiled. "I'll call you back."

"What's going on?" Andrew asked Sam.

"I have to go to Vegas for the weekend."

"Why? Can I come?" he asked.

"Not this time." Then she saw the disappointed look on his face. "Do you want to go to Vegas?"

"Yeah, I want the John Burke experience—the wig and everything."

Sam smiled at him. "The little black dress?"

"Yeah," he said, pulling her over and kissing her.

"Dad. Mom. Jeesh." Luke got up from the table and left.

"Does he have a swim meet tomorrow?" Sam asked.

"No."

Sam smiled. "Let me see if it's okay." She called Frank and let him know and then called Nick.

"I'm bringing a boy toy to play with," Sam told Nick.

"What?" Nick asked.

"I'm bringing Andrew. I didn't tell him anything."

"It's your plane. Okay," Nick said.

Sam gave him the details of where to meet them at the airport and hung up. "Okay, boy toy, go pack a bag."

"Awesome!" Andrew kissed her and ran off like a kid.

"Where is that wig?" Sam wondered.

Sam made reservations and then began to pack. She found the wig at her house in the closet. The little black dress was already at Andrew's. They took the kids over to Michael's and told him they were going to Vegas.

"You're not getting married, are you?" he asked.

"No. I'm not marrying any of you," Sam told him.

"Don't let her drink too much," Michael told him.

"Hey, I know the deal," Andrew said defensively.

"Don't get her drunk and try and marry her."

"I'm not getting married," Sam said again as they left.

* * * *

"Where are we staying?" Nick asked. He let all the appropriate people at work and in the chain of command know he would be gone for the weekend. His security was not happy, but they made accommodations.

Kimberly A. Biggerstaff © 2024

"How many times do I have to tell you? I took care of it. You'll have your privacy," Sam told him.

"Is this your plane?" Kevin asked.

"Yes. Come on, I'll introduce you to the pilot, Frank."

Sam took him up front to the cockpit. Andrew finally said something to Nick. He'd been wondering and decided to ask.

"What's the deal? Are you eloping?" he asked him.

"It's a classified mission," Nick told him.

"Fine. It's not like I work for the CIA or anything."

"Don't you make maps?" Nick said.

"Yes. But I went to FLETC (Federal Law Enforcement Training Center) in Georgia. Went on some missions. See this scar." He pulled his shirt up and showed them. "Got stabbed on an assignment by an IRA terrorist."

"Bullshit," Nick said, teasing him.

"It was at an Embassy party. A guy Sam pissed off wanted to hurt her, but she was on bedrest with Jess. I went and translated for Katrina. The guy had the terrorist stab me since Sam wasn't there. Almost died."

"Stabbed because of Sam. That I believe. Was that the terrorist she took down later in Ireland?" Nick asked.

"Yes."

"Mommy, look. I'm a pilot. I have wings," Kevin said, showing her.

"That's great, Kevin. Uh oh," Gia suddenly said, getting nauseous. Sam grabbed a puke bag and handed it to her.

"Eww. Mommy, are you sick?" Kevin asked her.

"No, I'm not sick."

"That is awesome. I love it," Sam said.

"What's wrong with you?" Nick said.

"I was always sick with every one of—" Sam stopped.

"I knew it," Andrew said laughing.

"Mommy, you puked," Kevin said.

"Oh, don't say puke," Sam said, going to sit as far away as possible.

"Andrew, could you give us a minute, please?" Gia said when she was able.

"Oh, yeah." He went back to sit with Sam.

"Kevin, come here." Gia explained to Kevin what was going on. She told him why they were taking a trip and why she was sick. She wasn't sure how he'd take it. But he was happy.

"Sam. guess what?" Kevin said, running up to her.

"What?"

"Mommy and Nick are getting married, and I'm going to be a big brother!"

"That's awesome. You'll be a great big brother. You have to protect your little brother or sister. That will be your job. And help your mom and Nick by listening and following directions."

"I'm a good marine," Kevin said. "Semper Fi!"

"Fly Fight Win!" Sam told him.

"What's that?"

"The Air Force motto. The Marines say Semper Fi. The Air Force says Fly, Fight, Win."

"Oh. Cool," Kevin said.

* * * *

"WOW! This is Awesome!" Andrew said. "Kevin, look, there's a pool and a pool table."

"It's like having another kid," Sam said.

"Can we go swimming?" Kevin asked.

"Wait. We're not staying here," Nick said.

"Yes, you are. You want the round bed or the regular?" Sam asked.

"No." Nick was adamant.

"Fine, we'll take the—" Sam began.

"We'll take the round one," Gia said. "Just go with it, please, Nick."

"Okay, for you," Nick said, relenting.

"Sam, who's that man?" Kevin asked.

"Our butler. He'll get us anything we want or answer any questions for us."

"We have a butler?" Andrew said. "Oh, this is AWESOME!"

"I want to swim. Andrew, will you swim with me?" Kevin asked.

"Uh, yeah."

"He needs a suit and a vest or water wings," Gia said. "I didn't bring swim stuff."

"Andrew, take Kevin and get him whatever he needs," Sam said. "Nick, I need to talk to Gia."

"Okay," he said.

Sam stopped him as he walked by. "Do you have a ring?"

"No. I was going to do that."

"Robert!" Sam yelled.

"Ma'am?" The butler appeared.

"He needs to buy a wedding ring. Will you give him some recommendations?"

"No problem, ma'am."

"Did you bring a suit?" Sam asked.

"Yes. One of the tailored ones."

"What about Kevin?"

"Oh, uh, I don't know," Nick said.

"I'll ask Gia."

"Okay, go on. We have planning to do." Sam went over to Gia as Nick, Andrew and Kevin left. "Okay Gia.

Kimberly A. Biggerstaff © 2024

What do you want? What kind of wedding? Gia?" Sam saw her sitting on the couch, crying. "Hey, what's wrong?"

"This is all too fast."

"Gia. Do you love him?" Sam asked.

"Yes."

"Then it's fine. Jonathan and Jess were both accidents. Oh, Marie was too. Wow, all the kids I gave birth to were accidents."

Gia laughed. "You're a good friend, Sam."

"Don't spread that around. I have a reputation to uphold."

"Barrett the Beast?" Gia asked.

"Yeah. How did you hear?"

"It was a security guard."

"Ha. I got arrested once at the Pentagon," Sam said, almost proud of it.

"You did?"

"Remind me. I'll tell you that story later. Do you have a dress, or would you like to go shopping?"

"I have one, but maybe we could go shopping. I need to get Kevin a suit. And I need a ring for Nick."

"Okay." Sam wrote it down. "Kevin's suit. Ring. Dress. Okay, now let me show you what I—no. Let's go shopping."

"It's late," Gia said.

"This is Vegas. They're open late. Come on. Robert!"

"Yes, ma'am." Robert appeared.

"We need to go shopping for dresses. Elegant dresses. Evening gowns or possibly wedding dresses."

"I know a place, ma'am."

"Do you want Nick in a suit or tux?" Sam asked Gia.

"Black Tux. The kind with a tie."

"Yeah, I like those too." Sam called Nick.

"What? Is she okay?" Nick asked.

"Typical expectant father. She's fine. You need a black tux. One with a tie."

"What about the suit?"

"This is her wedding; she gets what she wants. You do the honeymoon. A real one later." Sam hung up.

"Sam! Are you here?" Andrew yelled.

"Yes. What?"

"Kevin and I got what he needed," Andrew said and then just stood there.

"Okay, good. What?"

"I didn't know if you had other orders for me," he said.

"He needs a tux, but we can do that in the morning. Take him swimming. Then later, you can go gambling if you want."

"I can?" he said, making sure.

Kimberly A. Biggerstaff © 2024

"Yes. I'll give you the same amount I gave John."

He looked at her.

"Fifteen."

"Fifteen hundred?"

She laughed. "You'll lose that in ten minutes. No, fifteen thousand."

"Are you serious?" Andrew asked her.

"Yes."

"AWESOME! Kevin, get your suit on and wings!" Andrew yelled. Sam shook her head. Andrew kissed her. "You're the best."

"Robert!" Sam called.

"Ma'am."

"Make sure they eat something, please."

"Yes, ma'am. And here's the list of dress shops," he said.

"Oh, yeah, I know where this is. Thank you. Gia, ready to go?"

"Yes."

They went to the dress shop, and Gia found what she wanted. Sam picked out a new dress as well.

"Hello?" Gia said, answering her phone.

"I need your ring size."

"Six. What's yours?"

"Nine. You want me to get a black tux with a tie?"

Kimberly A. Biggerstaff © 2024

"Yes, please."

"Anything else?" Nick asked.

"Do you know where we're going to do this?" Gia asked him.

"Uh, not yet. What do you want? You need to tell me. Elvis? The Little White Chapel? That's where . . . somebody famous got married. But Sam said—"

"Gia, I'll help you find a place," Sam said.

"Never mind. We'll find a venue," Gia told him.

"Are you sure? Anything else?" Nick asked.

"No. It's fine."

"You know Sam's going to ask you what you want and then ask Robert," Nick said.

"So? She's my maid of honor. She's supposed to help me."

Sam grabbed the phone. "You better pick out a really nice ring, Nick." Then she hung up.

"Crap," Nick said.

"Sir?"

"Size six, but I'm not sure now. Maybe a bigger diamond," he said.

"Yes, sir." The salesman showed him more rings.

* * * *

"Wow, you look handsome," Sam said.

"I do?" Kevin said.

"You look great. Perfect for the best man."

"Mommy?" Kevin looked at Gia.

"You look . . . like your daddy when we got married. I love you, Kevin," Gia said, smiling at him.

"Mommy." Kevin got all embarrassed.

They went back to the hotel suite to get ready after they got everything they needed.

* * * *

Sam texted Andrew the address. Nick said he could come to the wedding. So Andrew, Nick and Kevin arrived at the venue thirty minutes before the time Sam told them.

"Are they here?" Nick asked Andrew.

"Yes. Do you have the marriage certificate?" Andrew asked.

"Yes. Kevin, do have the ring?" Nick asked him.

"Yes, sir." He saluted.

"Good work, Marine."

"Sir are you ready?" a woman asked.

"Yes."

Sam came down the aisle after the music started. Andrew smiled at her. Nick smiled as Gia walked slowly down the aisle.

"Wow. You look . . . you are the most beautiful woman I've ever seen," Nick said when she arrived next to him.

"You clean up good yourself," Gia said.

"Andrew. Close your mouth," Sam whispered.

"I was . . . she . . . I mean, you both look . . ."

"Stop talking," Sam said.

"Yes, ma'am."

* * * *

"Are we married now?" Kevin asked.

"Yes, we are, son," Nick said after they finished all the pictures.

"Congratulations to both of you," Sam said.

"Congratulations," Andrew said.

"What happens now?" Kevin asked.

"Uh, we'll go back and change and go find something to do. Your mom and Nick need some time alone."

Nick's security drove them back to the hotel, and Sam, Kevin and Andrew changed into their swimsuits. They went down to the cabana that came with the suite, and Andrew hopped into the pool with Kevin. Sam watched them from the cabana.

"Andy!" a man yelled.

Andrew looked. "Ron? Oh my gosh, Ron! Stay there on the steps, Kevin." Andrew got out and went over to Ron and shook his hand.

"Bullshit." Ron pulled him in close and hugged him. "I can't believe this. How are you?"

"Great. How are you? Everything going okay with the family?" Andrew asked.

"Yeah, well, I did what I had to," Ron told him.

"Well, you're not in jail and you're alive. That's something. Are you happy?" Andrew asked.

"Yeah. I moved to California and met a girl. You?"

Andrew looked over at the cabana. Sam waved. "Remember her?"

"Is that . . . ? No way."

"Yeah, we have a daughter and a son."

"No way. What happened to the blonde? Wasn't she her wife?"

"Yeah. Well, that's a long story, and her wife passed away a few years ago."

"Andrew!" Kevin called.

"Is that your son?" Ron asked.

"No. Our kids are at home. He's a friend's son. We came out to witness her wedding." Andrew waved at Kevin.

"Oh." Ron looked at Sam in the cabana. "Man, she still looks hot. Kept her figure after all these years."

"Hey. Knock it off."

"Sorry. Just looking. I can talk a good game, but I found the one for me. Over there." He looked at a woman sunbathing on a lounge chair.

"Nice. I'm happy for you, Ron."

Kimberly A. Biggerstaff © 2024

"Ron!" she yelled.

"Got to go, bud. It was great seeing you. Take care."
They hugged and Andrew got back into the pool with Kevin.

"Was that a friend?" Kevin asked.

"Yes, a very old friend," Andrew said.

"Andrew, doesn't Sam swim?"

"Sometimes. She got hurt in the war a long time ago.
She has scars and is shy about showing them."

"Oh. Was she on a plane?"

"No. Um. Maybe you should ask Sam or your mom to
tell you what happened." He picked Kevin up and tossed him
in the water. That was enough to distract him.

After a while, Andrew told him it was time for a
break. They got out and drank some water. "That was your
friend from Hawaii, wasn't it?" Sam asked.

"Yeah. Ron."

Sam didn't say anything. Andrew sat on her lounge
chair and leaned forward and gave her a kiss. "He said you're
still hot," Andrew whispered to her.

"Do you think I care what he thinks?"

"No. But it's nice to hear, isn't it?"

Kevin giggled as they kissed. "Sam, will you swim
with us?"

"Not here, Kevin. But maybe upstairs or at my villa
sometime."

They stayed at the pool until it was time for dinner. Sam texted Nick just to let him know they were coming up to change for dinner.

* * * *

"I love you, Nick," Gia told him. She smiled and kissed him. "But we may have a problem."

"What's wrong? Are you alright?" He started to think the worst.

"No, no. I didn't mean to worry you. I'm talking about Kevin. He might tell someone at daycare that he's going to be a big brother. Or worse, that we got married. You know how word gets around."

"I guess we should talk to him. Tell him it's a secret for now. Classified top secret. No one can know," Nick said. Unless you'd rather talk to him yourself."

"We're a family. He's your stepson now. We'll talk to him together," Gia said.

"Okay. Do you want to stay here in bed or get dinner? Or room service?" He ran his hand along her arm and over to her flat stomach. He smiled and kissed it. "My baby is in there."

"Yes and she's making me sick," Gia told him.

"Did you get morning sickness with Kevin?"

"A little. Hopefully, this won't last long or be too bad. It'll be difficult to hide at work."

Kimberly A. Biggerstaff © 2024

"Yeah, talk to Barb about that." Then he realized he had run off without telling her. "Oh boy, she's going to be mad at me."

"Because we did this?"

"Yes and that I got you pregnant," Nick said.

"Let's get dressed and have dinner with Sam, Andrew, and Kevin. I'll get ready and you can call her."

"No, I'll tell her in person. When we get back. I'll let Sam know we'd like to join them." He texted Sam and let her know.

"Nick?" Gia said.

"Yes?"

"The ring is beautiful. Thank you."

"We'll have to take them off when we go to work," he reminded her.

"I know. I'm going to wear it on a necklace under my uniform."

"Got it all figured out, have you?"

"Hardly." She laughed.

* * * *

They all had dinner together at Scotch 80 Prime. Sam was going to pay, but Nick insisted.

"Consider it the reception," Nick told her. "Or payback for the favors."

"No. I get to choose the payback," Sam told him.

Kimberly A. Biggerstaff © 2024

"I'm going to the casino," Andrew said. "Care to join me? I could use some luck."

"How much do you have left?" Sam asked.

"Just come with me. I need some help with some of the games. Wear the wig," he whispered.

Sam smiled. Then she looked at Gia.

"Go ahead. We've got Kevin. Thank you for watching him today," Gia said.

"Can I go swimming again, Mommy?" Kevin asked.

"Sure."

"We don't have suits," Nick said.

"I guess we'll have to get some in that little shop. Or we can just watch him and then go swimming after he goes to bed. Without suits," she whispered.

Nick smiled at her. "I like the way you think."

Chapter 13

On Monday, Nick went to Barb's office. "I'd like to take you to lunch today."

"That would be nice. Yes."

So Nick came back to her office at lunchtime, and they went to a restaurant off base. When they were almost finished, Nick finally told her.

"Barb, Gia and I . . ." But he had a difficult time finding the words.

"What is it? You've been wanting to say something this whole time. Just tell me."

He reached into his pocket and set his wedding ring on the table. "We went to Las Vegas and were married on Saturday."

Barb stared at the ring. "Crowded restaurant so I don't make a scene?"

"Please, Barb. I . . . love her, and I'm . . . going to be a father," he said in a low voice.

Barb stood and left. Nick knew she needed time. Then he thought he should warn Sam. Barb would tell John, and they would both be upset with Sam when they found out her involvement. He left a message on her voicemail.

"Did you know?" Barb asked Sam on Wednesday.

"He asked to use my plane. I let him. Andrew and I went along for our own fun," Sam told her.

"I suggest you leave," Barb said, going back to the papers on her desk.

"Don't you want him to be happy?" Sam asked her.

"Please leave," she said again.

Sam went to the door and opened it. "You're going to be a cousin," Sam said.

Barb picked up her stapler and threw it at the door just as Sam closed it.

"Jackson, she's mad at me. So . . . well, I wanted to warn you," Sam told the Captain.

"Yes, ma'am. Thank you," Jackson said.

* * * *

A week later, Gia was walking to the door of the Pentagon she always came through, and her heel caught in a broken piece of cement. She stumbled and grabbed her ankle.

"Are you all right, Gunny?" someone said, coming to her side.

"Uh, no. I twisted my ankle," Gia told him.

"Let me help you," the petty officer said. He helped her inside and asked the security guard to get a medic. Someone from the hospital came down with a wheelchair and took her down there. It was a bad sprain, and she stretched some ligaments and tendons. They gave her crutches and told her to stay off the ankle. She would have called Barb, but she was still mad. She certainly couldn't call Nick. She called her supervisor and let him know.

"Gunny, you can't drive like that. It's not safe. Do you have someone you can call?" a nurse asked her.

"I'll get a cab or something. Thank you." Gia took a cab to Kevin's daycare and picked him up early. But when she got there, Sam was visiting Barb and John's twins. She was on the list and sometimes went to help feed them. She saw Gia and went to her.

"What happened? Are you okay? The—"

"I'm okay. It's just a bad sprain. I won't be wearing heels for a while," Gia said.

"How'd you get here?" Sam asked her.

"Cab."

"You could have called me. Does . . . Mr. X know?" Sam whispered.

"No. I wasn't sure how to let him know," Gia said.

"I'll call him if you want. Let me take you and Kevin home. I have an idea I want to discuss with you two anyway."

Sam paid the cab driver and sent him away. Her driver took them to Gia's. Sam helped her get inside and made her sit down and elevate her leg.

"I've sprained and broken this ankle a few times. Just do what I say and what they told you. Stay off it as much as possible."

"Sam, they took an X-ray. I had to tell them I'm pregnant."

"Well, that will go nicely with my plan."

* * * *

"Honey, are you okay? The baby?" Nick asked when he arrived at her apartment. She told him what happened.

"We're fine."

Sam began to tell them her plan. "She's going to need a driver. You can't do it. I want to hire an actor to pretend to be your boyfriend. He can drive you and make appearances to distract and foil any rumors."

"What? No," Nick said. "Where's Kevin?"

"In his room, playing. Nick, maybe it's worth a try. Just for a month or so," Gia said.

Nick sighed. "Why are you doing all this?" he said to Sam.

"It keeps me out of trouble."

"Barb still mad at you?" Nick asked her.

"What do you think? Of course she is," Sam admitted.

"John?" Nick wanted to know.

"It doesn't matter to him. He's happy for you two, but he has to be on her side. I get that. It's fine."

Kimberly A. Biggerstaff © 2024

"An actor, huh?" Nick said.

"Yeah. Maybe an unknown from New York."

"I don't want him touching her," Nick said.

"He may have to, just a little, to make it believable. I'll try to find a gay guy. Will that work?"

"Yes. I don't want him falling in love with her," Nick said.

Gia smiled. "Nick, I love you."

"You, I trust. It's other men," he said.

Sam sighed and said, "She is so out of your league."

Nick gave Sam a look that told her to stop talking.

* * * *

"Uh, Gunny, do you have a minute?"

"Yes, Senior Chief."

It was a few days later, and Gia was back at work. She was still on crutches, although Sam found her knee scooter and lent it to her. It made it easier to get around.

"Chief?" Gia said again from her desk.

"Uhm, let's drop the rank for one minute. It's Jim. May I call you Gia?"

"Yes."

"Gia, may I take you to dinner sometime? Or maybe lunch?"

Gia smiled and touched the ring hidden under her uniform shirt. "Thank you, Jim. But I can't. I'm . . . involved with someone."

"Oh . . . uh, I didn't know. Okay," Jim said, going back to his desk.

"Thank you for asking though."

"I've been wanting to ask for months. I finally got the guts. But if you're seeing someone, that's okay. You really are, right? I mean, I can take it if . . ."

"Yes. I really am. Thank you again," she said, smiling at him.

"Good luck, Gunny," he said.

Gia smiled and scooted away to deliver some paperwork. Sam was right and this had better work.

Sam had contacted Michael's father, a director in California, and found a guy. She met with him and double-checked her two requests. She asked Marie to come meet him and to pour on the charm and flirt with him. Marie reluctantly agreed, and Sam was satisfied that he probably wouldn't fall for Gia. She spoke to him in Italian. That was her second request. He had to be fluent in Italian.

That afternoon, Sam called Gia and told her Antonio was waiting. He was perfect. Good-looking, tall, dark and handsome. And Italian. Sam wanted him to speak only

Italian, so he did so. It was the end of the day, so Gia gathered her things to leave.

"May I help you, Gia?" Jim asked.

"I . . . yes, thank you," she said. He took her backpack and carried it for her. They walked (she scooted/rolled) to the door and saw a man, Antonio, waiting there. He smiled and waved. She waved back. Sam had texted her a picture of Antonio so she would know what he looked like.

"Jim, this is Antonio."

Antonio gave her a peck on the cheek and said hello. Gia said in Italian, "Antonio, this is Jim. He works with me."

"*Buongiorno*," Antonio said.

"He only speaks Italian. He just returned from out of state," Gia told Jim.

"I see. Well, here you are. I'll leave you to it. Take care." He handed Antonio the backpack. Antonio smiled and said thank you in Italian.

* * * *

"So? How did it go?" Sam asked, calling later on.

"Fine. Tony picked me up and we got Kevin, and he brought us home and left."

"Good. Anyone see you? Anyone that matters?"

"A Senior CPO in my office carried my pack for me. It was perfect," Gia told her.

"Great, are you still having morning sickness?"

Kimberly A. Biggerstaff © 2024

"Yes. I'm sure the rumors will be flying tomorrow," Gia said.

"Is Nick home?" Sam asked.

"He just walked in," Gia said, smiling at Nick.

"Take care and call me if you need anything."

"Thank you, Sam," she said, hanging up.

"Nick!" Kevin yelled. He ran over to him.

"How was your day, Marine?"

"Outstanding, sir." He saluted him.

Nick saluted him back and then tussled his hair. "How's your mom?"

"Good. Nick, we need to get George more food. He's running low."

"Oh. Well, where do we go for that, and what does he need?" Nick asked.

"Crickets. The pet shop."

Nick cleared his throat. "Oh, okay. I'll ask your mom for directions and a list." Nick wasn't thrilled about getting crickets to feed George, but that was his job now. To take care of Gia, Kevin, and even George.

"Hey, sweetie. How are you feeling?" Nick kissed her.

"Just a little tired."

"Kevin and I need to resupply George's food. Can you write down the details for me?"

"Yes."

"You know, you could move in with me. My place is bigger," Nick suggested.

"What, the Commandant's House? I don't think so."

"The other house. The one I own," he said.

"Not yet. Let's wait a little while."

"I guess you're right," Nick said. "The stairs might be tough for you right now, anyway."

* * * *

For the next few weeks, things went well. Gia's ankle healed and she was walking fine.

"Major Harris, ma'am. How can I help you?" Gia asked, standing. She was surprised Barb had come to her office.

"Lunch?" Barb asked.

"Yes, ma'am. I'd like that," Gia said.

"I don't have time to go off base. Do you mind if we eat here?" Barb said.

"No, ma'am," Gia said. They walked down to the food court.

"How's your ankle?" Barb asked.

"Better, thank you. Sam lent me her scooter until I could put weight on it. I'm still rehabbing it. I won't be running the Marine Corps Marathon this year." Gia smiled.

"You ran the Marathon?"

Kimberly A. Biggerstaff © 2024

"No. I'm kidding. I did a half-marathon a few years ago before Kevin was born."

"Oh." Barb sat down at a table with her salad and Gia did too. "I'm sorry for the way I've been acting. I just didn't expect any of it." They kept their voices low.

"I didn't either. We didn't plan on the baby. We were careful, Barb. And Nick proposed as soon as I told him. Four months to go and he can retire."

"I heard a rumor you have an Italian boyfriend," Barb told her.

"That was Sam's idea. Please don't be upset with her. She's only trying to help," Gia said.

"I know. I've forgiven her. I'm just making her sweat a little. She's handling it better than I thought." Barb half smiled.

"Major, I don't know how to convince you that I love him."

"I know you love him. And I know he loves you. I see it every time I look in his eyes. I guess I've been the apple of his eye for so long that I may have gotten a little jealous. I'm sorry. He's been there for me when my parents couldn't. He's my uncle and I love him. I'm sorry, Gia, and I hope we can be friends."

"I'd like that. You're my niece now and Kevin's cousin." She smiled.

Kimberly A. Biggerstaff © 2024

"I've never had cousins. Although I think Kevin and the twins will play together more than us."

"And hopefully this little one." Gia patted low on her belly.

Barb smiled at her and squeezed her hand. "I'm here if you need anything . . . Aunt Gia."

* * * *

At four months, Gia had a small bump. "Are you sure there's a baby in there?"

"You've been to my appointments, and you know there is."

"Yeah, sneaking into the doctor's office like I'm a junk yard dog who knocked up the neighbor's prized dog."

"Nick, one month to go and you'll retire, and we can stop hiding."

"Yeah. One more month. Twenty-nine days, actually." But Nick was worried. The President had been increasing troops overseas in the mid-east. Especially the area around Israel. This president was the first to have Jewish ties. He understood how it would look but kept assuring the people of the nation that it was the right thing to do. The people loved him. He had a way of talking to the public on everyone's level. He got his hands dirty with the troops when he was an officer in the Air Force. He had been with Air Force Special Operations and worked with Delta Force, the Green Berets and the SEALs. He was retired after losing his right arm on a mission. He was elected senator and then ran for president. It wasn't even close. He brought the country together and instilled a sense of patriotism in America's youth.

But Nick felt war coming. If that happened, they would freeze retirements, even his. In wartime, he could be extended as a member of the Joint Chiefs.

"Gia, you know what's happening in the world. You know our position and can guess what's coming."

"No. Don't say that. Please." Gia was hoping time would pass and it wouldn't affect Nick's retirement.

"Gia, it'll be all right," Nick said, trying to reassure her.

"You're trying to make me feel better."

"Yes, I am. That's one of my many jobs." Nick smiled.

There was a knock on the bedroom door. "Nick," Kevin said, crying.

Nick got up and answered the door. "What happened, buddy?"

"I had . . . a bad . . . dream," he cried.

"Oh, come here." He picked him up and hugged him. "Do we need to recon for monsters?" he asked. Kevin nodded. "Okay, let's go. I'll take point. Watch my six." He put Kevin down, and they got down and crawled to Kevin's room. Nick checked around the corner and into the room. Then he looked back at Kevin and gave him a sign. Nick went in and cleared the room. A minute later, he came out. "All clear, Marine."

"Did you check the closet?" Kevin asked.

"Yes."

"Under the bed?"

"Yes," Nick told him.

"George's aquarium?" Kevin tried to think of any place a monster could hide.

"Yes. No monsters. No enemy."

"Thanks, Nick. You're the best." Kevin got in bed. "When can we move to your house?"

"I don't know. I want you to. Ask your mom." Nick pulled the sheet up and gave him a kiss on the forehead. "Sleep tight, Marine."

"Aye Aye, sir." Nick saluted him. Nick returned the salute. "Nick?" Kevin called as Nick was at his door. "You're the best stepdad ever."

"And you're the best stepson. Goodnight." He went back to the bedroom and crawled in next to Gia.

"All clear?"

"All clear," Nick said.

Gia kissed him. "You're the best."

"So I've been told."

Kimberly A. Biggerstaff © 2024

Gia playfully hit him on the arm and kissed him again. She moved on top of him and kissed him passionately. Nick moved her hair off her shoulder. "I am the luckiest guy in the world," he said, kissing her. "You are so out my league."

"Why does everyone say that?"

"It's true. You're so beautiful," he said.

"We'll see how you feel in a few more months when I'm big and fat."

"Well, I'll have to divorce you if you get too fat," he teased her.

She rolled off him.

"Hey, I was kidding. I will love you no matter what." He looked at her and moved his hand up her leg. He nuzzled her neck and began kissing it. But Gia didn't move. "Are you mad at me? I said I was kidding."

"So am I," she said, smiling and wrapping her arms around him.

* * * *

Nick had been working late for weeks. So when the President finally decided to send troops in, it came as no surprise. Everyone in the Joint Chiefs was in agreement.

"Mr. President, may I have a word, sir?" Nick asked after the meeting had ended. "Privately."

"Yes, of course, Nick."

Kimberly A. Biggerstaff © 2024

John gave him a good luck look. He knew what he was about to do.

"Sir, I have a problem."

"Have a seat, Nick. What's on your mind?" the President said.

"I've . . . been a good Marine. Obeyed the rules, followed orders."

"You wouldn't have become Commandant if you'd done otherwise."

Nick was having a hard time telling him what he'd prepared to say.

"Nick, would you like a drink? I understand you enjoy Redbreast or Macallum."

"Yes, sir." Nick chuckled. "You are a hell of a man, Mr. President. You do your research and can charm both men and women. You brought this country back from the brink of self-destruction."

The President smiled. "Don't flatter me, Nick. I'm just a man who loves this country and our freedoms. That means a man should be able to marry who he wants and not sneak around. Even a Marine."

"Your wife was a Marine. Wasn't she, Mr. President?"

"Nick, once a Marine, always a Marine."

"Semper Fi, sir."

"Fly, Fight, Win, Nick."

Nick just said what he needed to. "I fell in love with an enlisted gunnery sergeant. We're married and are having a baby in about four months. I was planning to retire."

"Nick, do you know how I got to where I am, besides a lot of luck?"

"No, sir."

"I've surrounded myself with the best people. I can read people, but sometimes I need help. It's not always easy. Do you understand what I'm saying?" the President asked him.

"Yes, sir," Nick said. The President had checked him out and already knew his situation.

"Nick, I need you. I'm your commander-in-chief, and I need the best for what we're about to do. You are one of the best."

"Sir. Fraternization is . . ."

"I understand why the rule exists and why it's necessary," the President told him. "Nick, if you stay, I will guarantee you will not be charged."

"My wife?"

"Neither of you," the President told him.

"Sir, it's becoming more difficult to hide. We're tired of it."

"Give me . . . six months. Please, Nick. I need the best."

"No offense, Mr. President, but I'm not sure you can."

"Nick, you have no idea what I can do. Six months and I will release you. I'm a man of my word, Nick."

Nick stood up and shook his hand. "Any other man, and I wouldn't believe it." He pulled him in close. "Six months. No longer, sir." Nick was satisfied until he had a thought. "Sir, may we make an amendment to our deal?"

"I'm nothing if not flexible. What do you want?"

"I'd like for you to go back and look at something. If you do that, I'll stay for . . . however long you need me."

"It must be important to you."

"Yes, Mr. President. It would mean a lot," Nick said.

"All right. You have a deal."

* * * *

"What happened, Nick?" John asked.

"I did what I had to."

"What does that mean?"

"He already knew and said he'd protect me." Nick turned and looked at John.

"He can't guarantee that," John said.

"I know. But for some reason, I believe him."

"And Gia?"

"She's going to have to understand." Nick sighed.

"Good luck," John told him.

* * * *

"Nick, I can't," Gia said.

"When this is over, we'll be free."

"This war will last for years. I'm tired of hiding," she said.

"So am I, but I trust him. I don't think it'll be that long. I will be there when you have this baby. I will cut his cord and kiss him on the forehead. Then I'll tell him how much I love him and you," Nick told her.

* * * *

For months, Nick worked long, hard hours, and it was taking a toll on him. Gia and Kevin noticed how tired he was. He became irritable and short-tempered.

One night, he called her. "I'm staying at my quarters on base tonight." He hung up.

The next day at work, Gia went to his office, but Nick wasn't there.

"Can I give him a message, Gunnery Sergeant?"

"No. Do you know where he is?"

"He went to grab a sandwich," his aide said.

"Thank you." She started to walk away and then turned to him and said, "You can tell him his pregnant wife will be waiting for him at her apartment tonight and he better come home."

Kimberly A. Biggerstaff © 2024

His aide stared at her. "Sure, Gunny, I'll tell him. Are you feeling all right?" He thought she was emotional because she was due any day. Her boyfriend must be out of town.

Gia turned and left. She went to the food court. It was crowded. She yelled, "Nick Foster! General Nicholas Foster!"

"Oh my god." He heard her yelling, and he walked over to her.

"Gunnery Sergeant, is there a problem?" he asked calmly.

"Yes, there is!" she yelled. "Nick Foster and I are married, and I'm having his baby."

"Gia, what the hell is wrong with you?" Nick said.

"Nothing. I love you." She kissed him. He dropped his sandwich and wrapped his arms around her, holding her and kissing her back.

"They're going to Court-Martial us," Nick said.

"I don't care," Gia told him, and they kissed again.

Everyone had stopped and stared at them. Barb was walking into the food court and then stopped and asked someone what was going on.

"The Gunny just announced that she and the General are married and the baby is his."

"Oh my god," Barb said. It was quiet. Then Barb started to clap. "Congratulations, General! Gunny!" Then, slowly, everyone began to clap.

Kimberly A. Biggerstaff © 2024

"Wow, that was like a scene from a movie," John said. "Good for them." He was in line, getting some food.

"I think we should go back to work," Nick said.

"Yeah. I don't think so. I think we might want to go to the hospital."

"What?"

"I've been in labor, and the contractions are close."

"What?"

"I'm having the baby right now!" she yelled.

"Oh crap!" Barb ran over to help. "Move it, General!"

"What?" Nick repeated.

"Get your wife to the hospital, Nick!" Barb ordered him.

"Oh, right, let's go." Nick woke up and helped her. "Oww! Dammit, Gunny, that's my hand."

"This is your fault!" Gia said.

Barb helped them and they got her to the hospital.

* * * *

"Congratulations. It's a girl," the doctor said.

"A girl." Nick smiled. They decided they wanted to be surprised as to the gender of the baby.

"Here, Dad, would you like to cut the cord?" the doctor asked.

"Definitely." Nick cut the cord, and the nurse took her to clean her up. "Wait." He kissed her on the forehead and said, "I love you." He went to Gia and kissed her. "I love you, honey. She's beautiful, just like you."

The nurse brought the baby to Gia and laid her on her chest. "Here you are, Mom."

"We have a daughter, Nick."

"We do." He couldn't stop smiling. "Sofia Francesca Foster. You'll be the first female Commandant of the Marine Corps."

"Let's get her to preschool first." Gia smiled.

Chapter 14

They finished the briefing, and everyone began to leave. "General Foster, please stay a moment," the President said.

"Yes, sir."

"How's your little girl, Nick?"

"Perfect, sir." Nick always lit up when he spoke about Sofia.

"And your wife?"

"Doing well."

"Very good. I'm happy for you. You've done a wonderful job for me, Nick."

But Nick thought this might be the calm before the storm. The good news that came before the rug was pulled out from under him. He swallowed the lump in his throat.

"I understand, sir. They're going to court-martial me."

"No. Nick, no. But I have heard some rumblings. You are well liked by your troops, so you have that in your favor. I just don't want to take any chances. Which is why, effective immediately, you are retired."

Nick smiled. "Sir, are you sure? I mean, we had a deal."

"Yes, I don't like to go back on my deals. I'm changing the terms. I said I'd protect you and your wife. I'm not sure I can. You've given too much of your life to the

Kimberly A. Biggerstaff © 2024

Corps and this country for something like this to ruin your career. You fell in love, Nick. You shouldn't be punished for that."

"I knew what I was doing, Mr. President. I'm willing to take my medicine."

"Nick, someone screwed up. Your original retirement paperwork went through. You've been retired all this time. And the extension paperwork seems to be missing," the President said.

"But sir . . ."

"However, I'd like to keep you on as a civilian advisor. I still need you, Nick," the President told him.

"For how long, sir?"

"Thought we had a deal. Until I say. And I'm looking into that other thing for you."

"Yes, sir. Thank you, sir. I'll stay for as long as you need as a civilian advisor."

"Congratulations, Retired General Foster."

"Thank you, sir." They shook hands. "I really appreciate this."

"Go home to your wife and children, Nick. I'll see you tomorrow morning, Mr. Foster."

"Thank you, Mr. President."

"Wear a suit, Nick," he said as Nick began to leave. "Oh, Nick." He tossed him a pin. "We'll have a proper ceremony later."

Nick caught the pin and looked at it. It was a Marine Corps Retired lapel pin. Nick smiled and left.

* * * *

Nick couldn't be happier. He drove to his house, the one he owned. Gia agreed to move in the previous month but had kept her apartment. When he arrived, Kevin came running and hugged him.

"Hi, Nick."

"Hello, Marine. Do you have a sit-rep (situation report) for me?"

"Yes, sir. Mom is napping. Sofia is good and Sam is eating."

"Good job, Marine," Nick told him.

"Hello, Nick," Sam said.

"Eating my food, Colonel?"

"Payment for helping with Kevin and Sofia," Sam said.

"Sam, Grace likes Cool Whip," Kevin said, letting her lick the Cool Whip from his bowl.

"Kevin don't feed the dog. She's a service dog, remember?" Nick told him.

"Sorry."

Kimberly A. Biggerstaff © 2024

"It's okay, Kevin. Just ask me next time," Sam told him.

"Did he eat something before the ice cream?" Nick asked.

"Yes. Barb sent a lasagna. I reheated it."

"Thanks for coming over and helping and for picking Kevin up."

"You're welcome. Well, I better go. My ride should be out there by now." She finished her bowl of ice cream, rinsed it, and put it in the dishwasher.

"See you and thanks," Nick said.

"Bye, Kevin," Sam said.

"Bye, Sam," Kevin said.

Nick went to the bedroom and kissed a sleeping Gia on the forehead. She stirred and opened her eyes. "Hi there."

"Hi. How are my girls?"

"Fine."

Nick looked over in the bassinet and saw Sofia. He smiled and put his finger down, and Sofia wrapped her hand around it.

"I have some good news," Nick said.

"Tell me."

Nick reached into his pocket, retrieved the pin and placed it in her hand.

"It seems my original retirement went through and no one knew. I've been a civilian all this time."

"Nick! That's wonderful!" She hugged him.

"But the President wants to keep me on as a civilian advisor."

"Oh. Well, that's okay. We won't have to worry about a court-martial, right?" Gia asked, relieved by his announcement.

"Well, I don't know why anyone would push it now."

"I guess we'll have to celebrate," Gia said. She reached her hand up and placed it behind his neck and pulled him close and kissed him. Then Sofia began to cry.

"Our daughter has other plans." Nick smiled.

Kimberly A. Biggerstaff © 2024

Chapter 15

Nick put on one of the tailored suits Sam bought him. Gia picked the shirt and the tie. "You look great," she said. "But one thing is missing." She placed the Marine Corps Retired lapel pin on his left lapel under an American flag pin he had already put on. "Have a great day, Mr. Foster." She gave him a kiss.

"Kevin!"

"Ready to go, sir." Kevin said. "Where's your uniform?"

"I'm retired now."

"Does that mean you aren't a general anymore?"

"No. I'm like . . . Sam. She's a retired colonel. I'm a retired general. You can still call me General."

"Oh, okay," Kevin said.

Nick dropped Kevin off at daycare and went to the Pentagon. He needed to clear out his office. There was a lot he needed to do now.

"General Foster, sir. I understand you've retired. It's been a pleasure working for you, sir," his aide told him. "If you need any help, let me know, sir."

"Thank you, Clark. You've done an excellent job for me. I guess I'll need some boxes," Nick said.

"Yes, sir. I've already been told you have an office in another part of the building. I'll have your things moved there."

"Oh, right, well . . . where is this office? Probably a broom closet somewhere."

His aide smiled. "I think you'll be pleased, sir." He handed him the office number.

"Well, this is . . ." Nick smiled when he realized the location.

"Sir, congratulations on your baby. What did you have?"

"A girl. Sofia Francesca Foster," Nick said, smiling wider. He took a picture out of his wallet and showed it to him.

"Aww. She's beautiful, sir. I have a four-year-old. Not looking forward to the teenage years," he said.

Nick said, "That's a little way off, but I get your point. Thank you, Clark. I'll grab a few things and head down to my new office."

John walked in and looked at Nick. "So, it's true. You retired."

"Thanks to the President, yes. But he's keeping me on as an advisor."

"Nice suit. Looks like one Sam would pick out," John told him as they walked into his office.

"Thanks. She did. She updated my wardrobe when I began dating Gia," Nick said, gathering some personal items.

"She has good taste in men's suits. Can I help?" John asked.

"Sure, grab those photos off the wall. You can walk with me down to my new office."

"They gave you an office here?" John was surprised.

"Yeah. I still need to figure out exactly what my role is."

As they were leaving, Nick said, "Don't be a stranger, Clark."

"Yes, sir. General." He snapped to attention as a sign of respect.

"Carry on, Clark," Nick said.

Barb was walking up the hallway and stopped in front of them. She saw the Retired pin on his lapel. "Why didn't you tell me?"

"It was sudden. The President told me yesterday at the end of the day."

"No ceremony? Just a pin and a goodbye?" Barb was disappointed.

"No, we can have an official ceremony later. As for goodbye, no. I'm an advisor to the President. Even got an office."

"How's Sofia and Gia?" Barb asked.

Kimberly A. Biggerstaff © 2024

"Great," he said, getting all mushy.

John smiled. "Four days old and she's got you wrapped around her finger." John looked at him. "Welcome to the club, Nick."

* * * *

"Nick, are you getting settled in?" the President said, stepping from behind his Secret Service Protection.

Nick automatically stood up. "Mr. President. Yes, sir."

"Take the morning and move into your office. This afternoon, I want you to sit in on a briefing with the Joint Chiefs. I'll have someone send you the details. You'll also need to get new credentials. Let me know if you have any problems or questions."

"Yes, sir. Thank you." Nick followed orders and went back to his old office. Clark had someone boxing up more of Nick's personal things. The Staff Sergeant helped him, and they took all of his things to his new office. It was smaller and Nick would have to take some things home. But he placed two photos on his desk. One was of him presenting Barb her Navy and Marine Corps Medal. The other was of him and Gia getting married. He'd been wanting to put that one out for months but couldn't. It didn't matter now. He phoned Gia.

"How are my girls?"

"Great. You caught me feeding her."

"I'm calling from my new office phone."

"They gave you an office?" Gia was surprised. "I thought you were just an advisor."

"I'm beginning to think it might be more. I don't know. Anyway, I just wanted to check in. I need another photo of Sofia. And Kevin."

"Decorating your office?"

"Yes. Hopefully, I'll be home at a decent hour."

"It's okay. Sam arrived about ten minutes ago."

"Doesn't she have her own kids to take care of?"

"Nick," Gia said.

"I know. I appreciate her coming and helping you. As soon as I can, I'll try and take some time off."

"We love you," Gia told him.

"I love you too. Bye."

Nick spent the next few weeks attending briefings and occasionally talking to the President. He had expected to be talking to the President more often than he was. But he kept quiet and wrote reports on his opinion about military operations, covert and overt, as requested by the President.

If Nick needed anything, he asked the Senior Chief Petty Officer (SCPO) in the office next door. One day he walked in, and the Senior Chief quickly closed a folder and stood up.

"Sir, may I help you?" Jim asked.

"Senior Chief . . . King, right?"

"Yes, sir," Jim said, wiping his brow.

"I realized I need some office supplies. Is there someone who can get me some staples, a stapler, paperclips and sticky notes?"

"Yes, sir. I'll get someone to get those for you. Pens too, sir?" Jim said.

"Yes, that'd be fine. Thank you, Senior Chief."

"Yes, sir. You're welcome, sir," Jim said.

Nick went back to his office and sat down. He thought about what he thought he saw. All he saw was Jim quickly closing a folder with a classified cover on it. Nick dismissed it, thinking he was being paranoid. Later on, a marine sergeant brought him the supplies he asked for.

* * * *

Gia had taken her twelve weeks and arrived back at work ready to go. It was difficult leaving Sofia, but she knew it had to be done.

"Morning, Gia. Welcome back." Jim said as she walked into the office.

"Morning, Jim. Thank you."

"How's your daughter?" he asked.

"Growing. It was hard to leave her this morning."

Kimberly A. Biggerstaff © 2024

"Yes, I remember my ex-wife saying the same thing about our kids," he told her.

"I didn't realize you have children."

"Two. A girl, ten, and a boy, eight. They live with their mother. Anyway, you have a lot of catching up to do," he said.

Although they were of the same rank, Gia technically outranked him by a few months. They had always gotten along, and other than when he asked her out, they didn't really have any personal interaction. Their professional relationship had always been fine. Jim was a Naval Intelligence Specialist, and occasionally they worked on the same projects.

"Is everything okay, Jim?" Gia sensed something different in him.

"Yes, fine. Well, maybe having the former Commandant right next door is making me a little nervous." He forced a smile.

"Next door?" Gia asked.

"Yes. Your husband's office is right over there. Didn't he tell you?" Jim was surprised.

"No, he didn't. I knew he had an office, but he didn't tell me where." She got up and went over and knocked.

"Enter," Nick said through the door.

"Mr. Foster." Gia smiled at him. "You didn't tell me you were right next door."

"Surprise," Nick said, smiling back.

"Nice office. Cozy."

"That means small. But I don't think many advisors get offices, so I guess I should consider myself lucky," he said. "Can we have lunch together?"

"Yes. Come get me," she said, leaving.

"Gia? Where are you going to . . . you know . . . pump?"

"The lady's room, probably."

"Okay."

"Why? Did you think I'd do it in my office?" Gia teased him.

"No, I don't know. See you at lunch," he said, a bit embarrassed he even asked the question.

Gia walked over and gave him a quick kiss. "Don't worry. My two ladies are only for you and Sofia," she whispered a bit seductively. Then she left.

"Wow. She is so out of my league. How did I get so lucky?" Nick asked himself.

He sat there for a minute and then went on about his day. At noon, he straightened his desk and went next door.

"Ready for lunch?" he asked.

"Yes. Just let me lock these files up." Gia went to the file cabinet and secured the material.

"I'll see you later, Jim," Gia said.

"Oh, yeah. Have a good lunch, sir, Gunny," Jim said.

"Off-base?" Nick asked her.

"Sure, that would be fine."

Nick drove them to a nearby restaurant, and they took a high-top table in order to speed up the process.

"How well do you know that Senior Chief?" Nick eventually asked Gia.

"Jim? Not that well. We've shared an office since I got here. But full disclosure, he did ask me out once."

"When?" Nick's jealousy popped up.

"After Sam got Tony over here. I turned him down of course." Gia smiled at him.

"I should hope so," Nick muttered in between bites of his chicken sandwich.

"What's wrong?" Gia noticed he seemed distracted.

"Nothing. I'm probably imagining it."

"Imagining what?"

"I'd rather not say anything until I can be sure. It has nothing to do with you. I promise," Nick told her.

"You know you can talk to me if something is bothering you, Nick."

"I know. And if I feel I need to, I will." He smiled at her. Changing the subject, he said, "This is nice. Having lunch together with no worries."

"Kevin said he wants to go to kindergarten with Finn and the other kids," Gia told Nick.

"He does? Where would that be?"

"Sam sends them to a private school. They all have gone there from Jonathan on down. Lex even sent his kids there. The Potomac Academy," she told him.

"How does Lex send four kids to private school? Or does Sam pay for it?"

"Nick," Gia said. "Ashley had a special scholarship. But yes, Lex eventually agreed to let Sam pay for what they couldn't."

"How do you know that?" Nick asked her.

"I spoke to Sam after Kevin told me. It's a very good school."

"I've heard. I've known officers and diplomats that have sent their kids there."

"So, can we consider it? Is it a question of the tuition because I still have some of Frank's life insurance."

"No. No, that's . . . you keep that. I can afford to send my son to a private school. But I would like to review everything about the school. Are you sure you want to send him to private school? The public school system is—"

"I'd like to consider it, Nick. Please. The classes are smaller, and he will already have friends."

"Finn is . . . an interesting boy. I'd like to know who his real mother is," Nick said quietly.

"What does that mean?"

"You can't believe Sam is their mother? She's . . . she's . . ."

"What? Too old?" Gia said.

"Well . . . yes," Nick admitted.

"She could have frozen her eggs. In fact, didn't she still have them when Emily was born?"

Nick was surprised that Gia knew as much as she did. They must have had some interesting conversations when Sam was helping with Sofia. "Well, then again . . . Sam is . . . interesting."

"Nick, I don't believe you. I thought you liked her."

Nick sighed. "Yeah, she's grown on me."

"You certainly have asked enough favors from her if you didn't like her. She's helped us out a lot, Nick."

"I know. I guess it's not her. It's that whole . . ."

"What?"

"All of them. That lifestyle. And Barb and John. It's . . . crazy."

"Are you sure you aren't jealous? We could ask her . . ."

"What! Absolutely not!" Nick got upset.

"I'm just kidding," Gia told him. "Despite her . . . lifestyle choices . . . you know she's a good person and will protect and defend her family and friends."

"Yes, I know. But aren't you curious about the triplets?"

"No. She already told me. They're going to tell Luke soon, and when the triplets are older, they'll tell them, too."

"Luke isn't hers either?"

"I didn't say that. Jess is the last one she had. She almost died giving birth to her."

"John told me what he had to do. Couldn't imagine doing that to you," Nick said, shaking his head.

"Yes, you would. I believe you'd do anything to save me, Sofia, Kevin, or any other babies that might come along."

"Other babies?" Nick looked at her.

"Just keeping the door open," Gia said, smiling.

"That's a discussion for another time."

"I agree. So if I get the information, we can consider sending Kevin to the academy?"

"Of course. I want the best for Kevin. For both of them," Nick said.

* * * *

"Colonel Barrett, I need to talk to you," Nick said on the phone.

"Why so formal, General Foster?" Sam asked him.

"It's important and not personal."

"I can come up to your office—" Sam began, but Nick quickly interrupted her.

"No. Don't come anywhere near my office or Gia's. Just . . . can you come to my house tonight about six?" Nick asked.

"Will Gia and the kids be there?"

"Of course they will. I need to run something by you based on your work experience."

"May I bring Finn?" Sam asked him.

"I suppose." Nick sighed.

"What's wrong with bringing Finn? Have you been talking to John? Finn is a good kid."

"I didn't say anything."

"Barb likes him. Kevin likes him."

"He's fine, Sam. Bring him. See you at six." He hung up. It was lunchtime, and Gia had to go over to Ft. Meade. Nick had made the call from his car. He went back inside, grabbed a sandwich and a drink and went to find Barb.

"Good afternoon, sir. How is civilian life treating you?" Jackson asked Nick.

"Not bad, Jackson. Takes some getting used to, but I'm doing all right."

"Your daughter?"

Kimberly A. Biggerstaff © 2024

Nick smiled. "I have some new pictures." He pulled out a piece of paper with pictures of Sofia on it in various positions. Since he couldn't have his phone there, he printed out photos to show.

"Aww, she's so cute," Archer said. "Sir," he added as an afterthought.

"Yes, she is," Nick said.

"Which reminds me, sir. Archer and I pitched in." He handed him a gift bag. "We thought it would be more appropriate if we waited until you retired. And we just haven't gotten a chance to bring this to you."

"Open it, sir." Archer was excited.

"Thank you." Nick took the gift bag and pulled out a onesie that said, 'My DADDY is a MARINE.' "Perfect gentlemen. I love it." There was a pink one that said, 'My MOMMY is a MARINE.' Nick laughed. "Gunny will love that." Then he pulled out a frame with the Marine Corps emblem.

"Those look familiar," Barb said. "Onesies and a picture frame."

"We do have one more thing, sir," Archer said. "I saw this recently online. It's from the Major and us." He handed him the bag.

"Wow! This is great!" It was a tactical diaper bag. They had loaded it with diapers, and it had a special place for

Kimberly A. Biggerstaff © 2024

wipes and an integrated changing pad. MOLLE straps to add stuff to it. It had two patches that said MOMMY and DADDY. "What's this?" Nick said, holding up what almost looked like a bulletproof vest.

"A tactical baby carrier," Jackson told him.

"Oh, this is too much. It must have—"

"Sir, consider it part of your retirement gift."

"Thank you, Jackson, Archer." He unexpectedly hugged them. "Thank you, Barb."

"You're welcome, sir. It was a pleasure serving in your Corps, General," Jackson said.

"Does John have one of these?" he asked Barb.

"No."

"Good. Don't get him one," Nick said. "I came to eat with you if you have time."

"Come on in." Barb walked back into her office.

"Thanks again, marines," Nick told them, taking everything into Barb's office until they got back and he could put them in his office.

"You've changed. For the good. It's nice to see you not so . . . rigid," Barb told him.

"Family changes you, doesn't it? How are the boys?"

"Good, you guys should come over one Saturday."

"Just let us know." Nick ate his lunch, and Barb updated him on the boys.

That evening, Nick let Gia know that Sam was coming over.

"May I ask why?"

"I need her opinion on something," Nick said. "Work-related . . . sort of."

"This thing you can't tell me about?" Gia asked.

"It's better for you if you don't. Plausible deniability," he said.

"I have a Top-Secret clearance, Nick."

"Trust me, please. It may be nothing. That's why I want to run it by Sam. Her experience may give me some insight."

Twenty minutes later, the doorbell rang. "She's punctual, I'll give her that," Nick said. "Hello," he said, opening the door.

"Hi, General," Finn said, saluting him. "This is for you." Finn handed him a six-pack of juice boxes. "Mommy said it's polite to bring something when you're going to someone's house."

"Thank you," Nick said.

"Finn!" Kevin yelled.

"Hi, Kevin."

"Want to feed George with me?" Kevin asked.

"Yeah! Cool!" They ran off upstairs to Kevin's room.

"This is for you," Sam said, handing him a bottle of Redbreast whiskey.

"Thanks. Look, I didn't mean anything by what I said. Finn is a fine boy."

"Actually, that's Alan. We fooled you."

"What?" He looked her in the eye. "No, it's not."

"No. But you thought about it for a second."

Finn, Alan, and Sky were the triplets. Born via surrogate for Michael and Sam. They used a donor for the eggs and expected two babies. Finn was a surprise because they had only seen Alan and Sky on the ultrasounds. Michael had never told Sam his mother was a twin. So it was a surprise that Alan and Finn were identical twins.

"Very funny."

"Hello, Sam," Gia said, carrying Sofia.

"Hi. Let me see my little friend," Sam said, looking at her. "Aww. I missed you."

Nick went and got two glasses and told her to join him in his study when she was done fawning over the baby.

"What's his deal?" Sam said.

"No idea. He won't tell me. I think he's trying to protect me," Gia said.

"Well, I guess I'll go find out," Sam said, giving Sofia back to Gia and heading to the study.

Nick handed her a glass of whisky and sat behind his desk.

"So, what's the problem?" Sam asked.

"I thought I saw something at work," he began.

"Can you be more specific?"

Nick sighed. "I think someone is stealing classified information."

Sam stared at him. "You're serious, aren't you?"

"I wouldn't kid about a thing like that. I'm talking about national security. We are at war, Sam."

"I know what's going on. I watch the news," Sam told him.

"The news?"

"And I hear things. I know people," she said. "Just tell me what you know."

Nick told her what he had seen. It had been twice now, and Jim was more than nervous anytime Nick came around.

"That's not much," Sam said.

"Which is why I wanted to run it by you and not the Feds," Nick said.

"Hmm. What does your gut tell you?" Sam asked.

"My gut?"

"Come on, Nick. You spent your life in the Corps. You saw war. You can't tell me in all that time you didn't trust your gut at times."

"Yes. I suppose you did, too," Nick added.

"Yeah, it helped me out on quite a few cases. And assignments."

"Mine is telling me I'm right."

"Well then, I guess we need to do some intelligence gathering." As Sam thought about the next steps, she watched Nick. "You're not telling me something."

"He works in Gia's office," Nick finally admitted.

"I see. So you **are** protecting her," Sam said.

"She wasn't even there when I started noticing. I don't want her involved."

"Okay. We'll start with the basics. Background check, finances, and stuff," Sam told him.

"How are we . . .?"

Sam gave him a look. "Don't ask questions. I still know people, and I'll keep this as quiet as I can."

"Thanks, Sam. I appreciate it."

"Anything else?"

"Uh, yeah, since you're here. It seems Kevin wants to go to that academy your kids attend when he starts school," Nick told her.

"I didn't say anything. Maybe Finn or someone else said something."

"I believe you. I just want to make sure about it."

"It's a good school. Small classes, more attention for the students. I can have them call you to set up a tour and answer any questions."

"You don't have to . . . oh, all right." Nick gave in because he told Gia he'd check into it.

"We sent Jonathan there because John wanted him to go. But the reasons back then are different than now. I've continued to send the kids there because they excel in that environment."

"Set up a tour for Gia and me."

"It doesn't hurt having a friend on the Board," she told him.

"You're on the Board?"

"Yes. Anything else?"

"No. I think that's enough for now." Nick finished his drink, as did Sam. They walked out to find Gia.

"Where's Sofia?" Sam asked.

"I fed her and put her down."

"Mommy, can I have a lizard?" Finn came running downstairs.

"No. Grace might eat him." She looked at Grace, her service dog, and said in Gaelic, "I know you wouldn't, but he doesn't need a lizard." Grace's ears twitched and she gave a quiet whine.

"Mommy, that's not nice," Finn told her.

"What's not nice?"

"Daddy says you shouldn't speak . . . that . . . if people can't understand you. It seems like you're talking about them," Finn explained.

Nick snickered. "Your father is right."

"I was talking to Grace."

"You said Grace wouldn't eat a lizard," Finn told her.

"Since when do you speak Gaelic?" Sam asked him.

"Andrew is teaching me," Finn said.

"I want to learn something," Kevin said.

"We can work on Italian. I spoke it to you when you were younger," Gia told him. "You and Nick can learn together."

"Great!" Finn said in Italian.

"Italian, too?" Sam asked.

"Only a few words," Finn admitted.

"Are you ready to go home?" Sam asked him.

"No," Finn said.

"Well, we need to go home."

"Mommy, can Kevin spend the night?" Finn asked her.

"Um, maybe Saturday night if it's okay with your dad, Nick and Gia."

"Can I call and ask him?"

"No, we'll ask when we get home," Sam told him. Finn began to pout. "If you pout, it's a definite no."

"Yes, ma'am," Finn said.

"You can play until our ride comes," Sam told him. Then she texted for their ride. She checked her calendar.

"Oh, I have an appointment Saturday night."

"At night?"

"More like a date with John and Barb," Sam said.

"I don't want to know," Nick said.

"Michael can watch them."

"Four kids?" Nick said, having doubts.

"Andrew is right next door. Jess and Luke can help."

"It's fine with me if Michael agrees," Gia said.

"So, it'll just be you, me, and Sofia?" Nick asked.

"I can make a special dinner. Or we can go out," Gia told Nick.

"Will you make your grandmother's spaghetti alle . . . clams?"

"Vongole," Gia said. "Yes. If I can find some decent clams."

"That sounds good," Sam said.

"You can't have any," Nick told her.

Kimberly A. Biggerstaff © 2024

"Man, you're possessive," Sam told him.

"Did he show you his Daddy Diaper Bag and Carrier?" Gia asked.

"No."

Nick smiled and went and got it. He put the carrier on and showed her the diaper bag.

"That is cool," Sam said as her phone dinged. "I'll peek in on Sofia and get Finn. Our ride is here. Take a picture of Sofia in that thing and send it to me." Sam went upstairs.

"Did you get whatever it was taken care of?" Gia asked him.

"She's going to help me verify something," Nick told her. "Uh, she's also going to arrange a tour at that academy for us."

Gia went to him and placed her arms around his neck. "Thank you." She kissed him.

"She's the one setting it up."

"Yes, but you agreed, so you get credit." She kissed him again, longer this time. "Unless you'd rather I kiss her," Gia teased, knowing he'd respond.

"Hell, no!"

Sam cleared her throat. "Kids in the room. We're off. Hopefully, we'll see you on Saturday. Or Michael will, if I don't."

"I won't see you Saturday, Sam?" Kevin asked.

Kimberly A. Biggerstaff © 2024

"I'm not sure. I'm supposed to go to Barb's and John's."

"Why don't I get to go to Barb's anymore?" Finn asked.

"You go when the other kids go."

"But I want to go by myself," Finn told her. "With you."

"We have to leave. We'll talk about it later. And don't pout."

"Yes, ma'am. Bye Kevin, bye Nick, bye Gia," Finn said.

"Goodbye, Finn," Nick said.

"See you later, Finn," Gia said.

"Later, dude," Kevin said.

"Later, dude?" Gia asked.

"Bye Finn," Kevin corrected himself.

Sam and Finn left as Nick and Kevin walked them out.

"Nick, will you help me put together a puzzle?" Kevin asked.

"Sure. Let's go," Nick said.

Chapter 16

Sam went to the George Bush Center for Intelligence the next day. As she walked into the main office, she saw Andrew's boss and smiled at him. He didn't show any emotion and barely acknowledged her. Sam had made a bit of an impression on him the first time she went to visit Andrew. She had kicked him out of his office and made love to Andrew on his desk.

He called security on her, but she left without incident. They knew Sam and since the Director had also shown up, she got away with it. Andrew's boss hadn't forgotten.

Sam walked into Andrew's office, knocking on the door. "Hello."

Andrew looked up from his desk. "Well, come for a visit? It's too early for lunch."

"I need a favor."

"A favor? From me? I hope it's not like the last one," Andrew said.

"What favor?" Sam asked him.

"The one where I had to . . . you know . . . Katie," he whispered.

"First of all, you . . . I . . ." Sam sighed. "I didn't come here to fight or ask you to do anything like that." She began

Kimberly A. Biggerstaff © 2024

to close the blinds. "But if you help me out . . . I'll make it worth your while." She locked the door and walked over to him.

"Are you trying to seduce me, Colonel Barrett?"

She set her hands on his chair and leaned over and nibbled his ear. "Maybe," she whispered.

Andrew began to unbutton her shirt . . .

* * * *

"Okay, what do you want?" Andrew asked her, tucking his shirt back into his pants.

"I need background and financials on someone."

"I don't do that," he said.

"You don't?" Sam said sarcastically. Then she got serious as she put her suit jacket back on. "You're still an officer. You have access."

"How do you know what access I have?"

Sam stared at him. "Seriously? I know a lot."

"Things have changed, Sam," Andrew told her.

"Are you saying you can't do it or won't?"

"Sam, I'm not Katrina. I can't just access . . ."

Sam suddenly got angry when he mentioned Katrina. "You're an ass." She opened the door and slammed it behind her, breaking the frosted glass. She strode out and headed to the Director's office.

"Ma'am," a man said.

Kimberly A. Biggerstaff © 2024

But Sam kept walking.

"Ma'am! You need to stop!" He yelled and touched her on the arm.

Sam stopped and glared at him. "Take your hand off me, right now," she said calmly but firmly.

He did but then said, "You need to come with me, ma'am."

"I'm on my way to see the Director," Sam told him.

"No, ma'am. You need to come with me."

Sam growled to herself and looked at him. "Lead the way, then," she said. But he motioned with his hand in the direction he wanted her to go and waited for her to go first. He took her to the security office.

"May I help you, sir?" the officer asked the man.

"This woman broke a window in an office. Check her out."

"Ma'am, may I see your badge and identification?"

Sam gave him the visitor's badge and her retired credentials.

The security officer sighed after looking at her credentials. He recognized her name. He ran her name through his computer. He kept glancing at Sam and the computer. The security officer looked at the man.

"Is there a problem?" the man asked.

"May I speak with you, sir?" The security officer stood and took a few steps away but still watched Sam. The other man walked closer, and the security officer began whispering to him.

"I don't give a shit. Do your job," he said and walked out.

* * * *

Nick wasn't sure whether to limit the time he spent in Gia's office or increase it to make it more difficult for Jim. Gia was there now, so it might be more difficult for him to do whatever he was doing. Nick wasn't sure how he was stealing the information, if he was.

He had lunch with Gia off base as a distraction. But Gia could tell he was still bothered by whatever it was.

"Nick," Gia said, but he sat, moving the food with his fork. "Nick." She touched his hand.

"What?"

"Are you sure you can't tell me what's going on?"

"I'd rather not," he said.

"Are you finished?" Gia asked.

"Yeah, I guess I'm not that hungry," Nick said.

"Let's go, then."

Nick paid the bill, and Gia took his hand as they went to the SUV. "You're in uniform, Gunnery Sergeant. No PDA (Personal Displays of Affection).

Kimberly A. Biggerstaff © 2024

"Give me the keys," Gia told him.

"I can drive."

"I'm taking you somewhere. Give me the keys."

He let her drive and was shocked when she pulled into a hotel parking lot. She leaned over and kissed his cheek and then whispered in his ear, "I'm getting a room. I'm going into that room, and I'll wait for you to come up. I want you to undress me slowly and kiss me and—"

"Gia!" Nick said as she moved her hand and fondled him.

"I'll text you the room number, Mr. . . . X." She smiled, grabbed her cap and purse and went inside.

"She's nuts. It's the middle of the day," Nick said to himself. "She won't do it. We'll be late getting back." Eventually, his phone dinged. "She did it. She got a room. This is crazy." But he got out and went to the room. He knocked softly and Gia answered.

"May I help you, sir?" she said.

Nick took a few steps inside. "I know what you're doing. I'm sorry I've been distracted. You didn't have to do this. I get the picture."

Gia just stood there. Then she walked over and began kissing him. "I'm going to undress you, Mr. X. Is this going to be a one-way encounter?"

"What's your name, ma'am?" Nick gave up and decided to play along.

"Call me Lola," Gia whispered as she pushed his suit jacket off and continued to kiss him.

* * * *

"See you later." Nick smiled at Gia as he walked her back to her office.

"Bye," Gia said, smiling back.

Nick gave Jim a look as he left. Jim shifted in his seat and looked down at the papers on his desk.

* * * *

Nick called Sam from his study when he got home later that evening.

"What is it?" Sam said angrily.

"I was just checking in. If this is a bad time—"

"I'm sorry. I wasn't able to get the information I wanted today."

"That's okay," Nick said.

"No, it's not." Sam was really irritated.

"Did something happen?"

"I got arrested at Langley," Sam told him. She was still mad at Andrew.

"What? Why?"

"I broke a window."

Nick sighed. "Why?"

"I was mad and slammed a door because someone wouldn't help me. Or couldn't. It doesn't matter. I'll find another way."

"Sam, it's okay. I'll just go to the Feds and let them handle it."

"I can do this. I can—"

"Sam, stop. Don't worry about it. I'll handle it," Nick told her.

"I don't quit," Sam said. "I'm not injured, so I don't quit." She hung up on him. "Michael!"

"Why are you yelling for me?" Michael came into the room.

"Bedroom, now."

"What?"

"Now or I'll go somewhere else. I'm still pissed at Andrew, and I . . ."

"Okay, I get it. But sometimes you make me feel like—"

"Do you want sex or not?" she asked.

"Hey, the kids are in the next room."

"Are you coming, or do I have to get a ride somewhere?" Sam was getting frustrated.

"Yes," he said.

"And don't pout. Finn gets that from you," Sam said.

* * * *

Kimberly A. Biggerstaff © 2024

Sam decided to call a friend. An undercover cop she had helped out. She was going through a rough time, and he asked her to help him with a case. Sam slept with him more than once. But she had to quit helping him when she had her brain aneurysm. "Hello?"

"Hi, I need a favor," Sam said. "I can meet you."

"A favor. Well, I did end up getting my man with your help, so I suppose I can do you a favor." Doug said. "Can you come to the station tomorrow morning?"

"Yes. Are you done with your undercover assignment?"

"No, I got arrested. It's part of my cover. Had to spend the night in jail."

"Is 9 a.m. okay?" Sam asked.

"Yes."

"How do you have your phone if you're in jail?"

"You don't want to know," Doug said.

"Eww."

"I'm kidding. I'm in solitary confinement and have friends. But I'll be able to see you," Doug told her.

"See you at nine," Sam said, hanging up.

"What are you up to?" Michael asked her, coming out of the bathroom.

"Helping Nick out with something."

Kimberly A. Biggerstaff © 2024

"Does this have to do with why you're mad at Andrew?"

"Yes. He wouldn't help me, so I have to go a different route," she said.

"Just . . . come home if you get horny," he said.

Sam smiled.

"Daddy," Sky called.

"Coming baby."

"You're such a good dad," Sam told him.

"Don't you forget it," he said, going over to the bed and kissing her.

* * * *

Sam went to the station and asked for Doug. He came out to meet her, dressed in his biker gear. He smiled at her.

"It's good to see you. You look . . . great," Doug said, looking her up and down.

"Thank you."

"How's the head?" he asked.

"Better. So you got your man?"

"We found the warehouse and the guy in charge of it. More work to do. Thank you again for your help."

Sam wanted to kiss him so bad she couldn't think.

"So, how can I help you?" Doug asked.

"Oh, uh, I need . . . background and financials on someone," Sam told him.

"Name?" he said, sitting at his desk. Sam handed him a piece of paper with Jim's info on it. Nick had given her his name and address.

"This him?" Doug asked.

"Yeah," Sam said, leaning in and reading the screen. Doug smiled as she hovered close to him. "Finances. Just to look, I know we'd need a warrant to act."

Doug did some more typing and let Sam read the screen.

"Huh. He's paying for something. Large withdrawals, besides an allotment. Probably alimony. No deposits other than his direct deposit military pay. He has an ex-wife and two kids that live with her."

"Credit cards," Sam and Doug said at the same time. He pulled up one.

"That's it. A hospital. Someone is sick or hurt," Sam said. "That's a good reason."

"Good reason for what?" Nick asked her.

"It's not a good reason to break the law. Let's just say I can understand why someone would break the law to pay hospital bills."

"Can I help you with this?" Doug asked her.

"No. Thank you, though. I appreciate this. You won't get in trouble?"

Kimberly A. Biggerstaff © 2024

"No," he said. Sam was still leaning over, hovering. "You smell great," he said. "I miss you."

Sam smiled and stood up. "I should go." She looked at the tattoo on his arm. "Anyone ever ask about that?"

"Yes," he said, looking at the signature she left on his forearm. He immediately had it inked over. "Some are impressed."

"Yeah, right," Sam said, not believing him. "You were nuts to ink my signature."

"I told you I was a fan," he said, standing. Then he opened his desk drawer and pulled out her book. "Would you sign it, please?" he said, standing too close.

"Uh, yeah," she said.

He handed her a pen and then the book. She sat at his desk and wrote something and signed it. When she stood, he again got a little too close. "Thank you," he said.

"Thank you. For your help." She was uncomfortable.

"Can I give you a ride?" Doug offered.

"No, my ride is waiting. I'll see you around," she said. But he walked with her. "You don't have to . . ." He suddenly pulled her down a hallway and pushed her against the wall and kissed her. At first, she resisted, but then Sam couldn't help but enjoy it. When he slowly moved his lips away from hers, he smiled. "I just needed a goodbye kiss," he said. Then he whispered in her ear, "You were the best I ever had." And then he walked back to his desk.

Sam stood there for a moment. "Dammit," she whispered. She left as quickly as she could. "Home, please," she said to her driver.

As soon as she walked in, she grabbed Michael's hand and led him to the bedroom.

* * * *

"I have some information," Sam told Nick that evening.

"I told you that you didn't—"

"Well, I don't always listen. I think someone is sick or hurt, and he's paying their hospital bills," Sam told him.

"Oh. That makes sense. I can understand that. Sort of. But I wouldn't sell out my country," Nick said.

"Would you consider it for Sofia or Kevin or Gia?"

"I see your point."

"People will do a lot when they're desperate or love someone. I think it's one of his kids." Sam was theorizing.

"So, what do we do?"

"I was considering a honey trap, but maybe something more direct."

"More direct?" Nick wondered.

"Confront him and tell him we know. Tell him to turn himself in, make a deal to catch the enemy, and hope they won't try him for treason or selling classified information."

"Do you think that will work?"

"Or . . . I could do both," Sam said, thinking out loud.

"What do you mean you?"

"I can make an offer for information . . ."

"No. That's too much. We need to tell someone and let them handle it," Nick told her. "If you get caught doing that without permission, you'll go to jail."

"After what happened at Langley . . . you might be right." Sam took a long, deep breath.

"What's the matter? Don't you know any FBI?"

"I did. He betrayed me and I killed him," Sam said.

Nick stared at her in disbelief.

"Self-defense. He tried to kill me first. We fought and the gun went off. I tried to save him. He . . . he had been . . . a friend long ago."

Nick sighed at the things she had done. Then he thought about all the things he didn't know. "Know any others?"

"I don't know. I'll check with Marie and John," Sam said. "Oh, what am I thinking? Knucklehead!" She smacked herself in the forehead.

"What?"

"He's Navy. NCIS. And I know just the person . . ." Sam called Jenny, Jonathan's fiancé. "Jenny. How's business? Are you ever going to be my daughter-in-law?"

Kimberly A. Biggerstaff © 2024

"Hello, Commander. Things are fine. I guess you haven't spoken to Jonathan."

"Why, what happened? You didn't elope, did you?"

"No. We broke up," she said.

"Oh, Jenny, I'm sorry to hear that. What did he do?"

Jenny laughed. "What makes you think it was him?"

"He cheated, didn't he?" Her silence was all Sam needed. "I'm sorry, Jenny. How long has it been?"

"Two months," Jenny said.

"Maybe he'll get his act together. I mean, if that's what you want. Want me to break his legs?"

Jenny laughed again. "I've missed you, Commander. I would love to have you as my mother-in-law. I think he just needs to work it out for himself, but thank you."

"Okay. I need to talk to you as an NCIS agent."

"Great. Let's meet," Jenny said.

"Are you busy now?"

"Now?" Nick whispered.

"Oh, well, I . . . tomorrow morning would be better. I'll buy you coffee."

"Um, this is delicate. Come to Nick Foster's place," Sam said.

"I've never heard of that place—oh, you mean General Foster? Sure. Give me the address."

"Are you okay, Jenny?" Sam asked.

Kimberly A. Biggerstaff © 2024

"Yes. Is 0900 (9:00 a.m.) okay?"

"Make it ten," Sam said. "You may want to sleep in."
She had a feeling Jenny was with someone.

"Goodbye, Commander," Jenny said, hanging up.

"Why did you tell her we're still broken up?"
Jonathan asked.

"Because I don't know if I'm taking you back," Jenny
said, getting out of bed. "You can't just show up and expect
me to take you back. You cheated on me."

"You just slept with me." He glared at her. "Fine. I'll
go back to base, and you can figure it out." He got up and
began to dress. "You know what, forget it. You don't want to
marry me. You've been messing with me. All this time
wasted."

"Wasted! Is that what you think of our relationship?
Wasted time? If that's what you think, then go back to your
girlfriend!"

"Maybe I will!" He stared at her. Then his face
softened, and he spoke calmly. "Jenny, please. I want to
marry you."

"You aren't ready to get married. We've only been
with each other since high school. I don't want to get
divorced in five years. Go back and date someone for a few
months."

Kimberly A. Biggerstaff © 2024

"I don't want to. I made a mistake. I'm sorry. I . . ." Then he realized something. "You . . . are you seeing someone?"

"We broke up, Jonathan," she said. She saw tears start to form in his eyes.

"Goodbye Jenny," he said, leaving.

* * * *

Sam was getting ready to leave Nick's when her phone rang.

"Jonathan?" she said, surprised.

"I screwed up, Mom. I think it's over for good," he said, clearly upset.

Nick and Gia left the room to give her some privacy. "What happened?"

"You know what happened. I guess I'm more like you than Dad."

"That's not a good way to start this conversation, son," Sam scolded him.

"I'm sorry. I just . . . I made a mistake. I apologized. I came to her, and we . . . I thought we made up. She said I wasn't ready to get married." He was speaking fast.

"Slow down and take a breath."

He took a deep breath. "She's seeing someone."

"Where are you?" Sam asked him.

"I just left her place. I drove up here to surprise her and apologize."

"Go to my house. I'll be there in a little while," she told him.

"Where are you?" Jonathan asked.

"I'm at Nick and Gia Foster's. The General, your former Commandant."

"Oh, right. Look. Forget it. I'll just drive back to Oceana." Jonathan was based at Naval Air Station Oceana in Virginia Beach.

"No, Jonathan. Go to my house. Please. I want to see you. Wait, why don't you come pick us up? Give your mom and brother a ride home."

"Brother?"

"Finn is with me."

"Oh. Okay, send me the address," Jonathan said, hanging up.

She texted him the address and went to Nick and Gia. "Sorry. Jonathan's having relationship issues."

"His girlfriend is the NCIS agent you called?"

"Fiancée. Yes. She's coming over here at ten tomorrow morning. I hope that's okay."

"Yeah, I guess. I feel like this is becoming a base of operations," Nick said, looking at Gia.

"We'll stay out of your way," Gia said.

"Jonathan's coming to pick me up and we'll go. Kevin is still spending the night tomorrow, right?"

"Yes. I'll take him over to Michael's at about six. Gia, do you have everything for that meal?"

"Yes." Gia smiled and Nick kissed her.

"Ah, young love," Sam teased.

"Young?" Nick said.

"Not your ages, the relationship," Sam clarified.

Sam's phone dinged. "I'm here,' Jonathan texted.

'Don't be rude. Get your ass in here and say hello,' Sam texted back. She went to the door and opened it.

"Mom, I'm not in the mood," Jonathan said.

"Just say hello and we can go."

"Maybe I should go to Dad's."

"No, you called me. You can see him tomorrow." They walked inside.

"Hello General Foster. Congratulations on the baby, marriage, and retirement."

"Thank you, Jonathan. Good to see you again." Nick had met Jonathan at his graduation from the Naval Academy. Nick put Sofia in his tactical baby carrier. "This is Gia and this is Sofia."

"It's nice to meet you, Mrs. Foster. Congratulations."

"Thank you. It's Lorenzo. I haven't changed my name. And you can call me Gia or Gunnery Sergeant, sir." Gia smiled at him. Jonathan couldn't help but smile back at her. "Nick, why did you put her in that?" Gia asked.

"I need to use it before she outgrows it."

"She's cute," Jonathan said.

"Here, you can hold her," Nick said, taking her out and handing her to him.

Jonathan was a bit surprised. But he carefully held her. He smiled. "I remember when Jess was this little." Sofia looked at him and moved some. She yawned. Jonathan had all kinds of thoughts going through his head. He thought he might have a baby of his own by now. He cleared his throat. "Here you go, sir." He handed Sofia back to Nick. "It was good to see you. Mom, I'll be outside." He quickly left.

Sam let him go.

"Sorry, I didn't mean to upset him," Nick said.

"No, I think that's exactly what he needed. I'll talk to him."

"I'll get Finn," Gia said.

"So, tomorrow at ten," Nick said.

"Yes," Sam said. Finn came running down the stairs. "Did you clean up?" she asked him.

"Yes, ma'am," Finn said.

"What do you say?"

"Thanks, Kevin, Nick and Gia."

"Am I still spending the night?" Kevin asked.

"Yes. Nick will drop you off at six," Gia told him.

"Bring a helmet if you have one. And any marine gear. We may biv . . . whack," Finn told him.

"Bivouac?" Nick asked curiously.

"Yes, sir. We have a tent and all kinds of stuff."

"Probably an air force tent with room service and beds," Nick teased.

"Daddy is Army. He knows how to biv . . . whack."

"Okay. I'll expect a report on Sunday," Nick told the boys.

"Yes, sir," they said in unison.

"All right, let's go. Your brother is waiting outside."

"Lex? He's home?"

"No, Jonathan."

"He's a Marine and fly's jets, Kevin," Finn said.

"Can I say hi to him, Mommy?"

"Yes."

They went outside and Jonathan picked Finn up. "Hey, brother. It's been a long time."

"This is my friend, Kevin." Finn told him. "This is Jonathan, my brother."

"What jet do you fly?" Kevin asked.

"F-18s."

"My Daddy was a crew chief for the V-22 Osprey. It crashed and he died."

"Oh, sorry to hear that. Flying is dangerous. But I'll bet your dad was the best crew chief in the Marines."

"Nick got me a toy Osprey," Kevin said.

"Cool. Now you need an F-18."

"Jonathan wants to be an astronaut," Finn said.

"Maybe someday," Jonathan said.

"Okay, let's go home," Sam said. She thanked Nick and Gia again, and they got in Jonathan's truck.

"How did he get a woman that looks like that?" Jonathan asked.

"It's one of the mysteries of the universe," Sam said.

Chapter 17

Jenny was right on time. Sam had timed it so Jonathan would see her. He was dropping her off and then going to John and Barb's.

"You planned this, Mom," Jonathan said.

"I need her services as an agent. Now remember what we talked about. Go big, Marine."

"Hello, Jenny. Good to see you." Sam hugged her.

"You too, Commander."

Jenny looked at Jonathan, who got out of his truck and leaned against it. Jenny started to turn to go inside. "Wait, Jenny. Can I have a minute?" Jonathan asked, walking towards her.

"Okay," she said.

"I just . . ." He stopped. "Mom," Jonathan said when he realized Sam was standing there watching.

"I'm going," Sam said.

When she went inside, Jonathan looked at Jenny. "I'm sorry. I want a chance to win you back. Will you go out with me tonight?"

"A date?"

"Yes. I mean, if you don't have plans already." He felt like it was his first time asking her. He kicked the ground with his foot.

"Okay. What time?"

"I'll pick you up at six thirty. Wear formal attire," he said.

"Formal? Like an evening gown?" Jenny asked.

"Or cocktail dress. A little black dress would be nice." He smiled. "Thanks for agreeing. See you at six thirty." He got in his truck and left.

Jenny shook her head. "There is no other guy, silly jarhead," Jenny said to herself. She went inside. "Nice to see you again General," Jenny said to Nick.

"Jenny. This is my wife, Gunnery Sergeant Gia Lorenzo," Nick said.

"Nice to meet you, Gunny."

"This is Sofia," Nick said, showing her to Jenny. "And that is Kevin."

"Hi. Do you have a badge?" Kevin asked.

"Yes, want to see it?" Jenny asked him.

"Yes, ma'am."

Jenny showed him her badge. "Wow, that's cool."

"Come on, Kevin. They have things to discuss. Coffee anyone?"

Everyone wanted coffee. Gia took Sofia and put her in her swing.

Nick led them to his study. "Please sit down." Sam and Nick explained what was going on as Jenny took some notes.

"So you just saw him quickly close a classified folder and then get . . . squirrelly?" Jenny asked.

"Yes, twice. And he's uncomfortable every time I go into the office."

"He made some large withdrawals from his account. No unusual deposits, but large hospital bills on his credit card," Sam told her.

Jenny looked at Sam. "Should I even ask how you know that?"

"Probably not," Sam said. "So, I was thinking a honey trap. I could put on my wig and go approach him with an offer . . ."

"What? No way." Jenny stopped her. "Ma'am. You reported it. I'll send it up to my boss."

"Jenny. Come on. You know that'll take forever, and he's . . ."

"Commander. Please. I'm not you. I can't get away with the sh—crap you did. Why didn't you go to the FBI?"

"I can't think of anyone I know."

"She killed the one she did know," Nick said.

"What does that mean?" Jenny looked at Sam.

"It was self-defense and a while ago."

Kimberly A. Biggerstaff © 2024

"Was that a guy named Brennan?" Jenny recalled.

"Yeah, how did you know?" Sam asked.

"I might have run you," Jenny said.

"You might have run me?"

"You're my future mother-in-law. You're the reason I'm an NCIS agent. Ever since I wrote that school report on you back at Kadena."

"Am I still your future mother-in-law? Thought you were seeing someone," Sam said.

"Seriously, Commander? Are you a jarhead like your son? There is no other guy," Jenny told her.

"Hey, don't be disrespectful, Agent Sloan."

"I apologize. Your son gets on my nerves sometimes."

"Yes, well, men will do that. Especially jarheads."

Nick cleared his throat. "If this is personal, I'll give you the room."

"No. Sorry, sir. I need to give my boss a heads up." Jenny wasn't budging on that point.

"Fine, but I want to help," Sam told her.

"We'll see," Jenny told her. "Just be patient, Commander. I'll be in touch."

"Okay. I'll try," Sam huffed.

"Fat chance," Nick mumbled.

"I heard that," Sam said.

"Agent Sloan, one more thing. My wife works in his office. But she was on maternity leave when I first saw what the Senior Chief did. I haven't said anything to her. Neither has Sam. I've kept her out of this, and she doesn't know anything."

"I understand sir," Jenny said. "But at some point, she may have to be interviewed."

Jenny offered to give Sam a ride and she accepted.

* * * *

Nick went back into his study and sat and thought. He was deciding whether or not to tell Gia or just wait. Eventually, Kevin poked his head in.

"Nick. Want to eat chow with me?" Kevin asked.

Nick smiled at Kevin's choice of words. "What's on the menu, Marine?"

"Grilled cheese sandwich and grapes or carrot sticks."

"Hmm. Okay." He got up and went with Kevin to the kitchen table. Gia set a plate in front of Kevin.

"Apple juice or milk Kevin?"

"I'll have what Nick has," Kevin said.

"Oh, uh, milk."

"Is being a marine hard, General?" Kevin asked.

"Sometimes. But it can be fun and rewarding. I was able to travel the world. I used to bring Barb special things from every place I was stationed."

Kimberly A. Biggerstaff © 2024

"I was born in California and now we live here. That's all I've been to."

"Well, maybe we can take a trip somewhere this summer," Nick said.

"Yeah! Can we, Mommy?" Kevin asked.

"Maybe," Gia said.

"Oh no!" Kevin remembered something.

"What's wrong?" Nick asked him.

"I need gear to take to Finn's."

"Are you finished eating?" Nick asked him.

"Yes, sir."

Nick got up from the table. "Come on. Follow me, Marine." Nick took him to the basement.

"Wow. I've never been down here," Kevin said.

"You don't need to come down here, okay. You can only come down here with me, clear?"

"Yes, sir." Kevin could see that Nick was serious about that.

Nick went to a box and found one of his old military backpacks. "Let's see what we have. I've collected a lot of stuff over the years." He began pulling things out. Canteens, ammo pouches, a helmet, web belts, and more.

"Wow! That's a lot of stuff, General."

"I've been in the military a long time. So, what do you think you need to take?"

Kimberly A. Biggerstaff © 2024

"A helmet," Kevin said.

"Here, let's put it in this backpack."

"Uh, this canteen." He handed it to Nick.

"That should be washed out, and then you can drink from it. Let's adjust this web belt." Nick made it as small as he could, but it was still too big.

"Nick, who's this lady?" Kevin asked, holding a picture frame. "She's pretty."

"Put that down!" Nick yelled.

Kevin dropped it in the box and ran upstairs crying. Nick looked at the picture frame. It was his wedding picture with Kaya.

"Nick!" Gia said coming down the steps. "Did you yell at Kevin?"

Nick was staring at the photo, wiping the dust off it. He barely heard her.

"Nick!" She said, walking to him.

"What?"

"Did you yell at Kevin? He ran upstairs to his room, crying."

"Oh. Um. Yeah, I guess I did. I'm sorry. I just . . ."

Gia looked at the photo. "Is that you, Nick?"

"Yes."

"You were a Lieutenant, and it looks like you were married," Gia said.

"I . . . was. I'm sorry, I didn't mean to yell at him. I'll apologize," he said softly, still looking at the photo.

"Nick, you never told me . . ."

"No, I didn't." He took the picture, unlocked an old footlocker, put it inside, and locked it again. "I'll apologize to Kevin," he said, starting up the stairs. "Um, I'd rather you not come down here, please."

Gia stood there for a few seconds and then followed him upstairs.

"Nick, please talk to me."

But Nick just went up the second floor to Kevin's room. He knocked and opened the door. "Kevin. May I come in?"

Kevin was under the covers, crying. "No! Go away!" he yelled, sobbing.

"I came to say I'm sorry," Nick said, waiting by the door. "Can I come sit down and talk to you? Please?" Nick asked. He waited and then asked again. "Kevin, please."

"Okay," he finally said from under the covers.

Nick walked over and sat down on the bed. "Kevin, I'm really sorry I yelled at you. It was wrong of me to do that, and I'm really sorry."

Kevin peaked out from under the covers. He wiped his eyes. "Marines don't cry. I can't be a marine."

"I'll tell you a secret Kevin. Yes, marines do cry. And I'm sorry I made you cry. I never want to hurt you, and I hope you can forgive me. I'm still learning how to be a husband and father. I'll make mistakes, and so will you. But we'll learn from them. I love you, son."

Kevin didn't say anything.

"Take your time and think about it, Marine." Nick got up and began to leave. Just before he got to the door, he felt the arms wrap around him.

"I forgive you . . . and I love you, too. I'm sorry I touched the picture."

"It's okay. I forgot it was there. It's not your fault, and you did nothing wrong," he told him.

"Nick, who was that lady?"

"Someone I knew a long time ago," Nick said. "Come on, let's see what Sofia is doing."

"She doesn't do much. She sleeps and eats and . . . you know," Kevin said.

"Yeah, I know." Nick smiled. They went downstairs and found Gia nursing Sofia.

"See. Eating," Kevin said. "May I go out back and play?"

"Sure. Be careful, Marine," Nick said.

Kevin smiled and went out the back door after Nick unlocked it for him. He went back over to Gia and sat in a chair near her.

"I apologized to Kevin, and he forgave me," Nick told her.

"Good," she said.

Nick could see that Gia was upset. They sat in silence for a while. Finally, Nick got up and went out back with Kevin.

"Push me, Nick!" Kevin asked as he got on the swing.

"Your mom is mad at me."

"Did you say you were sorry?" Kevin asked.

"I think I need to do more than that," Nick said.

Chapter 18

Nick took Kevin over to Michael's.

"Wow, that's a lot of gear," Michael said, looking at the military backpack.

"He said he needed military gear. I packed some old stuff I had. His civilian clothes are in his other backpack," Nick said, setting the pack on the floor.

"They should have fun. I've got the tent set up, and we'll make s'mores. He can have that, right?"

"Sure. He had some chicken nuggets before we came, but whatever you give your kids is fine." Then Nick asked him, "Can I ask you how you make up with Sam when you mess up?"

"Oh, hmm. Take her to dinner or cook a meal here. You know, the standard stuff."

"I get the feeling you don't screw up that much."

"I do, but she screws up more than me." Michael smiled.

"I need something for tonight. Hey, what kind of wine goes with spaghetti alle . . . clams. I forgot the word. She's making that if she's not too mad at me. I'll take wine and stop and get flowers and chocolates."

"Go with an Italian Pinot Grigio. And don't get a bunch of flowers. Get a single red rose. Skip the chocolates.

Stop at a jewelry store and get a charm for a necklace or charm bracelet."

"Is that what you've done?"

"Not yet. I'm saving it for when I really need it. But let me know if it works," Michael said.

"I guess I better get going if I'm going to get all that," Nick said.

"Spare no expense," Michael said.

"Yeah, I get it. Thanks," Nick said.

"Wait. Come with me," he said. They went to the elevator, and Michael took him to the basement.

"I didn't know you had an elevator."

"Kevin didn't tell you? The kids love it. How did you think I got upstairs?"

"I don't know. I never thought about it."

"I can use the stairs, but sometimes I use the chair, and I need the elevator for that. Sam had this whole house refurbished for me. The counters and cabinets move up and down. Everything is wheelchair friendly."

"Is this your man-cave?" Nick asked.

"Yeah. Sam has hers at her house. This is mine." He went to a wine rack and scanned it. He pulled a bottle off and gave it to him. "This is from Sam's vineyard in Tuscany. It's really good and will go great with your meal."

"Her vineyard in Tuscany?" Nick looked at the bottle.

Kimberly A. Biggerstaff © 2024

"Yeah. She said she bought it for me. Actually have my own label. But it won't go with clams. Trust me. You have to go to a wine shop and order this. You can't get it in the grocery store."

"I can't take this."

"Yes, you can. I have more. She gets them by the case."

"Okay, thanks. You saved me a trip."

Nick went to a jewelry store and looked at all the charms. Then he saw one he liked. It was a gold heart inscribed with "You are always in my heart." Now he had to get a rose. He checked his watch. She was probably wondering where he was. He decided to take his chances and head home. But on the way, he saw a house in the neighborhood with a rose bush out front. He rang the bell.

"Hello," he said when a man answered it.

"Um, I'm not selling anything. I . . . um was wondering if I could have one of your roses. Just one for my wife."

"Did you screw up?" the man asked.

"Yes, and I got wine and jewelry, and she's waiting with dinner. I messed up today and . . ."

"I get it. Yeah, take one. Come on," he said, taking out a pocketknife from his pants. "I sneak out here and cut one when I screw up too."

Kimberly A. Biggerstaff © 2024

"Thanks, let me give you some . . ."

"No, no. One rose is fine. We've all been there," he said.

"Thanks again. I hope this works," Nick said, shaking the man's hand. He noticed the tattoo on his forearm. "Semper Fi."

The man smiled. "Semper Fi, General."

"You know me?"

"Been out for a while, but I keep up with what's going on in the Corps. Good luck, sir."

"Thanks." Nick went back to his SUV and drove the few blocks home.

He took everything inside. Gia had already set the dining room table. There were candles, and it was set for romance. He was a bit surprised, thinking she was mad at him. He could smell the food. He set the wine on the table. He had them gift wrap the box with the charm in it. He set it above her plate and placed the rose on top. He sat down and waited. His phone dinged and he read the text. 'Go put on a suit.'

"A suit?" he said to himself.

'Ok. Whatever you want,' he texted back. He ran upstairs and changed into a suit. He wondered where she was but went back downstairs, sat and waited. 'Pour the wine and light the candles,' read the next text.

Nick sighed but did it. Then Gia came out and served the meal. She was wearing her long raincoat. "What's under the coat?" He smiled.

Gia didn't say anything and sat down. She was still mad. She stared at him, waiting.

"It smells delicious." Then he added, "I'm sorry. It was a long time ago. I wasn't ready to tell you. I don't talk about it because it's too painful." He waited, but she didn't say anything. "I know you would probably understand, but—"

"Stop. Please eat before it gets cold," she said.

He picked up his fork and tried the spaghetti. "It's delicious. But I can't enjoy this knowing you're . . . mad . . . at . . . me." He watched as she stood and took off the raincoat. She was wearing a little black dress.

"Close your mouth and eat, Nicholas."

"Yes, ma'am." Nick thought to himself how beautiful she was and how lucky he was to be married to her.

They ate in silence until Nick was finally ready to tell her. "She taught a Japanese language class on-base in Okinawa. We dated for a year and got married. Then she got pregnant." He took a breath and spoke slowly. "It was during a checkup that they found the cancer. She wanted to try and wait for the baby to be born before starting treatment, but it was aggressive, and . . . they didn't make it."

Kimberly A. Biggerstaff © 2024

"Nick. You don't have to—"

"No, it's okay. I should have told you long ago. I'm sorry I didn't. I couldn't date for a long time, and when I tried, it just . . . no one ever made me feel the way she did . . . until I saw you." He looked at her and continued. "From the moment I saw you, Gia, I couldn't get you out of my mind. Rank didn't matter. I . . ." He got up out of his chair at the head of the table and knelt beside her. He picked up the rose and handed it to her. Then he gave her the box. "This says how I feel."

Gia set the rose on her lap and opened the box. "Nick, it's . . . perfect. I love it and I love you." She kissed him. "I'm sorry about your family. I know it was hard for you to tell me that, but you can tell me anything, Nick. Our relationship went fast, but I love you, Nicholas Eric Foster, and you're always in my heart, too." She leaned in and they kissed. "Thank you for telling me. I'm sorry I was upset."

"No, you had every right to be. I should have told you about her. I've just pushed it down for so long . . ."

"It's okay, Nick. I understand," Gia said.

Sofia's cries came through the baby monitor. Nick smiled and stood. "I'll check her," he said.

"She probably just needs changing," Gia told him. Nick went upstairs and changed Sofia and put her back in bed.

"Sleep tight, sweetie," he said, kissing her. He went back downstairs, but Gia wasn't there. The candles were out, and the plates were gone. "Gia?" he called. But she wasn't around. He went back upstairs, and when he went to the bedroom, she came out wearing a black negligee. He saw the charm on a necklace around her neck.

"Boy, you're fast, Gunny," Nick said.

"Permission to get frisky, General."

"Granted. By all means, granted," he said, taking his suit jacket off as she approached.

* * * *

Gia got out of bed and put on a robe. "Where are you going?" Nick asked her.

"I'm going to put the rest of the food away."

"I'll help clean up," Nick said, getting up and putting his shorts on. They went downstairs and put the food away and cleaned up.

"Dinner was great. Thank you for cooking," Nick said, kissing the back of her neck.

"You're welcome."

"Gia, I think the Senior Chief is stealing classified information," Nick blurted out.

"What? Jim?"

"Yes. It's what all this secret squirrel stuff is about. I was trying to protect you, but I don't want to keep things from you anymore."

"Nick, that's a serious allegation."

"I know. I wasn't sure and that's why I contacted Sam."

"I never saw anything," Gia said.

"It may have started when you were on maternity leave," Nick said. "Do you know anything about his ex or kids?"

"No, just that he has a boy and girl that live with their mother. What should I do?"

"Nothing. Just be aware."

"I can't believe he would do that," Gia said.

"We're still not sure. Jenny is NCIS. She's going to run it by her boss."

"I'm glad you told me, Nick." She gave him a kiss. "All done down here."

They went back up and checked on Sofia, who was sleeping soundly.

"Want to make another one?" Nick asked.

"No. I mean, I . . ."

"I'm just kidding. It's too soon. I want to enjoy her for a while," Nick told her as they walked to their bedroom.

Kimberly A. Biggerstaff © 2024

"We can talk about it later. Much later," Gia said, wrapping her arms around his neck. As they kissed, Nick untied Gia's robe and slid his hands around her waist. He gently ran his hands up her smooth back and then pushed her robe off.

"Are you squared away, General?" Gia asked him.

"Yes, Gunny, I'm good to go," he said, sweeping her up and carrying her to the bed.

* * * *

Sam called Nick a few days later. "Has Jenny or anyone contacted you?"

"No," Nick answered. "I told Gia."

"I thought you—never mind. It's fine. We should just go with my plan."

"Sam, no. Don't do anything yet. Just give Jenny another few days."

Sam growled. "Oh, okay fine. I'll wait."

"You miss it, don't you?" Nick asked her.

"Miss what?"

"The cases, going undercover."

Sam sighed. "Sometimes, I guess I do. I like figuring things out. Hang on, I'm getting another call. It's Jenny! Call you later." She hung up.

Nick smiled and hung up. Gia walked into his office at the Pentagon.

Kimberly A. Biggerstaff © 2024

"Talking to your girlfriend." Gia teased him.

"Girlfriend?"

"Sam," Gia said.

"Yes. How did you know?"

"Just a guess. You always get a scowl on your face when you talk to her."

"I do not," he said.

Gia laughed.

"It's a little early for lunch," Nick said, looking at his watch. "Everything okay?"

"Yes. I just wanted to see you." Gia smiled at him and leaned on his desk, right next to him.

"I'm glad you're not getting tired of me," Nick said, smiling back. He placed a hand on her knee and slid it up her skirt. "I love it when you wear your skirt," he whispered.

"Aww, isn't that cute," Sam said, walking in. "Want me to close the door so you two can have fun?"

Gia stood up quickly and turned around, and Nick quickly removed his hand.

"I thought I told you to stay away from my office," Nick said. "And didn't I just get off the phone with you?"

"Relax. It's not a problem. I was . . . nearby."

"I better get back to work," Gia said.

"I can leave and guard the door," Sam offered.

"Maybe you'd like to watch, Colonel," Gia said in Italian as she smiled and left.

Sam laughed. "Well, sometimes—" she began in Italian.

"What do you want, Colonel?" Nick said, interrupting Sam as she watched Gia walk away. "Hey, stop looking at her ass."

"I still don't know how you landed her." Sam had wandered into the hall as she watched Gia and came back inside Nick's office.

"You and me both. Why are you here?" Nick asked her.

"I missed visiting you at the office. How was your date on Saturday?"

"Very good," he said.

"Did Kevin have fun?" she asked him.

"Yes, he had a great time. Wants to do it again. Wants me to get a tent so Finn and Alan can come spend the night."

"That's great. I'm glad the boys get along. Kevin's a good kid."

"Yes, he is. How was your . . . date?" Nick asked, knowing she had spent Saturday with John and Barb.

"Good. I know you don't like it, so don't feel obligated to ask."

"Were you always . . . like this?" Nick wondered.

"Like what?" She smiled, trying to get Nick to say what he meant.

"You know what I'm talking about. All these people and together with . . . threesomes and . . ." Nick was embarrassed, which is what Sam intended.

"No. I was faithful to Katrina for years. Well, except when John seduced me in the sandbox."

"What!" Nick was appalled.

"It's in the book, isn't it?"

"I . . ."

"We didn't go far. I stopped it after he got under my shirt."

"I really don't need to know that."

"I know, but I like seeing you blush," Sam said, smiling.

"I don't know how your wife managed to put up with you," Nick said.

"I'm great in the sack," Sam said.

"Get out of my office," he said.

"Oh, crap," she said.

"What now?"

"Grace is alerting. Can I have my seizure in here?"

"Are you kidding me?" Nick asked.

"No, I'm not. I could go next door."

"No, what do you need?" Nick didn't have a clue.

"Just some space." She stood up and moved the chair she was sitting in. "Just make sure I don't hurt myself or hit my noggin." She laid down on the floor.

"Is that what you do? Lay down and wait."

"Yes. Would you rather I fall down?"

"No. How long?" Nick asked her.

"Grace gives me about ten minutes or so."

Nick went back to work on the computer. When he heard a noise, he peered over his desk. "Holy . . ." Nick had never seen anyone have a seizure before. He didn't like it and tried not to watch. It lasted about forty seconds but felt longer for Nick. He went over and looked at her. Grace had her paws over her legs.

"Nick, what is she doing?" Gia asked after she opened the door.

"She just had a seizure."

"Oh. What are you doing?"

"Nothing. You don't do anything. Other than making sure she doesn't hurt herself," Nick told her. "Have you ever seen one?"

"No."

"Not fun to watch," Nick said. "Why did you come back?"

"Need to borrow a highlighter."

"Right drawer," he told her.

"Thanks." She walked around Sam and Grace. After a while, Grace began licking Sam's hand, and eventually Sam sat up.

"Do you need anything?" Nick asked.

"Water," Sam said.

"Gia, there's a bottle in the bottom drawer," Nick told her. Gia tossed the bottle to Nick, who gave it to Sam.

"How often do you have those?" Nick asked.

"One or two a day. Sometimes I skip a day or two. Good girl, Grace." Sam retrieved a treat from Grace's pack and gave it to her.

When Sam was ready, Nick helped her up and she sat in a chair. "Mind if I sit here for a moment?"

"No, take your time."

"Grace lets me know when I can get up." She took a sip of water.

"Are you having lunch with Barb?" Nick asked.

"Yes."

"You have lint on your pants," Nick told her.

"I have a lint roller. I'll get it," Gia said, going back to her office.

"Why are you staring at me?" Sam asked Nick.

"Sorry, that's the first time I saw a seizure."

"Oh. Fun stuff, huh?"

Nick walked around and sat at his desk, not saying anything. Seeing Sam vulnerable like that made him think.

"Here you are," Gia said, handing the roller to Sam.

"Want to do my ass?" Sam said in Italian.

"Hey, stop flirting with my wife," Nick told her.

"You're no fun, Nick."

"Yes, he is," Gia told her.

"Well, maybe you and I can have lunch someday and you can tell me," Sam said. "Did I get it all?"

"Looks good to me," Gia said in Italian.

"Are you flirting with her now?" Nick asked Gia.

"I better go. I may have to take Barb to a hotel," Sam said.

"Would you not say things like that in front of me? That's my niece," Nick reminded her.

Sam waved as she put her suit coat back on and left.

"Hmm, ready for lunch?" Gia asked.

"Why are you smiling like that?" Nick asked her.

"Thinking about a hotel lunch."

"Stop listening to Barrett," Nick said.

"You're turning me down?"

"I didn't say that," Nick said, getting up and closing the door.

Kimberly A. Biggerstaff © 2024

Chapter 19

Gia was working on her computer when Jim suddenly spoke. He had been unusually quiet the past week. "Gia?"

"Yes?"

"How far would you go for your kids?"

"What do you mean?" she asked.

"Forget it."

"Jim, if you need to talk, I'll listen."

He waited a few minutes. "My son is in the hospital."

"Jim, I'm sorry."

"It's his heart," Jim said. "Gia, I . . . can I tell you something?"

Gia was afraid he was going to tell her what he'd done. "Jim, if you tell me you've done something, I . . ."

"No, I . . ."

"Jim, turn yourself in," Gia told him.

"What? Why?"

"If you did something illegal, it's better to turn yourself in now, before they catch you."

"What? I haven't done anything," he said.

"You haven't. Nothing?"

"No." Then his face changed, and he realized what she thought. "The General thinks I'm selling classified information, doesn't he?"

"Jim, I said don't tell me."

"Gia, I haven't. I'm not a traitor . . . but . . . I was approached."

"You need to report it. Right now," she told him.

"I did think about it . . ."

"Jim!"

"I know. You're right," he said.

"Hold on." Gia got up and went to Nick's office. "Come over here. Now."

Nick followed her over. "Tell him, Jim."

Jim stood up. "Sir. I was approached to sell classified information, but I haven't. I swear to you, sir. I would never betray my country. See, my son is in the hospital, and it was tempting, but no, sir, I haven't."

Nick looked at him. "You need to report the contact."

"Yes, sir."

"Hold on." He called Barb's office. "Is Sam there? Tell her to come down here now. It's important."

"Sir, I need to call—" Jim began.

"Just wait," Nick told them.

They waited. Nick poked his head out of the office every now and then. "Over here."

"Did you miss me, Nick?" Sam asked.

"No. You need to hear this," he said, letting her into the office and closing the door.

Kimberly A. Biggerstaff © 2024

"Colonel Samantha Barrett, this is Senior Chief Petty Officer Jim King."

"Ma'am. It's a pleasure to meet you. I read your book and the second one too. They use some of your cases at our school."

"Don't believe everything they told you," Sam told him.

"Senior Chief, tell her," Nick said.

"Sir . . ."

"She knows I suspected you," Nick told him. "I consulted her."

"Oh, well, ma'am, I was approached by a foreigner to sell classified information. But I haven't done it. I swear, I would never."

Sam looked at him. "Why should we believe you?"

"Ma'am, I love my job and this country. I would never betray it."

Sam walked behind him. "Not even for family?"

"No, ma'am. I thought about it, but I can't do that. Wait, how did you know—"

"It's not important," Sam said. "Tell me what happened."

They listened as he told them how a woman approached him one day when he had left the hospital. He had taken a few days of leave and went to see his son. She made contact again after he returned to work.

Sam began asking him questions. She asked for a description of the woman. After a few questions, she asked the same one: "Did you take any money or any payment?" She asked him over and over again. She also asked, "Did you share any classified information?" Then she'd say, "Not even for family? For your child."

Gia started to say something when Jim began to sweat and get flustered. But Nick touched her hand in a silent "no." He watched Sam work as she questioned Jim. He was impressed with the way she worked. She knew when to pause, when to raise her voice and when to whisper. She would speed up and slow down. She was relentless, and he could tell she was enjoying it even though her face didn't show it. She should teach a class on interrogation. He wished Barb had been there. Although Barb had her own talents for interrogation.

"All right. I believe you," Sam finally said.

"Was that necessary? He told you everything," Gia said.

"Yes, it was necessary. I needed to be sure he wasn't lying. Besides, the Feds and NCIS will do the same. We need to call Jenny. She's going to be pissed at me."

"You interrogated me without reading me my rights," Jim said.

"I'm retired. I have no authority," Sam said. She glared at him and asked, "Did you lie to me?"

"No, ma'am."

"Call NCIS over at Quantico. Ask for Agent Jennifer Sloan," Sam told Jim. "Tell her I told you to call her." She waited. "Now, Senior Chief," Sam ordered him.

"Yes, ma'am," Jim said, picking up his phone.

As Jim called, Sam walked back over to Nick and Gia. "Did you enjoy the show?" Sam asked.

"No," Gia said.

"How do you think they get some of the intel you analyze? That was nothing to what the agency does," Sam told her.

"I'm not naïve. I know what happens out there. It doesn't mean I have to like it," she said, walking out.

"She'll be okay. I'll talk to her," Nick said.

"Don't go far, Gia," Sam called.

"I'll be in Nick's office," she said.

"That was . . . impressive. You really were good at your job. You enjoyed it, didn't you?" Nick asked Sam.

Sam smiled. "Yes. I miss it."

"Ma'am? She wants to talk to you," Jim said to Sam.

"Now, I'm going to get my ass chewed," Sam said, taking the phone from him. Jenny didn't hold back. She was pissed at what Sam had done and told her to stay there with all of them. When she hung up, she said, "I hope Jonathan never pisses her off like I just did."

They waited for Jenny to arrive with her partner. When she arrived, she said something to her partner and then went to Sam. "With me, ma'am," she said through gritted teeth.

"We can go in here. Gia, you can go back to your office," Sam said as they went to Nick's office.

"Give her hell, Agent," Gia said, leaving and closing the door behind her.

"Look, I know you're pissed, but—" Jenny suddenly hugged her.

"Thank you, Commander," Jenny said.

"What? I thought you were mad at me."

"I have to do that in front of them. This is the best case I've gotten."

"What have you been doing over there?" Sam was stunned by her reaction.

"I'm the lead agent this time. This is great. But you shouldn't have done anything. Did you interview him?"

"Well, uh, I had to make sure he wasn't lying."

"Shoot. I would have loved to see you interview him," Jenny told her.

"Nick was impressed, but Gia didn't like it."

"So, tell me what he told you," Jenny said.

Sam told Jenny everything, and they went back next door after she told Sam she had to still act mad at her. Jenny and Sam knew what had to happen. They needed to catch the woman in the act. Sam was itching to be involved. The problem was Jim didn't know when she would contact him again. They'd have to put a tail on him. The time she contacted him in DC was when he was at the grocery store. They'd have to be careful. They got a description of the woman and said they'd get a sketch artist so they could try and figure out who she was. They waited for the artist, and Jim asked if he could inform his supervisor.

"What the hell is going on here?" a naval commander said, walking into the office. Jim and Gia snapped to attention. "Senior Chief?"

"Sir, this is Agent Sloan and Agent Lake from NCIS."

"Commander, we need to talk," Jenny told him. She took him to Nick's office and briefed him. She returned alone. "Okay. Senior Chief, from now on, you will have a tail. We'll be watching to see if she makes contact. She'll be watching you as well, but we'll be careful. Hopefully she won't spot our people."

"He needs a wire," Sam muttered.

Jenny continued, ignoring Sam, "General, you and the Gunny wait for me. We'll need statements from you."

Sam slowly went over to Agent Lake. "So, you let her take the lead on this," Sam said, knowing he was her supervisory agent.

"You brought her the case, Colonel," Lake said.

"You know me?"

"I know of you. You're a bit like your father. A legend in your field."

"A legend? First time I heard that." Sam scoffed.

"Expecting words like notorious or infamous?" he asked.

"Maybe. Barrett the Beast."

He gave a slight laugh. "I heard what happened over at the agency. You're not banned. They seemed to have lost the paperwork or deleted it."

"How would you know that?" she asked.

"I have my ways."

"You know someone over there."

"They wanted to teach you a lesson," he said.

"I have never asked for special treatment, and I paid for the window."

"You don't have to ask for special treatment. They're afraid of you. Even today. Barrett the Beast gets around." He smiled at her.

"Who do you know?" he asked.

"My husband can be an ass sometimes. He bragged about how he took you to security."

"Your husband? Oh yeah, he was a jerk. I was on my way to see the Director."

"Despite making them write you up, he did you a favor."

"How's that?"

"You need to tread carefully with this Director. She may act like a fan, but she's made it clear she doesn't like your . . . antics."

"Antics? Well, I guess I do get out of hand sometimes. But I haven't been up there in a while."

"Personally, I think she's jealous. She admires you but doesn't want to admit it," he said.

"How's Sloan doing?" Sam said, changing the subject.

"She's going to be a very good agent. She's always reading up on the latest techniques and researching the old-school ways, too. Seems to prefer your old cases. I'll bet she's read every one of them ten times. Knows everything that's not above her pay grade. I just need to make sure she doesn't go rogue like you tend to do."

"Old-school? Some of that stuff is still relevant," Sam said.

"I know. That's why they teach it at FLETC. Sloan could do worse than having you as a mentor."

"I'm not her mentor. I barely see her," Sam said.

"She talks about you all the time. She's been studying you for years. She told me she wrote a report on you back in high school."

"Kid stuff. She's engaged to my son."

"I know. She's head over heels for him. Been asked out by nearly every guy in the office. Straight guys. Turns them all down. Very faithful."

"That's nice to know. She's a great girl."

"Agent Lake," Jenny called him.

"Hey, keep her safe, or the Beast will get you," Sam whispered in his ear before he walked over to Jenny. After briefing Lake, they were getting ready to leave when two more agents showed up. Jenny told Nick and Gia to go to NCIS to give their statements.

"Colonel, let's go. You can ride with us," Lake said.

"What?"

"We need your statement."

"Aw, come on. I gave you a verbal one."

"Not good enough. Besides, we need you to sign some waivers if you're going to assist us."

Sam perked up and smiled. "Awesome," she said quietly. The other two agents stayed with Jim. Jenny took the sketch with them back to NCIS.

"Can I see the sketch?" Sam asked, following them.

"No," Jenny said. Then she handed it to her.

Sam stopped in her tracks.

Chapter 20

When Nick and Gia returned from giving their statements, a message was waiting for Nick. "Sir, the President would like to see you. If you'll come with me." Nick went with him to the White House.

"Nick. How is everything?" the President asked him.

"It's become interesting, sir. Did you place me there on purpose, sir?"

The President smiled. "Nick, how would you like to spend more time with your daughter?"

"Sir?"

"You served me well. You're done. Thank you, General. There'll be a retirement ceremony for you on Friday."

"Oh, well, thank you, sir." Nick didn't quite know what to say.

"Bring the kids. I'd like to meet them."

"Yes, sir." He shook his hand and felt the coin. The President gave him his coin. It must be over. "Sir, are you sure you—"

"Take some time off, Nick. You deserve it. And I know how to find you if I need you."

"It's been an honor, Mr. President," Nick said.

Nick was taken back and went to his office. He stepped next door and asked Gia for some boxes.

"Boxes? Why?"

"My job is finished. Retirement Ceremony on Friday."

"What do you mean? The President fired you?"

"No, I didn't get fired. He let me go. He's done with me." Nick smiled.

"Done with you? What?"

"Stop questioning it and get me some boxes, Gunny." He went into General mode.

Gia stared at him.

He cleared his throat and softened his tone. "Please. I get to spend more time with the kids."

"Don't order me," she told him.

"Sorry," he said. "I need some boxes."

"I'll get your boxes." She picked up the phone and called someone.

"Thank you," Nick said. Gia stuck her tongue out at him. "That's not very professional," he said.

A few minutes later, Gia went to his office. "Your boxes are on the way. I expect dinner when I get home."

"Yeah, sure," Nick said, chuckling. Then he saw her face. "Oh, you're serious. Uh, okay. But you may not want me cooking all the time. I'm not half as good as you."

Kimberly A. Biggerstaff © 2024

"We'll see. Pick the kids up?" Gia asked.

"Yes, I'll get them," he said.

"Someone needed boxes, Gunny?" a Corporal said.

"Yes, General Foster," she said, walking out.

Then he saw the Corporal watching her. "Corporal!"

"Sir?" he said but kept watching Gia.

"That's my wife, Corporal!"

"Yes, sir. You're a lucky man, sir," he said.

"Give me the boxes and return to your post." Nick was irritated.

"Yes, sir," he said, leaving.

"Maybe I need to stay here. Too many people checking my wife out." He went back to Gia. "How long before you can retire?"

"Eight years."

"Eight? I thought you told me six once?"

"It's eight, minimum."

He sighed. "Start wearing slacks."

Jim and the agents smiled, trying not to look at them.

"Excuse me?" She stood up. "Come with me," she said. They walked back over to his office, and she shut the door. "What do you mean wear slacks?'

"Do you know how many men I see checking you out? Not to mention Barrett."

Gia smiled. "You're jealous."

Kimberly A. Biggerstaff © 2024

"Damn right. I know how these men think. Barrett is another story . . . but I don't like—" She stopped him by kissing him.

"You have nothing to worry about. Sam is just having fun because she knows it bothers you. As for the others"—she pushed him against the door and kissed him again—"I'm yours, Nick Foster. No one else but you."

He took a breath. "I still think you should wear pants. Wear camouflage," he said, inching her skirt up.

"I'll take it under advisement," she said. "I have to go to (Ft.) Mead. See you at home. Don't forget dinner."

"McDonald's okay?"

"No," Gia said, backing away from him.

"You're going to leave me after you did that?"

"We already christened this office," she said.

He smiled, remembering it was just before lunch. Gia waited for him to move so she could leave.

"I have work to do," she said.

"See you later," he said.

* * * *

Nick took two boxes with him. He picked the kids up, and they went to the grocery store.

"Kevin, I need to make dinner. What should we have?"

"Why? Is Mommy mad at you?"

"No. She just asked me to make dinner since I'll get home first."

"Hot dogs?" Kevin suggested.

"No."

"Hamburgers."

"No."

"Uh . . . chicken nuggets?"

"No."

"I got nothing, Nick," Kevin told him, shrugging.

Nick smiled. "Let's look around, and maybe we'll figure something out."

"Pizza?"

"No, I think she expects me to make something. Not just heat it up and serve. What other things does she make that you like?"

"Uh, ravioli is good."

"She makes that from scratch. Not enough time."

Kevin groaned. "Hey, meatloaf. And I can help. Mommy lets me put in the soup mix, and I mash it together with my hands. I wash them really good before we start."

"I should hope so. Meatloaf. Hmm. Okay. We need ground beef. Oooh. Look at this one." He was searching on his phone and showed Kevin a photo of a meatloaf and its recipe.

"Yum. That looks good. Let's make that one."

"Agreed. I don't know what we have at home, so we'll buy everything in this recipe. Ready for our mission?" Nick asked.

"Ready, sir."

Sofia made a noise from the carrier Nick was wearing.

"Her sock is coming off, Nick," Kevin said.

Nick fixed her sock, and they continued their mission.

"Hey, that's a cool baby carrier. May I ask where you got it?" a young man asked Nick. "Getting ready to have a little boy myself."

"Yeah, I'm a marine, and my niece and her fellow marines thought I'd like this for my daughter. Look at the diaper bag. There. Tactical Baby Gear."

"My stepdad's a general. Retired," Kevin said proudly.

"Cool. Thanks, General. And thanks for your service," the man said.

"Thank you," Nick told him. "Do we have all our supplies?" Nick asked Kevin.

"Yes, double-check," Kevin said.

They went through the list. "All accounted for. You want anything?"

"Um . . . I don't know." Kevin shrugged his shoulders again.

"Doesn't Mom give you treats or anything special in your lunch?"

"How about a comic book?" Kevin asked. "No, a ship."

"A ship?" Nick asked.

"Yeah, Finn has army men and planes. I only have the one plane Daddy flew on. Were you ever on a ship? I want your ship."

"Yeah, I served on some ships long ago. We need to go to a toy store for that or find one online. They have some books here. Let's go find you one, and we'll look for a ship later."

"Okay."

Kevin found a book and picked a baby book for Sofia. They paid for everything and went home. Then they got to work making the meatloaf. Kevin helped.

"All right, good job, Marine," Nick said after putting the meatloaf in the oven and setting the timer.

"We better clean up. Mommy doesn't like a messy kitchen," Kevin told him.

"Yeah, we did make a mess."

They cleaned up and sat down. "Thanks for your help, Kev."

"Don't call me Kev."

"Oh, okay. Can I ask why?" Nick asked.

"Daddy called me that," Kevin said softly.

"I'm sorry. I won't call you that," Nick told him.

"I like it when you call me Marine."

Nick smiled and rubbed the top of his head. "Then that's what I'll call you, Marine." Sofia began to cry. "Time to check her."

"Can I look for a ship on your computer?"

"Uh, yeah. You know how to spell it?"

"I'm four. Yes, I can spell ship." Then he spelled it.

"Sorry. That's great. I'll write down the ships I was on." Nick wrote down the ship's names and their designations. "I'll bring my laptop out here, and you can sit at the kitchen table." He got the laptop and got him started. Then Nick ran upstairs and changed Sofia's diaper. He brought her back down and set her in her swing. When the timer went off, he put the glaze on the meatloaf and put it back in the oven.

"Mashed potatoes, Nick," Kevin called.

"Right. Thanks, buddy. It's going to have to be instant."

"I'm home," Gia called. "Wow, something smells good."

"Hi, Mommy. Nick and I made dinner," Kevin said, running to her and hugging her.

"Hamburgers?" she guessed.

"No."

"Pizza?"

"No." Kevin laughed.

"I give up."

"We made a special meatloaf. We went to the store and bought all the stuff and came home and made it. I helped mix all the stuff in it. Nick cried cutting something."

"He did? Was it onions?"

"Yeah."

"You didn't tell him my trick?"

"I forgot."

"Hi, sweetie." Nick came in and kissed Gia on the cheek.

"Hello. So you really made something."

"You told me to. Could I have gotten away with—"

"No. I'm starved and it smells great," she said.

"Go change and we'll set the table. It's almost ready. Glass of wine?"

"Yes. No. I need to go pump first."

"Okay."

Gia got some clean bottles and went upstairs.

Nick and Kevin set the table and waited for Gia to come back.

"Okay, I'm ready." Gia sat down in her usual spot after transferring the milk to special bags and placing them in the freezer. Nick served her the meatloaf, mashed potatoes, gravy, and green beans. "Wow, that glaze looks great," she commented.

Nick and Kevin waited for her to try it. "Oh my gosh," she said as they watched.

"What? Did we mess up?" Nick asked.

"No. This is delicious. Wow. A-plus, boys." Gia smiled.

Nick and Kevin high-fived. "Don't expect that every day," Nick told her.

"What were you doing on the laptop, Kevin?" Gia asked.

"Nick's buying me a ship."

"A ship?" she asked.

"A model of one I served on. Have you ever served on a ship?"

"Just the one I told you about, so far."

"Oh, right. I forgot. So far, that sounds like . . ." Nick swallowed his food. "Did you get orders?"

"Can we talk about it later?" Gia said, not wanting to change the mood. But it didn't work.

"Uh, yeah." Nick was quiet for the rest of the meal.

"Kevin, you made a great meatloaf. Thank you," Gia told him.

"It was fun, wasn't it, Nick?"

"Yeah, it was fun, Marine," Nick said gloomily.

Kevin cleaned his plate and even had two slices of meatloaf. "May I be excused?"

"Yes," Gia told him. "Why don't you go play in the other room." Kevin ran off. "I'm sorry. I didn't want to tell you like that. It's a TDY. Six months or so."

"I guess . . . it's part of the job. We'll be fine," Nick said. "When and where."

"When is soon and where . . . is classified."

"Are you kidding me? I was Commandant—"

"Nick. You know where the ship will be headed," she said. She looked at the list of ships Nick wrote out for Kevin. "I think Kevin should get this one." She pointed to one, and Nick knew it was the one she would be deployed on.

"How soon?" he asked again.

"Next week."

He took a breath. "Okay. We'll be fine. I'll take care of the kids. I can do that."

Gia hugged him. "Yes, you can do this."

"You need to be careful. Stay away from the sailors and marines," Nick told her.

"Nick."

"I have to say that."

"I understand." She smiled at him.

They finished cleaning up the kitchen and put the leftovers away. "How about that wine now?" Nick asked her.

"Definitely," Gia said.

Nick poured them a glass, and they went and sat down in the family room. Kevin was looking at his new book. "When are you going to tell him?" Nick whispered.

Gia sighed. "I guess now is as good a time as any. Kevin, come here, baby."

Kevin walked over and stood in front of Gia. She moved over and asked him to sit between her and Nick.

"Kevin," Gia began. She looked at Nick for help.

"Kevin, being a Marine means you have to go where the Corps needs you," Nick said. "The Corps needs your mom somewhere else."

"We're moving?" he asked.

"No, honey. I need to go alone. It's called a temporary duty, and I'll come back when it's over."

"You're leaving us?"

"I have to . . . it's my job. But you have Nick and Sofia. And I'll bet you can stay with Finn and Alan sometimes."

"Can we talk on the phone?"

"Yes, sometimes. And video chat and write letters. It might be hard where I'm going, but I will talk to you every chance I get." She pulled him close and whispered in his ear, "I need you to take care of Nick and Sofia for me."

"When are you leaving?" he asked her.

"Next week. So we need to make sure Nick has everything he needs and knows how to take care of you and Sofia."

"Okay," Kevin said. "I'll miss you, Mommy."

"I'll miss you too," Gia said, hugging him.

"We can do this, right, Marine?" Nick asked him.

"Right, General." He saluted him. "Are you going on a ship, Mommy?"

"Honey, I can't tell you. It's a secret," she said.

"Okay." Then he whispered, "Can I have a model of it?"

Nick and Gia smiled at him, and Gia hugged him again.

* * * *

Gia wrote everything she could think of down for Nick. Sam said she would help when she could, but she was obsessed with finding the woman who contacted Jim. Barb and John would help, and Michael said Kevin could spend the night whenever he wanted.

"We didn't get to tour the school," Nick told her.

"I trust you. Go check it out, and if you think it's good for him, then enroll him."

"Okay."

"I'm going to miss his first day of Kindergarten." Gia's eyes welled up. "And Sofia's first tooth and crawling and . . ."

Nick held her tight as they lay in bed. She'd be leaving the next morning.

"I will take lots of pictures and videos." He kissed her. "I've been meaning to ask you something. Are you taking the First Sergeant or Master Sergeant route?"

"I'm . . . not sure. I still have some time to decide."

"I think you should go for Master Sergeant. You're too good at your job. Although you'd probably be a good first sergeant. Taking care of the troops."

"You're biased."

"Yes, but it's true. You are very good at your job."

"I love you," she told him.

"I love you, too. Stay away from the men and wear pants. That's an order," he said, smiling.

"Yes, General," she said, turning towards him. "You know, if I got pregnant . . ."

"No. As much as I love you, no. Not now."

"I know. I just . . . I'm going to miss you. One more time for the road?" She smiled.

"Um. I think I can manage that," Nick said.

Chapter 21

Nick took Kevin and Sofia to tour the school. He asked lots of questions and was satisfied after making sure Kevin liked it.

"How was it?" Gia asked.

"It's really nice. The academic program is great, and Kevin wants to go there. There's all kinds of extracurricular things he can do."

"He's going to kindergarten."

"I guess I got a little more excited about than I thought I would," Nick said.

Gia smiled. "Is he nearby?"

"Kevin, your mom wants to talk to you." Nick moved away from the screen.

"Hi, Mommy!"

"Hey, baby. I miss you," Gia said.

"I miss you too," Kevin said.

"Are you helping with Sofia?"

"Yes. I have chores to do."

"Chores?"

"Yes. I help with the laundry and the garbage and set the table and clean my room and Nick pays me an . . . what's it called?"

"Allowance," Nick said from offscreen.

"Yeah. I like the school, and Finn and Alan will be in my class. Sky will be there, too."

"That's great. I love you."

"I love you too, Mommy," Kevin said.

"Gia, they need you," a voice said.

"I have to go," Gia said to them.

"Bye, Mommy."

Nick came back with Sofia. "Wave to Mommy."

"Bye, sweetie. I love you guys."

"Be safe," Nick said as she blew a kiss.

* * * *

A couple of months went by, and the next time Gia and Nick spoke, something didn't seem right.

"Gia, what's wrong?" Nick asked her.

"Nothing," she said softly.

"Don't do that. Please tell me."

"I'm just tired and I miss you all so much."

Nick let it go this time, but he knew something wasn't right.

"Thank you for all the videos. Sofia is growing so fast. Is everything going okay?" She changed the subject.

"Yes. We're all doing great, other than missing you."

"Don't forget to video the first day of school. He has to wear uniforms, right?" Gia said.

Kimberly A. Biggerstaff © 2024

"Yes. We got them and all his supplies, a new backpack, and a lunchbox too."

"Thank you, Nick. You're making it a little easier. I need to go. I love you," she said.

"Gia, remember what I said. You can tell me anything."

"Nick, I can handle anything that comes up, and if I can't . . . I'll let you know. Goodbye." She disconnected the call.

Gia grabbed her gear and went to her workstation. As she was walking, Commander Graham blocked her way. "Hello, Gunny."

"Commander."

He placed his hand against the bulkhead and cornered her. "I just can't stop thinking about you. You know, there are lots of places—"

"Commander, I told you I'm married and not interested."

"You are too pretty for just one man," he said, placing his other hand on her waist.

"Remove your hand, or I'll report you," Gia said.

"Ha, yeah right. I can ruin your career. It'll be a 'he said, she said' thing." He saw someone coming, so he moved. "Another time," he said, walking away.

Kimberly A. Biggerstaff © 2024

Gia took a deep breath. He was right, and even if she reported him, chances were she'd never get any good assignments or evaluations. Maybe she should tell Nick and see what he thinks. No, he'd get mad and try to take care of it. She decided to try and find out if there were other women he'd done it to. She couldn't be the first. But she'd had enough of him.

She went to work and tried to avoid him. But he always sought her out. She tried to stay in groups or walk with at least one other person. But it wasn't always easy.

"Brittany, can I ask you something?" Gia said to her bunkmate. "Have you had any . . . issues . . . with anyone on board?"

"Issues?" Brittany stopped reading her book.

"Yes. You know . . ."

"Why? Have you heard something?" Brittany asked.

"No, I . . . I'm sorry. Forget it." Gia changed her mind.

* * * *

"Gia, can I talk to you?" Brittany asked a few days later.

"Sure."

"The other day, were you talking about . . . Commander Graham?"

"Uh, yes. He . . . made a pass at me. Saying things and he touched me on the waist twice. I told him I was married and wasn't interested, but he didn't stop," she told her.

"You're not the first," Brittany admitted.

"You too?"

"Yes. But . . . I can't risk my job. We don't have proof."

"I guess we'll have to figure something out. We can't let him get away with it," Gia said.

"Gia . . . I like you, but . . . I was glad when you came on board."

"Because he moved from you to me?"

"Yes. I'm sorry about that. I mean, I don't think any of us should put up with that. If you can figure out a way without ruining our careers, I'll help you. It's just that I send money home to my parents. They need help with the family farm. I can't afford to be blackballed and lose this job."

"I'll see what I can come up with," Gia said, going to sleep. She felt better knowing she wasn't the only one. Now, to come up with a plan.

The next free time she had, Gia went to the library. She was surprised, but she found Sam's book and checked it out. She wanted to see if she could find anything that might help her. She tried to skim over the parts she didn't need but found it difficult. It was a really good book and very interesting. She was eating lunch when a woman sat down next to her.

"Gunny, you're not alone," the petty officer said.

Gia stopped reading, and suddenly there were three other women nearby. "What's going on?" she asked.

"We have been in your shoes. We just wanted you to know."

"I'm going to figure something out." Gia tried to reassure them.

"We better go. That's a good book," another petty officer said.

"She's a friend," Gia said.

"You know Colonel Barrett?"

"Yes. She babysits my son sometimes."

"Colonel Barrett babysits? I just can't see that."

"She's a really nice person. Just don't piss her off," Gia said.

"That I believe," a marine staff sergeant said. "We shouldn't be seen all together like this. Let us know, Gunny."

Later, when she finished her shift, she video called Sam. "I need some advice."

"You and your husband will never be able to pay me back for all these favors and advice I give you," Sam said.

"This is the first time I've asked," Gia said.

"You're a package deal."

Kimberly A. Biggerstaff © 2024

"Hi, Gunny." A head popped on screen.

"Hi. Are you Finn or Alan?"

"Finn."

"No, you aren't," Sam said.

"Mommy, you can't tell us apart?" he said.

Sam looked at him. "You're Alan. Nice try. That's Alan."

"I'm Alan," he said, laughing.

"Hi, Gunny!" Finn said. "We tried to fool you."

"Hello, Gunny," Sky said.

"Mommy!" Kevin said.

"Hello. Kevin? What are you doing there?"

"Staying with Sam and Michael. Sofia too," Finn said.

"What's going on? Is Nick okay?" Gia was suddenly worried.

"He's fine. Well, physically. Go play, kids. I need to talk to Gunny," Sam said.

"Sam, what's going on? Where is Nick?"

"Okay, don't get mad at me. He's on his way to see you?"

"What? Oh my god! I'll kill him. How can he get here?"

"He asked the current Commandant if he could go on a Morale and Welfare Tour. So, tell me what you need. You didn't tell him."

"I told him I could handle it myself," Gia said.

"Then why are you calling me?"

"I can't afford to make a mistake. My career is on the line, along with that of some other women."

"It's a man! What's he done? Oh, did he make a pass?"

"A little more than that, and I'm not the first. He's an officer."

Sam sat back in her chair. "Shit."

"Swear jar, Mommy!" Finn yelled.

"Sorry."

Gia explained the situation. She told her she read her book to get ideas, but she wanted to get it straight from the horse's mouth. "So, what do you think?"

Sam sighed. "All these years in the service, and this is the first time this has happened to you?"

"I never said that. But no one bothered me when I was with Frank. Can you suggest anything?"

"The easiest thing would be to try and record him doing it. Blackmail works. I once had David make a guy believe he and his friend were Chinese spies to keep him from reporting Lex and Laura before she was an officer. No, you could get in a lot of trouble if something goes wrong." They heard a crash offscreen. "Jiminy Christmas, Finlay Joseph Kincaid!"

Kimberly A. Biggerstaff © 2024

"It was Alan, Mommy!" Finn yelled.

"Can I get back to you?" Sam asked.

"Yes. When did Nick leave?" Gia asked.

"This morning," Sam answered.

"Thank you. Oh, Sam. You have some fans here," Gia told her.

"Oh, yeah? Maybe I'll send them some autographed books."

"See you later, and thank you for everything," Gia said, smiling.

"Stay safe, Gia, and kick him in the balls if all else fails." They disconnected.

* * * *

"I think we should start a rumor that he's gay. He'd hate that. Or that he has a small d*** ," Brittany told Gia later that day.

"No, I think I have a better idea." Gia smiled.

Chapter 22

Twenty-four hours later, Brittany opened the door and said, "Gia, you will never believe who came aboard." She stopped and stared at the man in uniform in their quarters. She snapped to attention.

"Carry on, Staff Sergeant," Nick said.

"Staff Sergeant Brittany Henry, this is General Nick Foster, my husband."

"Honored to . . . meet you . . . sir. Did you say . . . husband?"

"Yes," Gia said.

"A pleasure to meet you, SSgt. Henry," Nick said. "Would you mind giving us a few minutes?"

"Yes, sir, no problem, sir."

"Brittany, could you not say anything about us being married, please?" Gia asked.

"No problem," she said, leaving and securing the door.

Gia turned from Nick. "I told you I could handle it."

"You didn't seem surprised to see me. Why is that?" Nick asked.

"I spoke with Sam yesterday. Saw Kevin," Gia said.

"Why did you call Sam?"

"To get her advice. Nick, you shouldn't have come. And how did you get permission?"

"I was activated and I'm on a Morale Tour."

"Activated? What's wrong with you?" Gia was angry.

"It's only for a couple of weeks. I made a deal to check out the Marines in this area. Then I'm going home to the kids. Oh, here. I took the kids for pictures." He handed her a photo of him, Kevin, and Sofia.

"Aww. She's getting so big. I'm still mad at you," Gia said, playfully hitting him on the chest.

"You're not going to tell me, are you?"

"Not until I have to," Gia said, sitting on her bunk.

"How did you manage to get these quarters?" Nick asked.

"Just lucky," she said.

"I'll say." He moved close and kissed her.

"General. That's not allowed."

"I missed you so much." He wrapped his arms around her waist and went to kiss her again, but she pulled away. "I knew it. Who is it?" he demanded.

"Please, Nick," she said as she started to tear up.

He looked away from her. He waited and then, with a lump in his throat, he said quietly, "Well, I guess we can discuss the details when you get back. I hope you'll let me keep Kevin sometimes," he said sadly.

Kimberly A. Biggerstaff © 2024

"What?"

"I knew you were out of my league. I hope you'll be happy with whoever—"

She suddenly slapped him. "What the hell is wrong with you?"

"Ow. What was that for?" he asked, touching his cheek.

"I love you. I'm not seeing anyone, you idiot. In fact, I'm trying to keep a damn officer away from me."

"What officer?" Nick was mad again.

"I'm not telling you. I said I'd handle it," Gia said.

"Arggh, you are so frustrating. But I love you." He went to touch her but hesitated. "Did he . . . ?"

"No. Just saying stuff and well, he touched my waist twice. But I'm not the first. There are others on board."

"Bastard," Nick said.

"Nick." Gia hugged him. "There is no one but you." She kissed him and it turned into a very passionate kiss. Nick reached under her MARPAT (Marine Pattern; camouflage) uniform top and untucked her shirt so he could touch her skin.

"Even in this camouflage, wearing pants, you are beautiful," he said, smiling at her.

"General Foster to the Captain's Mess. General Foster to the Captain's Mess," a voice announced over the intercom.

"Dammit," he said.

Kimberly A. Biggerstaff © 2024

"Have fun, General."

"If you need anything, just let me know."

"I'll be fine," Gia said.

"Of course you will. You're a marine," he said.

"No, I'm a Foster," she said, smiling at him.

He opened the bulkhead door and left. He made his way to the Captain's Mess. "General Foster, I'm Captain Willoughby. Welcome aboard. You already met my XO (Executive Officer). These are some of my other officers." The Captain introduced the men. "This is Commander Graham. And this is Chief of the Boat, McDaniels."

"Sir."

"A pleasure to meet all of you. Captain, I was having a look around and found two enlisted marines sharing quarters that looked like officer quarters."

"Chief?"

"Yes, sir. We're shorthanded in some areas, and . . . was it two females, sir?"

"Yes," Nick said.

"Those quarters are unoccupied, and the Marines are on temporary duty with us. I upgraded them for morale."

"Good idea, but I don't like hearing that you're shorthanded," Nick said.

"Well, that's why we called in the Marines, sir," the XO said.

Nick laughed. Graham whispered to another Commander.

"What is it, Graham?" Nick demanded.

"Nothing, sir. You have some very fine marines." Then he softly added, "Fine-looking." Nick heard him and scowled.

"Graham, are you on watch?" the XO asked.

"Yes, sir."

"Better get going," the XO told him.

"Yes, sir." He snapped to attention and left.

"He's still young. Sewing his oats, as they say," the XO tried to explain. "I'll speak to him, Captain."

Nick didn't say anything but didn't have a good feeling about the Commander. He might be the officer Gia was talking about.

* * * *

"Gunnery Sergeant Lorenzo, you are looking extremely fine today," Graham said, blocking her path.

"Commander." That was all Gia said.

"I was just telling the General what fine marines he has."

Gia thought about telling him Nick was her husband, but he'd only stop messing with her and move on to another woman. So she kept quiet about that. But Gia was getting tired and frustrated with him.

Kimberly A. Biggerstaff © 2024

"Excuse me, Commander. I need to go," she said.

"What's you hurry? You're off duty for another . . . few hours." He checked his watch. I heard the Chief upgraded you and you only have one bunkmate. Or I know some places the sailors go." He had once again backed her against the bulkhead. He glanced around and smiled at her.

"Move out of my way, Commander. I said no more than once. I'm happily married and not interested. I'm going to report you."

"No one will believe you, and I can ruin your career. God, you're beautiful." He touched her on the chin. "Did you ever think of modeling? I'd love to take some nude photos of you." He placed one hand on her hip and one on her neck and forcibly held her so he could kiss her. Then he touched her breast.

"Take your hands off my wife!" Nick began to pull him away as Gia kneed Graham in the balls. Graham groaned and Nick began to swing at him, but Gia stepped in front of him and partially blocked his swing with her arm.

"General, NO! We got him," Gia said. Unfortunately, she caught part of his punch on her cheek.

"Oh, Jesus, Gia. I'm sorry. Are you okay?" Nick asked.

"Son of a—" She stopped herself and held her cheek.

Brittany appeared from behind a corner and held up a phone. "I got it all, Gunny. Right here on video. And I guess you are a witness, General."

Nick was pissed. "Take her to the infirmary. I'll take him to the brig."

"I need . . . a medic," Graham said, doubling over and holding his groin. "Fucking bitch."

"Ask for one in the brig," Nick said as he steered him into a pipe. "Oops, sorry about that."

"I'm okay. I can go myself. Follow him and make sure he doesn't do anything stupid, please," Gia told Brittany.

"Yes, Gunny. I'm sorry you had to go through that."

"I'm sorry you and the others did too. Hopefully, we got enough to take care of him. You better go."

Gia went to the infirmary for an ice pack. She was cryptic as to why she needed it. The medic gave it to her.

Nick took Graham to the brig. "I'm turning this man in for . . . making sexual contact towards an enlisted female."

"Uh, yes, sir," the sailor said.

"I'm an officer. You should confine me to quarters," Graham said.

"No, you're an animal, and you belong behind bars," Nick said. "I'll take responsibility for bringing him here."

"Get me a medic, sailor," Graham said.

Kimberly A. Biggerstaff © 2024

The sailor looked at the General. "Get him one." Then he saw Brittany. "Sergeant, what are you doing here?"

"Gunny asked me to follow you and make sure you didn't . . . you know."

"He's safe as long as he's in there," Nick said.

"Yes, sir."

"Did you say she's your wife?" Graham asked. "What's it like tapping that? Bet she's a great lay, right, General?" Graham knew he was done for and just mouthed off.

When the medic came, Nick told him, "He got kneed in the groin. I think he needs a prostate exam too." Then Nick whispered something to him. The medic looked at Graham with contempt.

"Hey! What did he say?" Graham asked the medic. "He lied. I don't need a prostate exam. I'm fine."

* * * *

Nick pressed the charges so Gia didn't have to. But after word got around, more women came forward and reported Graham for what he had done to them. He scared a couple of the lower enlisted women so bad they had sex with him. The charges began to pile up.

The Captain was embarrassed and angry that this officer had gotten away with it for so long on his ship.

Kimberly A. Biggerstaff © 2024

"General, I apologize for what happened. I don't condone that behavior, and we will step up our efforts to prevent this from happening."

"I don't think we can totally eliminate this behavior. But we need to make sure the reporting process is simple and no one has to worry about repercussions. Reporting a crime shouldn't ruin a career when you're a victim."

"Yes, sir."

* * * *

"I'm sorry I got involved in that mess. I should have let you handle it. I guess I just . . . worry about you and feel like I should be protecting you. I'm old-fashioned that way," Nick told Gia. "But I'm still glad I came and was able to see you."

"I like the fact that you worry and want to protect me. But you need to listen to me when I tell you I can handle something."

"I know. I'll try to do better. I haven't had anyone to take care of in such a long time. Times have changed, and I need to catch up."

"I'm not saying I don't want you to protect me," Gia said.

"I get it. I'm sorry."

"I love you, General Foster. Now go home and take care of our kids," Gia ordered him.

Kimberly A. Biggerstaff © 2024

"I need to finish my tour. One more week. I'm proud of what you did. Those women wouldn't have come forward without you. Be safe, Gunnery Sergeant Lorenzo." He gave her a quick kiss, not caring who saw or that they were in uniform.

* * * *

When Nick returned, he went to see the new commandant. "Congratulations, Nick. I heard you helped root out a sexual predator."

"It wasn't me, Jake. My wife deserves the credit. And those other women who put their careers on the line to come forward."

"I'd say you were biased, but regardless, you both did a great job. I read your reports concerning our troops' morale on those ships. Glad to hear the Marines are happy for the most part."

"They're marines. They know when to suck it up."

"Do you think they told you what you wanted to hear? After all, you were commandant."

"I tried to reiterate to them that I wanted the truth. Any problems would be dealt with appropriately. There were a few issues, but nothing the Chief or XO on those ships can't handle."

"Good. Would you like to continue and tour some more?" the Commandant asked him.

Kimberly A. Biggerstaff © 2024

"No. We had a deal. I need to go home and be with my kids," Nick said firmly.

"Thanks again, Nick," he said, extending his hand.

"Thank you for letting me go. I know it was a big request," Nick said, shaking his hand.

"Yes, well, let's just say that when someone in the White House found out, I didn't have much of a choice. Take care, Nick."

"Hey, you got a few coins?" Nick asked before he left.

* * * *

"I'm looking for Gunnery Sergeant Lorenzo," Jonathan said to the Chief of the Boat.

"Hold on, sir," he said, looking at his computer.

"She's on duty. Not sure you have clearance to go where she is, but this is it." He wrote down where she was and gave it to him. He went to where she was and used the phone to call inside.

"Gunny, you have a visitor outside," a Petty Officer told her.

"I'll kill him if he's back," she said, getting up and going to the door. When she opened it, she was met with a smile.

"Captain Burke? What are you doing here? It's good to see you."

"Hello, Gunny. It's good to see you too."

"Did Nick send you?" Gia asked.

"No. I've been assigned here. Get some carrier landings and, you know . . . real-world stuff."

"Maybe we can talk later over coffee, Captain," Gia told him.

"Sure. I'd like that. See you, Gunny," Jonathan said, leaving.

Gia went inside and secured the door. "Captain?"

"He's the son of some friends."

"Captain Burke. Why does that name sound familiar?"

"Hmm, I don't know." Gia smiled. She figured it wasn't really her place to tell others who his father was.

* * * *

"Scuttlebutt says you took down a sleazeball squid," Jonathan said.

"I had help," Gia told him. "How did you know I was here?"

"The General sent word. This is pure coincidence that I got assigned here," Jonathan said. "Hey, do you know anything about this ghost my mom is chasing?"

"Ghost?" Gia asked.

"Yeah, something you guys were involved with. A guy in your office," Jonathan said.

"No, you'll have to ask your mom or Jenny. I think it's an ongoing investigation. Is your mom still helping them?"

"I think so. Dad says she is obsessed with finding this woman. Thinks she knows her. But that's all I got out of him."

They talked for a while and then went their separate ways. Gia had only met Jonathan that one time he came to pick up Sam and Finn, but it was nice to see someone from home who knew the same people.

Both Gia and Jonathan were very busy. Every once in a while, they managed to grab a coffee or a few minutes to talk.

"So when are you and Jenny getting married?" Gia asked him.

"I thought it was going to be soon, but then I got sent out here."

"You should just go do it. Fly to Vegas or something," Gia suggested.

"Our moms don't want that. They told us."

"Can you have a small one?"

"I think so, they just don't want us running off."

"Next time you get time off and go home, do it. Tell Jenny to have her dress or uniform ready, and you always have yours ready. You could have someone get certified to perform the ceremony. You know online or whatever."

"I get it. Have it all planned so we can do it whenever."

"Right," Gia said.

"Thanks, Gia. I'll talk to Jenny," he said.

Jonathan went back to his quarters that he shared with other officers.

"Hey Burke, you better be careful about fraternizing with that Gunnery Sergeant," a fellow pilot told him.

"She's friends with my parents. I'm not fraternizing and I'm engaged."

"Optics, man. Just be careful."

"Did someone say something?" Jonathan asked.

"Scuttlebutt says she may have flirted with that officer."

"Bullshit. She's not like that. And he was a dick. There were other women."

"I'm just telling you . . ."

"And I'm telling you. She's not like that. She loves her husband," Jonathan said.

"You have to admit, she's really hot."

"Don't you have a sortie coming up?" Jonathan said, trying to end the conversation.

"See you, Starboy."

"Fly safe, Rocky," Jonathan said.

Jonathan laid in his rack and began to read the book he borrowed from the library. But he started to think about Gia. "Oh, come on . . . idiot. Jenny, Jenny, Jenny. Think about her. No, don't think about any of them." He couldn't concentrate, so he changed and went to the gym. He lifted some weights and ran on the treadmill. He went back to his quarters and took a shower and tried to go to sleep.

"Jonathan? Can we talk?" Gia asked.

"Sure."

"Would you walk with me?" she asked as they went down the corridor. They kept walking, and he wasn't paying attention to where they were going. He barely heard what she said. The corridor became darker, and finally he couldn't help himself. He placed his hands on her shoulders and kissed her.

He sat up and looked around. "Dammit."

"Dreaming about your girl, Starboy," Rocky asked him.

"Shut up," he said, laying back down.

* * * *

Jonathan decided to stay away from Gia for a while and concentrate on flying. A few days later, she sought him out.

"Captain Burke? Do you have a minute for a coffee?" Gia asked.

"No, sorry, Gunny," he said, walking away.

Kimberly A. Biggerstaff © 2024

Gia didn't think much of it, but after a few weeks, she wondered if she had done something. She found him and stopped him. "Captain Burke. I need a minute, sir," she said almost as an order.

"What is it, Gunny?"

"Did I do something?"

Jonathan looked around. "No. I just heard some scuttlebutt and thought it would be better for both of us if I kept my distance," he told her.

"Scuttlebutt, right," Gia said. "Thanks for telling me." She turned and walked away.

"Dammit," Jonathan said to himself.

Gia went back to her quarters. She was told they might be picking up one or two female officers and she and Brittany would have to move.

"Gunny, what's up? Bummed about having to move?" Brittany asked.

"No, I mean sure. We were lucky to get these."

"Yeah. Back to the dorms," Brittany said.

"Brittany, have you heard anything about . . . me and Captain Burke?"

"Uh, yeah, but I know there's nothing going on, and I tell them that," Brittany said.

"Great, thanks," Gia said. "His mother is Colonel Barrett. She'd probably make me disappear," Gia said.

"Wow. Imagine having her for a mother." Then Brittany said, "You know how the military is. It's just gossip. How much time do you have left here?"

"Two months."

"Stay strong. Two months and you can go home to your husband and kids. How is your daughter?"

Gia smiled. "Want to see the latest video?"

"Of course."

Gia pulled up the video she had saved on her phone and showed Brittany.

* * * *

Gia was working and didn't know what had happened until later.

"Gunny, you might want to go to the infirmary," Brittany told her.

"Why?"

"A pilot was injured," Brittany told her. "Captain Burke."

Gia didn't hesitate and went off to the infirmary. Jonathan was sitting up and being checked out. He saw Gia and smiled.

"Gunny, may I help you?" the nurse asked.

"No, I . . . just . . . no thanks," she said.

"Gunny!" Jonathan called.

Gia had started to leave but turned.

"Gunny, a word, please," Jonathan said.

"Sir?" Gia walked over to him.

"I'm okay. The arresting cable snapped, and I caught a gust that threw me in the drink. Had to eject. Minor injuries," he told her.

"That's good, sir. Too bad about your plane."

"Yeah. Maybe I can get my mom to buy me another one." He laughed but then grimaced at the pain. "Guess I'm grounded for a bit. I'll probably have time for more coffee," Jonathan said, letting her know he was sorry and wanted to have a coffee with her. He missed talking to her.

She just smiled and walked away.

"You know she's married, sir," the medic told him.

"Of course I know. Her husband worked with my father."

"Your father?"

"Yeah, General John Burke, Air Force Chief of Staff," Jonathan said proudly. For some reason, at that moment, he didn't care who knew who his parents were. He was glad to be alive.

* * * *

"So, you're okay?" Jenny asked.

"Yeah, I may be half an inch shorter. But yeah. I'll heal," Jonathan said. "Jenny, I don't want to wait anymore. I want to get married as soon as possible."

Kimberly A. Biggerstaff © 2024

"I do too," Jenny said.

"You do?"

"Yes. As soon as we can," Jenny said. "I'll take care of everything. Just stay safe and make better landings."

Jonathan gave a chuckle. "It wasn't my fault. I've been cleared. Just need to wait and pass my flight physical. Uh, Jenny. Will you tell my mom?"

"Jonathan James Burke. No, I will not tell your mommy that you crashed a multi-million-dollar jet."

"Okay. Just asking," he said. "Man."

"I love you, Jonathan."

"I love you more, Jenny."

Chapter 23

Nick and the kids were waiting at the base. They had driven down, and Nick had gotten a hotel room on base.

"How do I look, Nick?" Kevin asked.

"You look great, Marine. Does your sister look okay?"

"Yeah, for a girl. Mommy will be surprised."

"What about me? Squared away?" Nick asked.

"Yes, sir. Nick! Look! Is that her?"

Nick smiled. "Go get her, buddy."

Kevin ran to her and jumped into Gia's arms. "Oh, I missed you so much, Kevin." She hugged him and started to cry. She saw Nick holding Sofia and walking closer. But he stopped and set her down. Gia set Kevin down and watched as Sofia took two steps and fell. She crawled to Gia, who picked her up and kissed her and hugged her tight.

"Ma." Then she looked at Nick and said, "Dada."

Nick hugged Gia and kissed her. "We missed you, Gunny. Welcome home."

* * * *

A couple of weeks later, everything was back to normal. Kevin was in school, and Gia was back at work after taking a week off. It was Saturday and Nick was reading a book. The doorbell rang and he went to answer it.

"May I help you?" Nick said to the man. He was probably a few years older than Nick. He was nicely dressed in slacks, an oxford shirt and sport coat.

"I'm looking for Gia Lorenzo or Gia Conti."

Conti was Gia's maiden name. "May I ask what this is about? I'm her husband."

"I just have this letter for her," he said. He began to get uncomfortable. "Maybe you should give it to her." He offered it to Nick.

"Nick, can we—oh, hi," Kevin said, standing next to Nick.

"Hi," he said, looking at Kevin.

"Go get your mom, Marine," Nick told him.

"Yes sir." Kevin ran off to get Gia.

Nick could tell the man was nervous. But Nick was also being careful. It was awkward for both of them. "How do you know Gia?"

"I . . ."

"Nick, what's up?" Gia asked.

"You have a visitor," he said, stepping a little to the side.

"Yes?" Gia looked at the man.

When he saw her, he was floored. He nearly fell off the step.

"Are you okay?" Nick asked, grabbing his arm.

"Yes. Sorry." He looked at Gia. "Are you Gia Conti from Naples?" he asked, but after seeing her, he knew it was her.

"Yes. Do we know each other?"

"No. I didn't know . . . I wanted to give you this." He handed her a letter. "Everything is in there. Well, most of it. I just wanted to say I'm sorry this took so long. The ball is in your court." He smiled and left.

"Wait, who are you?" she called after him.

But he ran across the street and got in his car and drove off. Gia closed the door and looked at the letter. Nick was standing nearby. "Old boyfriend?"

"Funny. I have no idea. He was old enough to be my father. Maybe he knew my grandmother in Italy. He knew my maiden name and where I lived."

"Open the letter."

It was thick and when she opened it, she found a photo. "Oh, my god." Her hands started shaking.

"Gia, what is it?"

"This . . . this is my mother and . . ." Gia started but couldn't finish.

"That man. He's older now, but that looks like him. Come sit down," Nick said. He took her to the couch and then went to get her a glass of water. He gave her the water, and she took a sip.

"I think this calls for something stronger," she said, staring at the photo.

Nick went and fixed a glass of scotch and set it on the side table. Gia took it and drank it all.

"Easy there. You're out of practice." Nick looked at the photo. "You look like her. Now I know why you're so beautiful."

Gia grabbed his hand. "Sit here with me."

"Of course."

She began reading the letter. She had to stop a few times to regain her composure. When she finished, she folded the letter and put it back in the envelope.

"Gia, are you alright?" Nick asked her.

"He's my father," she said.

Nick wasn't sure what to say. "Um, how do you feel about that?"

"I don't know. I knew he was a doctor. But that's all. My mother and grandmother never told me anything. I stopped asking after a while. Every summer, we'd go overseas and help in the missionary camps. I played with the kids," Gia told him. "I wasn't there when . . . we were getting fresh water from a new well we helped build. They came in and stole the medicine and supplies. They said mom was trying to reason with them, but one got angry and . . . shot her."

"I'm so sorry, honey." He hugged her.

"I was ten. That's when I was sent to live with my grandmother in Naples."

"What did he say in the letter?"

She handed him the envelope. "You can read it." She stood and went to get another glass of water.

Nick pulled the papers out and began reading. Gia's mother and this man fell in love one summer, and each summer they would live and work together. The third summer, he told her he was joining Doctors Without Borders and he wouldn't be coming back to that location. They split up amicably. He wrote her a couple of times but never received a reply. She never told him she was pregnant. He said if he had known, things would have been different. He moved on with his life but never forgot Gia's mother. He heard she had been killed and felt guilty for years. He thought he should have been there. When Gia's grandmother died, an attorney contacted him with a copy of Gia's birth certificate and a letter telling him about Gia. It took him a while to decide what to do. Then he had to search for her. He knew she had moved to California and married Frank Lorenzo. It was in the letter her grandmother sent him. Eventually, he found her living in Arlington. Then he had to work up the nerve to contact her. He decided to write the letter and let her decide. His cell phone number was on the last page, along with his email. He was in town for one more week.

Nick stood and went to the kitchen. "What do you want to do?"

"I don't know. I need to think about it," she said.

"Whatever you decide, I will support you," Nick said, placing a hand on her shoulder. Gia turned and hugged him, resting her head on his shoulder. He held her until Kevin came in.

"Nick, George needs food."

"Okay, buddy," he said.

Gia let go of him. "It's okay. You guys go. Maybe I'll take Sofia for a walk or something."

"Gia. Just don't . . . I mean, he's probably a nice guy, but . . . you don't know him."

"I won't do anything without telling you," she said.

"Um, why don't you come with us?" Nick said. "Or take her in the backyard. She likes the swing and the little playhouse."

"You don't want me to leave the house?" she said.

"We don't know anything about him."

"Okay. We'll stay here." Gia smiled at him.

"Thank you," Nick said.

Kimberly A. Biggerstaff © 2024

After he left, Gia looked the man up online. He was still a doctor and had a practice in Wyoming. She phoned Sam.

"Hello Gia. When can I babysit my favorite Italian baby?"

"Sofia is fine. And I don't need a babysitter right now."

Sam sighed. "But you need something."

"I'm sorry, but you're my friend, and I trust you with this. Are you still chasing ghosts?"

"Chasing ghosts?" Sam asked.

"That's the way Jonathan put it."

"Yes, I am. But it's slow going. What do you need?"

"Background on someone," Gia said.

Sam sighed.

"It's a doctor who lives in Wyoming."

"Wyoming? Hold on a minute. You'll have to ask him."

"Ask who?" Gia asked.

"Hello, Gia. How's life back on land?" Andrew asked.

"Fine."

"Is there something I can help with?"

"I guess. I'd like background on someone. He lives in Wyoming," Gia told him.

"Background." Andrew sighed and looked at Sam. "You're testing me."

"Testing you?" Gia asked, confused.

"Sam, not you, Gia. You know what, yes, give me the name and what you know."

"You ass," Sam said, walking away.

"Swear jar, Mom!" Luke called.

Gia gave him his name, cell phone number, email and the name and address of his practice.

"Age?"

"I . . . don't know. About Nick or Sam's age. Maybe somewhere in between?"

"Is this . . . personal or something bad? Like a stalker or spy?"

"No, nothing like that. He . . . I think he's my father. I never knew him, and he showed up today with a letter and a photo of himself and my mother."

"I see. I'll see what I can do for you. Do we have time?"

"Yes. But he leaves in a week. I'd like to make a decision in the next day or two."

"I understand. I'll call you," Andrew said.

"Is Sam okay?" Gia asked.

"Yeah, she's mad at me. She asked me to run background on someone about seven or eight months ago. I said no and she got arrested."

"Oh, that might have been for Nick's thing."

"She didn't say. She just got mad."

"Why are you helping me?" Gia asked.

"Because I like you and you asked. Also, I don't want her going to that cop. And I knew it would piss her off."

"Dad!" Luke yelled.

"I'll call you, Gia," he said.

"Thank you."

"Where did your mom go?" Andrew asked Luke.

"The bedroom," Jess said.

Andrew smiled and walked off toward the bedroom.

* * * *

Gia took Sofia into the backyard and placed her in the baby swing. Later, she placed her about halfway up on the slide and caught her as she slid down. Sofia laughed and giggled. They were still outside when Nick came home.

"So, is Sam checking him out?" Nick asked.

"How did you know?" Gia asked.

"It's what I would have done."

"Actually, Andrew is running him," Gia told him.

"Dada," Sofia said.

"Hi sweetie. Are you ready to go inside?" Nick asked her. He picked her up, and they all went inside.

* * * *

Andrew called Gia at work on Monday morning. "I have that information you requested. Care to meet for lunch?"

"Yes. Tell me where."

Andrew was waiting at the restaurant when Gia arrived.

"Thank you for doing this, Andrew. I hope Sam isn't too mad at you."

"No, I did something else for her." He smiled. "Brian Stephen Van Horn. Born in Grand Forks, North Dakota. Fifty-nine years old. Here, you can read it. He's a good guy on paper. Med school, summers in—"

"Africa. It was a missionary camp. My mother would go every summer until she . . . was killed."

"Gia, I didn't know that. I'm sorry," Andrew said.

"That's how they met, at the missionary camp. But they broke up before she knew about me. I was ten when she died and went to live with my grandmother in Italy." Gia read the papers.

"One traffic ticket that was dismissed because he was taking someone to the hospital. Like I said, a good guy on paper."

"Why do you word it like that?" she asked.

"Because some people are clean on paper but just haven't gotten caught yet. The kid next door who is secretly killing puppies and grows up to be a serial killer."

"Andrew."

"Look. I'm waiting for a—" His phone rang. "This call. Excuse me." He stood and walked out. Gia kept reading the paperwork. Harvard Medical School. Top of his class. Worked at a hospital in Boston, then moved to Wyoming and bought a ranch. He opened a small practice in Cheyenne.

Andrew returned and sat down. "I called the local police in Cheyenne. They love him. No problems. He's a good guy and a very good doctor."

"The police? Really?"

"Relax. It's good to talk to the locals. Anyway, if you decide to give him a chance, I won't stop you." Then he decided to share something personal. "You know, when I was young, my dad and I didn't get along. He sent me to military school. They didn't even acknowledge my existence for a while. I regret that. Although who knows how my life would have turned out if he hadn't done what he did. Did you know my father was Sam's CO in San Antonio?"

"No," Gia said.

"Yeah. She was shocked when I told her who I was. We had already slept together."

Kimberly A. Biggerstaff © 2024

Gia chuckled. "Well, I can only imagine. Thank you for doing this."

"No problem. Glad to help," Andrew said.

* * * *

"Nick, I'm going to call him," Gia announced at dinner.

"Okay. Are you going to meet him?" Nick asked.

"Oh, I uh . . . I suppose but . . ." Gia hadn't thought that far ahead.

"He already knows where we live. You could invite him for dinner," Nick said.

"No. I'd like to talk to him alone. I mean in public."

"Have him meet you at a restaurant tomorrow for lunch," Nick suggested.

"Okay, good idea."

"May I be excused?" Kevin asked.

"Yes, good job, Marine."

Gia looked at Sofia and then at the floor under her highchair. "Too bad George doesn't eat what falls on the floor." Gia smiled and tickled Sofia.

"Yeah, maybe we need a dog. A bulldog and name him Chesty," Nick said.

"Mama," Sofia said.

"Aww. Good girl," Nick said.

"You did a great job with them when I was gone. I can't believe she took to me so fast," Gia said.

"I showed her your picture every day and talked about you. We even watched videos."

"Thank you," Gia said, looking at him.

"I'll clean up. Go do what you have to do," Nick said.

Gia went to Nick's office and closed the door. "Mr. Van Horn? It's Gia Lorenzo. I was wondering if we could meet for lunch tomorrow."

"Yes, I'd like that," he said.

* * * *

They met at a restaurant near the Pentagon. He stood as she approached.

"You're a marine?" he said. "I didn't know."

"Yes. I joined right after high school. I was always fascinated by the sailors I saw in Naples."

"You didn't want to go to college?"

"I have my degree. I was seventeen when I graduated high school. I wasn't ready for college. The Marines gave me a chance to grow up, mature and travel some."

"Your mother always talked about traveling. I think it's why she went on the missions," he said. "You have her eyes and hair."

"You're a doctor?"

"Yes. What else did you learn?" he asked her.

"What do you mean?"

"If I were you, I would have checked me out. The sheriff and I are friends. He called and said someone was asking about me. It's fine. I don't blame you."

"I'm sorry. You have to be careful nowadays. Yes, a friend checked you out. I didn't know he'd call the sheriff."

"It's fine. I understand. I'll tell you anything you want to know."

"Did you love her?"

"Straight to the point. Yes, I did. I asked her to join Doctors Without Borders and come with me. But she wanted to stay in that village. She said they needed her. She got attached."

"We went every summer. I played with the kids," Gia said.

"Can you tell me what happened to her?" Brian asked.

"I was ten. Rebels came in to steal medicine and supplies. I was with some other kids getting fresh water at a new well. It was over by the time we got back. They said she tried to reason with them and was protecting a little boy they wanted to take with them. They shot her."

"I'm . . . so sorry," he said, swallowing the lump in his throat. "I should have been there."

"It's not your fault," she told him. She could see he still felt guilty about not being there.

"I didn't know about you," he said.

Kimberly A. Biggerstaff © 2024

"Would it really have mattered?"

"Yes. I loved her. I tried to write, but she didn't write back. Did she ever find anyone else?"

"No. She dated sometimes but never married. There was one I thought she might marry, but it didn't work out. What about you?" Gia asked.

"Um, I married later. I have a son. But we divorced after two years of marriage. I never forgot about your mom."

"I have a half-brother."

"Yes. This is him." He showed her a picture on his phone. "Peter. This is his wife. They just got married. How long have you and your husband been married?"

"Oh, just under a year. He's my second husband. My first husband died in a plane crash in California. He was a marine too. The little boy you saw is our son, Kevin. He's five. Nick and I have a daughter, Sofia."

"Two grandchildren." He smiled. "I have a small ranch with a couple of horses. I always hoped to have grandkids who would visit and I could teach them to ride." His face changed, and the smile was gone. "I don't understand why she didn't tell me." He wasn't mad. He just wanted to understand.

"I don't know. I used to ask about my father when I was little. But all she'd say was that he was a doctor and needed to help people. I didn't know my grandmother was planning on contacting you. She died a couple of years after Frank and I married and before Kevin was born. Even though she didn't tell me anything, she never said anything bad."

"Sounds like she didn't say much at all." He reached into his jacket pocket and pulled out a tattered piece of fabric. It looked old but was very colorful. "One of the women in the village gave your mother a dress made from this fabric. When I left that last summer, I found this little piece of fabric in my suitcase. She put it there." He got choked up. "I'm sorry I didn't get to see you grow up. But it looks like you've turned out fine." He wiped a stray tear away.

"I remember that dress." Gia recalled. She wore it for a few years and then stopped."

Brian pulled out a small wooden spoon and set it on the table. "This was carved by one of the men in the village. He told me that when I decided to marry your mother, I needed to present a dowry. It's their tradition. He told me to give this to her. I want you to have it." He pushed it closer to Gia. "I was going to give it to her, but . . . she wouldn't go with me. She didn't want to volunteer with Doctors Without Borders. She loved those people. She had a good heart."

* * * *

"Hello, Nick," Sam said.

"What the hell are you doing here?" Nick asked.

"I could ask you the same question."

Kimberly A. Biggerstaff © 2024

"She's my wife. I have every right to make sure she's okay."

"Where are the kids?" Sam asked.

"Kevin is in school, and Sofia is right here," he said, moving the blanket over her head. "You can see her. Why did you ask?"

"My . . . patch was in the way," Sam said, sitting with him. "I'll join my friend," she said to the hostess. "She's going to be upset with you for watching her."

"She probably wouldn't know. But you and your dog aren't exactly incognito."

"She's fine. So that's her father?" Sam asked.

"Yeah. I guess he's a nice guy. What are you doing here?" Nick asked.

"Eating. I have to eat."

"How did you know she was here? You were checking on her, too," Nick said.

"No. Well, so what? She's my friend," Sam admitted.

Nick smiled. "Thank you."

"Be quiet." Sam glanced around. Then she saw a woman with long blonde hair. She had her back to Sam and was at the bar. "Nick, see that blonde at the bar?"

"No."

"Please. I need your help," Sam said, pleading.

Nick looked and saw her. "Yeah. I see her." He looked back over at Gia.

"I think she's the one who contacted Jim."

"What? You still chasing her?" Nick asked.

"Yes. Now go talk to her and get her to turn this way," Sam said.

"No."

"How many times have I helped you?"

"Dammit. Fine." He got up and went to the bar. "Hi, there."

"Hello," she said with an accent.

"Can I buy you a drink?" Nick asked.

"Do you always pick up women with your child?" she asked him.

"I heard women like it," he said quickly.

"You are cute. Go back to your wife."

"Yeah. I think I will. Say, where are you from?"

"A small town in Russia," she said.

"Oh, I went to St. Petersburg once. Beautiful city. Went to . . . the Hermitage Museum and the Faberge Museum and other places," he told her so she knew he wasn't lying.

"For work or pleasure?"

"I was studying European History." He smiled at her. "I'm Grant."

"Grant. I'm Anastasia." She smiled at him.

"It's a pleasure to meet you. Your English is very good. How long have you been here?"

"Just a few months. I learned at university. I teach English there. Or taught. I'm . . . retired."

* * * *

"Come on, Nick, I didn't say to get her life story or pick her up," Sam said to herself.

"Sam, what are you doing?" Gia asked.

"Oh, hi Gia. I'm having lunch."

"Right," she said suspiciously. Then she saw Nick at the bar. "You guys are spying on me."

"Now, why would we . . . yes. We were worried about you. I need to check something," Sam said, standing.

Gia followed her over to Nick.

"What are you—" Sam started.

"Amy and Jill. I want to introduce you to—" But when he turned around, she was gone.

"Dammit," Sam said. "Where did she go?"

"What are you two doing? And why do you have Sofia?"

"What was I supposed to do with her? How did it go?" Nick asked her.

"This is ridiculous. Nick, did she look like this?" Sam showed him a photo on her phone.

"Yeah. Where did you get that?" he asked.

"That's my wife," Sam said.

"But . . . she's . . ."

"Dead. So who was that woman?" Sam said.

"She said her name was Anastasia. She was from a small Russian town. She learned English at her university and taught it there. That's all I got."

Sam looked at him. "Hmm. Maybe I'll turn you into a spy yet."

"No, you won't. Go home, Nick," Gia said. "Bye-bye, sweetie," she said to Sofia, touching her head.

"Mama," Sofia said.

"It's her," Sam said, walking with Nick. She stopped and made a call. "Charlie, I want the truth. Is she dead?"

"Sam, she died in your arms. You know she is," Charlie told her.

"I am telling you there's a woman who looks exactly like her. And I have a witness." She handed Nick the phone. "Tell her."

"Sam showed me a photo of her wife, and this woman looked like her. Same hair and facial features. She spoke with a Russian accent and said she was from a small Russian town."

Sam took the phone back. "See, I'm not crazy or hallucinating. She told Nick her name was Anastasia."

Kimberly A. Biggerstaff © 2024

"I don't know what to tell you, Sam," Charlie said.

Charlotte (Charlie) was Sam's stepmother. She did occasional work for the CIA. She was helping Katrina (Sam's ex-wife) bring in a foreign agent when Katrina was killed. But Sam knew the agency could fake a death. They had done it before, with her father. It was for his safety. So it wouldn't be that far-fetched to think they had done it with Katrina. Fake her death and send her into hiding with a new identity.

"All right, Charlie. How is everyone?" Sam asked.

"Fine. One is finding it difficult to keep up with the other. But everyone is in good health."

"Good. Give them my best and let me know if you learn anything about this."

"Take care, Sam." She hung up.

"Would you like a ride?" Nick asked Sam.

"Yeah, to Langley," Sam said.

"Okay. Mind if I tag along until I have to pick Kevin up?"

Sam looked at him. "You enjoyed playing spy, didn't you?"

"Yeah, but . . . I'm just curious. You said she's the one that made contact with the Senior Chief."

"Crap. Yeah, I need to tell Jenny I saw her. We saw her," Sam said.

Kimberly A. Biggerstaff © 2024

As they drove to Langley (CIA headquarters), Sam called Jenny. She told her where she saw the woman and that Nick talked to her.

"At this rate, she may bạn me from the wedding," Sam told Nick.

"It was a coincidence we were there."

"I know and she does too." She called Andrew.

"I'm close and need to come talk to you and the Director."

"Make an appointment," he said.

"I'm making one now. Why are you—oh. I will make it worth your while."

"Are you going to break anything?" he asked.

"Not as long as you don't . . . p-i-s-s me off," Sam said.

"Why are you spelling? Got a kid with you?" Andrew asked her.

"Nick and Sofia."

Andrew sighed. "All right, I'll come get you."

When they arrived, Andrew signed them all in. "Have you ever been here before, General?"

"No. No reason. Don't you make maps?" Nick said just to irritate him.

"You know I do. We had that conversation. I like that carrier and diaper bag."

Kimberly A. Biggerstaff © 2024

"Yeah, all the guys do," Nick said.

Andrew took them to his office and introduced Nick to his team. "The boss is on vacation. So we're lucky."

"He doesn't bother me," Sam said.

"No, you bother him," Andrew said.

"Hi, Colonel. Don't tell me you had another kid," Katie said.

"No, he's just a friend. This is Nick and his daughter, Sofia."

"Aww, she's a cutie," Katie said.

"Nick, stay here," Sam told him. She and Andrew began to go into his office. "Hey, you said your boss is away?"

"No, Sam."

She smiled. "Come on," she said, opening the door. She pulled him inside and locked the door. After closing the blinds, she kissed him.

"Is she . . . ?" Nick started to ask.

"Yeah, we're used to it. The first time was . . . well, she kicked our boss out of his office and did it in there on his desk. He was so mad. Called security. But the Director came down and nothing happened."

"She seems to get away with a lot," Nick said.

"With good reason, I think. Barrett the Beast," Katie said. "You look familiar. Have we met?"

Kimberly A. Biggerstaff © 2024

"I don't think so. I used to work at the Pentagon."

"Are you in the service?"

"Marines," Nick told her.

"Nick Foster, Commandant of the Corps," Katie said.

"Yes. Retired now and playing Mr. Mom."

"That's great."

"So, you guys make maps? I probably looked at many of them."

"Yes. I can't show you anything. Sorry."

"No, that's okay. So how does Andrew fit in?"

"He's our team leader. He's great. I think they're going to promote him."

"Did he get stabbed on a mission?" Nick knew he did. He just wanted to hear the story from someone else.

"Um. Yes. An Irish terrorist. It was supposed to be the Colonel. But she got her in the end. She always gets her man . . . or woman."

They heard a ruckus from the office. Katie smiled. "The first time they were in there, she was very loud. I think she did it on purpose. Just to shock us all."

"She's nuts. Too many concussions," Greg said.

"You're still mad that she broke your jaw."

"Still can't chew right," he said.

"And you're still ugly," Katie told him.

"Why did she break your jaw?" Nick asked him.

Kimberly A. Biggerstaff © 2024

"She was going through a rough time, and he commented on her appearance. She heard and hit him."

"She had a cast on her hand, too," Greg said.

"Even I know better than to say something about the way a woman looks," Nick said.

"She's still nuts," Greg said.

"Need another trip to the hospital, Gregory?" Sam said as she came out of the office.

"No, ma'am," he said, slinking back in his chair.

"Let's go," Andrew said, putting his suit coat on.

"Where are we going?" Nick asked.

"To see the Director," Andrew answered.

"I'll stay here," Nick said.

"No, you spoke to her. You have to come."

Nick shook his head. "What have you gotten me into, Barrett?"

"You're the one who saw you know what and called me. So, you started this," Sam told him.

"No, I was placed there. On purpose . . . by the President," Nick said quietly. But Sam's ears were fine.

"What? The President put you in that office on purpose?" Sam said.

"I believe so. He seems to know a lot more than your average president."

Kimberly A. Biggerstaff © 2024

Sam began to get angry. Andrew stopped and stepped in front of her. "You need to listen to me. Don't go in there and demand answers. She's not like other directors. She is NOT a fan of yours. She doesn't like you, and she will probably tell you that. So, just try and . . . not be you."

Sam growled, "What the hell does that mean? Do they know something? Do you?"

"No. I don't know anything. I would have told you. All I mean is . . ." He took a breath. "Sam, please. I like my job and . . . I was going to surprise you, but . . . I'm up for a promotion. My boss's job. And Katie will probably get mine. Please."

She looked at him. "Okay, fine. I'll behave. But I want some answers."

"Just try and not be Barrett the Beast."

"You are getting on my nerves," Sam told him.

Andrew whispered something in her ear.

"No, you won't. Really? You promise," she asked.

"Yes."

"All right. But you better," Sam warned him.

They went into the outer office. "Andrew Cassidy and visitors," he told the Director's secretary.

"One moment please." They sat down and waited while she called. "You may go in, Mr. Cassidy." The woman smiled at him.

Kimberly A. Biggerstaff © 2024

"She likes you," Sam told Andrew. "Stay away from her."

"Jealous, Samantha?" he said, smiling.

"What is with you? Don't call me Samantha," she told him.

"Quiet. And remember what I said," Andrew told her.

"Andrew. So good to see you," the Director said. She practically drooled over him.

Sam looked at Nick and growled.

"Director, I'm looking forward to that party. It's been a while, and I hope you'll save me a dance. Ma'am, this is General Nick Foster, Retired. Immediate past Commandant of the Marine Corps."

"A pleasure to meet you, General Foster." She shook his hand. Then she directed her attention to Sam. "Colonel Barrett. What have you gotten yourself into this time?"

Sam held her tongue and tried to be polite. "Director. A suspect in an NCIS case has appeared, and she resembles a former CIA officer. A dead officer."

"Interesting," the Director said. "And you want to know if she's really dead. Or if this is another . . . Mr. Trask situation?" She sat in her chair and leaned back. Almost taunting Sam.

Normally, Sam would have trounced her. Made a crude comment, threatened her, done something. But for Andrew, she stood there, not saying anything.

"Director. General Foster made contact with her and said she resembles this officer," Andrew told her.

"Who?"

"Katrina Rogov," Andrew said.

The Director stopped rocking in her chair. "Everyone out, right now. Cassidy, you stay. General, Colonel, wait outside."

Sam clenched her fists and turned on her heel and almost slammed the door, but Nick caught it.

"I thought I made it clear I don't want that woman's name mentioned in my office," the Director said.

"She's who we need to find. Or someone who looks like her."

"She's dead and she sullied the reputation of this office," the Director said.

"That was years ago, and she did what she did to protect her family. She served this agency well, and so did Colonel Barrett. Barrett lost an eye catching the man that poisoned Katrina."

"I've read their files . . . and her book. I know what they did."

"Then why are you being such a bitch about them?" He finally stood up to her.

The Director smiled. "I would throw anyone else out of here for talking to me like that." She leaned back in her chair. "You were so young at Oxford. Remember that bed and breakfast in Stratford-Upon-Avon?"

"I remember," he said, trying not to smile.

"Have you always liked older women?" she asked him.

"Are you jealous of her, Claire?" Andrew asked.

"You had to stay with your assignment. I had to stay in England. It wouldn't have worked."

"You didn't answer my question," he said.

She smiled. "Tell the FBI about the woman. We don't deal with domestic cases. See you at the party. I suppose she'll be your plus-one."

He turned and left without saying anything. "Where did they go?" he asked the secretary.

"General Foster had to pick his son up. The Colonel said, and I quote, 'I'm going to the Pentagon to get laid by a marine.' Unquote."

Andrew smiled at her and left.

* * * *

"Hi, Nick," Kevin said, running to him.

"How was school, bud?"

Kimberly A. Biggerstaff © 2024

"Great! We're learning about the weather."

"That's important when you plan missions or are on a ship at sea or in an airplane."

"Will you take me on a ship?" Kevin asked, buckling his seatbelt.

"I'll see what I can do," Nick told him. They drove home, and Nick asked if Kevin had any homework.

"I have to color this page," he told him. Kevin got some crayons and sat at the kitchen table and did his work. He finished and went and got a coloring book and colored it for a while.

"May I go outside and play?" Kevin asked when he was tired of coloring.

"Sure, be careful," Nick said.

"Dada," Sofia said.

"What's up, sweetie?"

Sofia grabbed his leg and pulled herself up. She made a noise, and he picked her up.

"Want to help with dinner?" He tickled her. Nick was enjoying being Mr. Mom. But he thought about today and caught himself smiling. He had fun. Then he heard the side door open.

"Hi. How was work?" Nick asked.

"Fine. How was your work?" Gia asked.

"Are you mad because I went to the restaurant?" he asked her.

"A little."

"I just wanted to make sure you were okay. We don't know him."

"Andrew checked him out. Not even a traffic ticket. I'd like to get to know him, Nick. He's my father."

"Just take it slow. I don't want to see you get hurt."

"What happened with that woman?"

"You were there. She disappeared."

"And then what?"

"What do you mean?" he asked.

"I mean, then what did you do? I'm getting to know how Sam thinks. She won't let it go."

Nick sighed. "I gave Sam a ride to Langley. She took me inside, and we met with the Director. For about a minute, and then I left to pick Kevin up from school."

"Why are you getting involved in this?" she asked him.

"I was involved in this the moment I suspected Jim of stealing classified information. I spoke to her. They'll probably want a statement. That's all."

"You have a family and you're not a spy," Gia said, reaching for Sofia.

"Mama."

"Come on, honey," Gia said, taking Sofia upstairs with her.

Gia changed out of her uniform as Sofia sat on the bed with a toy.

* * * *

The next morning, Nick got a call. "Hello?"

"May I speak with Nick Foster?"

"Speaking." Nick listened as the man told him he was with the FBI and they needed a statement from him regarding the woman. "Sure, I can come up there."

Nick went to the office that he was told to go to and gave his statement. Then he ran some errands. He was at the grocery store when he heard a voice.

"Hello again. Grant?" she said.

"Uh, hello," he said. Nick looked at the blonde-haired woman. "Anastasia, right? You're not stalking me, are you?"

"No. I have an apartment nearby."

"Oh. So, what are you doing in Washington? Business or pleasure?"

"A little of both. I came for a job interview. Taking in the sights while I'm here. You wouldn't happen to know a tour guide?" She smiled at him.

Nick smiled back. "I'm not sure my wife would appreciate me showing a beautiful woman around town."

"I understand. Well, maybe we'll run into each other again," she said. She began to walk away.

"Wait. It's nearly lunchtime. May we buy you lunch?"

"Yes, that'll be nice. I don't know anyone in town."

"Oh, at the bar, I thought you were with friends," Nick told her.

"No. I like to talk to people. I . . . feel comfortable here."

"Do you need to take anything home for the freezer or fridge?"

"No. You?" she asked.

"No, let me pay for this and you can follow us."

"Fine."

They paid for their groceries, and Nick put Sofia in the SUV. On the way to a nearby restaurant, he called Sam.

"Guess who I'm taking to lunch at Theismann's?"

"I'm not in the mood, Nick."

"Well, you better get up here, fast. I don't know how long I can keep Anastasia here."

"What? Theismann's? I'm on my way," Sam said. "Sorry, Eric, I have to go." She happened to be up at the daycare eating with Eric and Eddy. Sam told the ladies she had to leave. Her driver was waiting, and she had him take her over to Theismann's. She looked around for Nick's SUV and saw it. So they were inside. She went to the bar and sat down after a quick scan. They must be at a table. She ordered a beer. She took a few sips and then decided to look for them. But suddenly, she was nervous. She sat there and drank her beer. Finally, she got up and went to find them after downing a shot of whisky.

She saw Nick facing her and Sofia in a highchair next to him. The woman was laughing over something he said. Sam slowly walked up to them. "Hi, Nick. What's so funny?"

"Sam, how are you? I was telling Anastasia my real name and why I lied."

"Good."

"Sam, this is Anastasia." He looked at Anastasia and said, "This is Colonel Samantha Barrett."

"Nice to meet you," she said, looking at Sam.

Sam was taken aback. The resemblance was uncanny.

"Uh, you too," Sam said, staring at her.

"Sam, would you like to sit down?" Nick said.

"Yes, please join us," Anastasia said.

Sam sat down. She couldn't take her eyes off her.

"Is something wrong, Ms. Barrett?" Anastasia asked her.

"You remind me of someone. You look a lot like her. And call me Sam."

"May I ask where you were born?"

"Tarutino, Russia."

Kimberly A. Biggerstaff © 2024

"Is that near Moscow?" Sam said in Russian.

"Yes, about 109 kilometers southwest. You speak Russian?"

"Yes. It's one of many languages," Sam said. "Do you have a sister?" Sam asked in English.

"No. Not that I know of."

"What do you mean?" Sam asked.

"I was adopted right after I was born. They said my mother was very young. But my parents, the ones who raised me, were wonderful."

"Excuse me, ma'am." A man came up and spoke to Anastasia.

"Yes?"

"My name is Agent Jordan and I'm with the FBI. Would you come with us, please?"

"Nick, what did you do?" Sam asked.

"I had to call them, Sam."

Anastasia smiled. "It's all right, Nick. I would have been disappointed if you hadn't reported me. May I show you my identification?"

"Yes. Slowly, please," Agent Jordan said.

Anastasia slowly pulled her identification out and showed it to him. "Anastasia Rostova." He smiled and sarcastically said, "Great. These are diplomatic credentials."

"She's a diplomat. You can't take her," Sam said happily.

"Stay out of this ma'am. Who are you?"

"Colonel Samantha Barrett."

"We don't want Rostova. But that one is on our list, Agent Jordan," the other FBI guy said.

"What list?" Sam asked. "Why don't you want her?"

"We need to talk to you. Come with us and make a statement."

"No," Sam said.

Anastasia touched Sam's hand. In Russian, she said, "It's okay. Go do what you have to." Anastasia gave her a card. "Call me, please." She looked at Nick and stood. "Thank you for lunch, Nick Foster. No . . . hard feelings. Is that how you say it?"

"Yes," Nick said, standing. "I'm sorry I had to . . ."

"I understand. It's fine. I . . . might be in touch."

"Come on, Barrett. Let's go," Jordan said, touching her on the arm.

"Take your hand off me," Sam said angrily. "I'll be down later."

"Sam." Anastasia took a step closer and suddenly kissed her. "Go with them. Tell them the truth."

"I don't know the truth. Who are you?" Sam had a tear in the one eye that was showing.

"Yes, you do," she said, walking away.

"Let's go."

"God dammit." Sam yanked her arm away and punched Jordan in the nose.

"Oh, boy," Nick said.

"All right. You're under arrest," Agent Barstow said.

"Shit. My hand. What are you doing? I need my dog. I have seizures," Sam tried to explain as his partner handcuffed her. But Jordan was pissed and bleeding. His partner, Agent Barstow, led her away. Grace tried to follow.

"Come on, Sofia, we can't leave her."

"Hey, take this dog!" Jordan yelled to him.

"It's a service dog, and if she gets hurt having a seizure, you're liable for her injuries or death," he said, following them. "Where are you taking her?" Nick asked.

"Who are you?" Barstow asked.

"Foster, I called you guys. Let me see your badge," he said, suddenly suspicious. They kept walking.

"Sir, your check," the server said.

"Here." He pulled out a credit card and handed it to the server. Take it. I'll come back for it," Nick said, following the men and Sam.

"Call Andrew and John," she called to Nick. "My hand is broken, you ass. Ow. They aren't FBI, Nick!"

"Shit." He went to his SUV and put Sofia in her car seat as fast as he could, trying to keep an eye on them. He got in and began following them. "Call Andrew at work," he said using the voice recognition.

"Hello?"

"Andrew, it's Nick. Sam's been kidnapped . . . I think."

"What? Did she put you up to this?" Andrew asked. "She's still mad, isn't she?"

"I'm not kidding. Two men said they were FBI, but they never showed ID."

"Is Grace with her?"

"Yes."

"Grace has a tracker. Don't worry, I'm leaving now." He hung up.

"Call John at work."

"General Burke."

"John, Sam's been kidnapped by two men posing as FBI."

"Nick? Very funny," John said.

"I'm not . . . why do you . . . Andrew said Grace has a tracker," Nick said.

"You're not kidding?"

"No. He's following her via the tracker. I'm following them." He changed lanes. "Where are you going? Crap."

"I'm on my way, Nick. Go home. We got this," John said, hanging up.

"No way. I'm not letting her out of my sight if I can help it." He looked in the rear-view mirror. "Our first car chase, Sofia."

She giggled at him. They drove for half an hour. Nick watched and slowed down as they pulled into a parking lot. He watched as they took Sam into an office building. But the building was old and condemned. Nick parked on the street where he could watch. He sat and waited.

He jumped when there was a knock on his passenger window. It was John. Nick unlocked the door and John got in.

"What the hell are you doing, Nick?" John asked.

"She's my friend. What if Grace's tracker went out or something? She's in that building with two men. She hit one and hurt her hand."

"Hey. Let me in," Andrew said. Nick unlocked the door, and Andrew got in the back. "Hi, Sofia. Did you come to help Daddy?"

Sofia smiled and said, "Dada."

"She's in that building. Two men," John said.

"Nick, tell us what happened from the beginning," Andrew said.

"I was at the grocery store shopping when that woman came up and began talking to me," Nick went on, telling them what occurred.

"Katrina died. It can't be her," John said.

"Sam asked where she was born and if she had a sister. She said she was adopted at birth. Do you think Katrina had a twin sister she didn't know about?" Nick asked them.

"I guess it's possible," John said.

"But who the hell are these guys?" Andrew wondered. "Sorry, Sofia." She clapped and giggled. "Your first mission. Rescue Sam."

Nick called Gia. "Hey, something's come up, and I can't pick Kevin up. Can you get him?"

"Yes, are you okay? Is Sofia?"

"Yeah, I just . . . can I tell you later?" Nick said.

"Yes," Gia said and they disconnected the call.

"Nick, you can go. Andrew and I got this," John told him.

"No, you guys might need backup."

"You have Sofia."

"I would never put her in danger," Nick said. "I'll wait here. I can call the cops or whoever you want."

"What's the plan, John?" Andrew asked.

"Oh, my god. Andrew . . . do you see what I see?" John was shocked and stunned as the woman approached the SUV.

"No, that's . . . impossible, isn't it?" Andrew said.

The woman stopped at Andrew's door, and Nick unlocked it so she could get in. Andrew moved over, still staring at her. John was staring the entire time as well.

"John Burke, Andrew Cassidy, this is Anastasia Rostova."

"Hello, gentlemen. Nice to meet you," she said.

Suddenly, John got out of the SUV and went to the back of it. He didn't know what to think. He knew it wasn't her. It couldn't be.

"Was it something I said?"

"You look . . . Who are you?" Andrew asked.

"Anastasia Rostova," she said.

"You have to be her twin sister," Andrew said.

"Who?"

"Katrina Rogov. Maiden name Davis."

John opened her door. "Show me your right shoulder," he demanded. "The front of it."

She looked at him. "I'm not her."

"Show me, now," John said.

She unbuttoned two buttons on her blouse and pulled her shirt away so he could see her shoulder. No scar.

"Your stomach. Here," John said, pointing to the spot of Katrina's bullet wound.

She untucked her blouse and again showed him. "Satisfied?"

"No. But you're not her." He looked at Andrew. "She doesn't have the scars Katrina had."

"I'm not her. I told you." She tucked her shirt back in and buttoned the two she had undone. "But she may have been my sister. I don't know. I was adopted at birth."

"Katrina never said anything about being adopted."

"Maybe she wasn't. Or didn't know," Anastasia said.

Nick had been watching and listening. "John, a word please." He got out and went to John on the sidewalk. "I don't understand any of this. Jim described her as the woman who asked him to steal classified information. But she showed those men diplomatic identification. It's why they didn't take her. Oh, but then they said they didn't want her. They asked Sam to go make a statement. She told Sam to go and tell them the truth. Then she kissed her."

"You didn't say she kissed her before."

"I wasn't sure it was important. I just want you to know everything. Sam is still in there."

"Thank you, Nick. You can leave whenever you want," John told him again.

"No. Not yet."

Kimberly A. Biggerstaff © 2024

John smiled and patted him on the back. He went back to the SUV and got in the passenger seat where he was before. "All right, we need some answers from you. Nick said you have diplomatic ID. Let me see them."

She gave him the wallet. "They're real."

"You tried to get an American to sell classified information."

"That was a deception. I wouldn't have taken it. I needed a way to draw General Foster out."

"Me? So you knew who I was when I told you my name was Grant?" Nick asked her.

"Yes. But you were never my target."

"I needed Colonel Barrett."

"That's a round-a-bout way to get to her," Andrew said.

"You're all important. And I was trying my best. I'm a diplomat, not a spy," she said.

"What is your end game? What do you want?" John asked.

"I need to talk to Colonel Barrett."

"She's not available," Andrew said.

"Who are those men?" John asked.

"I don't know. They aren't with me. I'm alone."

"Great. We've got two things going on here," Andrew said.

"So we don't know why those men have Sam?" Nick clarified.

"If she doesn't know, then no," John said.

"Nick, I think Sofia needs changing," Andrew said.

"Oh, right," he said, getting out and going to the rear of the SUV with his tactical diaper bag.

"Hey, that's a cool diaper bag," John said.

"Yeah, you can't get one," Nick said.

"Why? Did Barb give you that? That's not right," John said.

Nick changed Sofia in the rear of the SUV. "There. All good, sweetie." He gave her a kiss after cleaning his hands with hand sanitizer.

"There's a dumpster over there, Nick." Andrew pointed to it. "Can I hold her?"

"Sure." Nick handed her to Andrew. "Aww, they make you want another one, don't they?"

"No. No more babies for anyone in this family," John said.

"Hey, it's none of your business if I want another kid," Andrew told John.

"It is if you use Marie again," John said.

"Marie?" Nick asked. "Is that how Luke was conceived? I wondered about that. What about Michael's kids?"

"Yes, we used Marie's egg for Luke," Andrew told him. "But he doesn't know yet. So, don't say anything."

"So, Luke is really your grandson, John?"

"Yes," John said.

"What about Finn and the others?" Nick asked.

"Yes," he said.

"Well, that explains a lot. I always thought there was something weird about Finn."

"What the hell does that mean? He got that OCD stuff from Barb."

"That's not contagious. I'm just messing with you," Nick said.

"Boys, we have a problem," Anastasia said.

"Sorry," they all said.

"We need to get in there," Andrew said.

"Nick! Nick!" Kevin said, jumping up and down.

"Kevin! What are you doing here? Where's—"

"I'm right here, Nicholas. What are all of you doing?" Gia asked.

"How did you find me? Did you track me?" Nick asked.

"There's a tracker in the diaper bag. You know that," Gia reminded him. "I wanted to make sure you and Sofia were okay."

"We're fine. I told you that."

"Then what are you doing? And who is your friend? You look . . . No."

"Gia, this is Anastasia. We think she might be Katrina's twin sister," Nick said.

"Katrina? As in Sam's ex-wife?"

"Yes," John said.

"She looks like the woman that Jim described," Gia said.

"Yes, that was me. It was a ruse. I never would have taken any information."

"I don't want to know anything. I'm taking Sofia home with me. I was going to invite Brian over for dinner."

"What? No. Not alone."

"He's my"—she looked at Kevin—"you know . . . and I want to get to know him."

"Do it tomorrow. Sam's been kidnapped. She's in that building with two men that we know of."

"Nick . . ."

"He's telling the truth. We don't know who has her or why. But they're in that building," John said.

"I'm taking Sofia and Kevin home."

"Aww, Mom. Marines don't leave people behind. We have to rescue Sam," Kevin said.

She looked at Kevin.

"Yeah, Mom, come on," Andrew said.

"Don't you make maps?" Gia said.

"Come on, get a new joke," Andrew said, pouting. "I got stabbed by an Irish terrorist.

"Big deal. I took a bullet for Sam in the back and got shot in the stomach and the . . ."

"The ass," Andrew said.

"Swear jar, Andrew," Kevin said.

"Here's a five," Andrew said, giving him a bill from his wallet.

"Still injured more times than you. And I can still take you college boy."

"Let's go, old man," Andrew said.

Andrew and John started their bickering like they usually did. "Stop it, both of you," Gia said. "Why don't you do that to get in the building."

"What?"

"You need a way in there, don't you? Either chase him in there or do your fighting as a distraction so they'll see what the commotion is," Gia said.

John and Andrew looked at her. "That might work," John said.

Nick smiled proudly. "Good work, honey."

Gia gave him a look that told him she was still mad at him. "You should change out of your uniform, John. Is that your go bag?"

"Yes."

"Do you guys have any . . ." Gia started, but Kevin yelled.

"Guns! You gotta gun, John?" Kevin asked.

"Kevin. We have to be tactical, and that means quiet. We don't want to give away our position, Marine," Nick said.

"Oh, yeah. Sorry, General. We need camouflage," Kevin whispered.

"We . . . are going home," Gia said. She took Sofia from Andrew. She looked at Nick. "Because Sam has done so much for us, you can stay," she told Nick. "But if he gets so much as a scratch, I will kick both of your asses. Understood?"

"Yes, Gunny," John said.

"Yes, Gunny," Andrew said.

"Swear jar, Mommy," Kevin said.

"Go get in our vehicle, Kevin."

"Semper Fi, Nick," Kevin said, holding his fist up for a fist bump.

"Semper Fi, Marine," Nick said.

"Fly, Fight, Win, John," Kevin said.

"Fly, Fight, Win, Kevin."

He looked at Andrew. "What do you say?"

"The Work of a Nation. The Center for Intelligence. That's the official motto."

Kimberly A. Biggerstaff © 2024

"I don't know about that," Kevin said, making a face.

"There's an unofficial motto that goes like this: 'And you shall know the truth and

the truth shall make you free.'"

"John 8:32," Gia said. "Good luck." She went to the SUV and got the kids strapped in. She came back and handed Nick a small duffle bag. "Stay safe, Marine," she said, kissing him. "I love you."

"Love you, too. I'll be careful."

"Remember what I said, wingnut and . . . map maker," Gia said.

"Why don't I get any respect?" Andrew asked.

"I like her," Anastasia said.

"What's in the bag?" John asked.

Nick opened it and found a small can of pepper spray and a Smith & Wesson .380 Bodyguard and two extra clips with hollow points (ammunition).

"Wow. I love your wife," John said.

"Why does she have a gun? I didn't know she had a gun," Nick said. "And stay away from my wife."

"Smart woman in this city," Anastasia said.

"Man, you are jealous," Andrew said.

"Look at her," Nick said.

"Yeah, she is way out of your league. How did you land her?" Andrew asked him.

"Shut up," Nick said.

John grabbed his go bag and began to unbutton his shirt.

"Hey, do that out there," Nick told him.

"Why?"

"There's a lady in the car," Nick said.

Anastasia smiled.

John took his backpack and left the vehicle. He went down an alley and changed into his civilian clothes.

"Andrew, do you have other clothes?"

"In my SUV," he said. "Excuse me, Anastasia." He smiled at her as she moved to step out of the vehicle so he could get out. "You know, Sam's son has a daughter named Anastasia. We call her Stasia."

"I prefer Ana," she said.

Andrew went to change as John came back. "Where's he going?"

"To change," Anastasia told him. "You and Colonel Barrett are close, yes?"

"Very. We have a son together, and she adopted my . . . daughter."

Anastasia waited for him to say more.

"Katrina is her mother."

"Oh. So, you and . . . ," Ana began.

"It's complicated," John said.

"Yes, I get that impression."

John's phone rang. "Hello?"

"Do you know where Sam is?" Michael asked.

"I was going to call you, Michael." He stepped away and explained to Michael what was going on. "Don't worry, we'll get her."

"I can ask Kelly to babysit and come help."

"No, I think we'll be okay. I'll let you know if we need the army."

"Be careful, John," Michael told him.

"We'll get her back," John said and then hung up. "Andrew, are you ready to do this?" John asked him.

"Yes. Give me the gun," Andrew said.

"No, you can have the pepper spray."

"I'm qualified—"

"Just take it," John said, tossing the small can at him.

"Andrew," Ana said. She handed him a folding knife. "I would like that back.

"Nice. Yes. I'll return it," he said. "Thank you."

John rolled his eyes. They discussed their plan, and John told Nick if they weren't back in fifteen minutes to call the police.

"Phones on vibrate," John said.

They started walking to the building through its empty parking lot. They began arguing when they got close. It wasn't difficult. Andrew was the youngest of Sam's men, but he was second after John. If there was a hierarchy, it was John, Andrew and then Michael. Andrew and John always had something between them. A sort of competitiveness. And when they started, it would sometimes end up with both of them on the ground, wrestling.

As they got inside, they got louder. Andrew stumbled over some trash on the floor, which John laughed at and made fun of him for.

"I'm ready to go, old man."

"I can still beat your ass with one hand tied behind my back."

"No, you need it for your cane, gramps."

"You need a diaper change," John said, pushing a door open and seeing Sam and the two men at a table. John raised his weapon, and Andrew raised the can of pepper spray.

"Hello boys," Sam said. "Took you long enough."

"What the hell are you doing?" John asked. "Are you okay?"

"Schooling these boys in poker."

"What is . . . schooling?" one said in Russian.

"Teaching you," Sam replied in Russian.

"We thought you were kidnapped," Andrew said.

"I am. But they don't want to hurt me. Put the gun away. Ha, full house, I win," the men cursed in Russian.

"Nick said they spoke English and posed as FBI," John said.

"FBI, The X-Files. Good show," one of the men said in English. "Good acting, yes?"

"Yeah, you had us fooled," Sam said.

"She hits good for a girl," the one with a swollen nose said.

"I broke my hand again," Sam told them.

"Sam! What is going on?" Andrew yelled.

In Russian, she said, "That one there is the one you want." She pointed to John.

The men stood and walked toward John. He raised the gun again and said, "Back off, Russky."

"Cousin! We are your cousins," one said in Russian.

"I'm not your—what?" John replied in Russian.

"Your mother and our father were brother and sister. You are Petyr, no?"

John got very serious. "No, I'm not," he said and walked away.

"I don't understand," one of the men said. "He's not happy to find family?"

"I'll talk to him," Sam told them. She went after John.

"Hi, I'm Andrew," said Andrew, introducing himself as if it were normal.

"John, wait," Sam called.

He kept walking out, with Sam following.

"Hey, they got her," Nick said. "Uh, oh, that doesn't look good." He and Ana watched as Sam and John argued. Finally, she strode angrily towards them with Grace by her side.

"Are you okay?" Nick asked, getting out.

"Yes, I'm fine. Take me to the hospital for my hand," she said, going to the passenger seat.

"Hello," Ana said. "Colonel Barrett, I need—"

"Not now. Just give me some time," Sam said angrily.

"I'll go. You have my number, Colonel Barrett," Ana said, getting out. "Please call me."

"What was she doing here?" Sam asked.

"She said she needed to talk to you. We figure she's the twin sister of your wife."

"I suppose John checked the scars?"

"Yes, she didn't have them."

"Ana!" Andrew called. He caught up with her and gave her the knife back. "Thanks. Didn't need it. Where are you going? I thought you had to talk to Sam."

"She isn't in the mood," Ana told him.

"What is he doing?" Sam asked, watching Andrew.

Kimberly A. Biggerstaff © 2024

"Giving her knife back to her."

Sam opened the window and yelled, "Hey, Hawaiian boy! Stop flirting and go home!"

"She has anger issues I think," Ana said, looking at Sam.

"Yes, she most definitely does," Andrew agreed.

"Does she get jealous?"

"Sometimes, yes. Why?"

Ana smiled and kissed Andrew a very long kiss.

"Bastard," Sam mumbled.

"I think she made the first move," Nick said.

"I don't care. It's his fault," Sam said.

"You should call Michael and let him know you're okay," Nick said.

"Why are you still here, Nick?" Sam asked. "And did you lose a kid?"

"You're my friend. I owe you," he said. "Gia tracked me and took Sofia."

"Nick, give this back to your wife. Thanks for your help," John said, handing him the gun and clips. "May I have that bag?" John was on the driver's side. So Sam picked the bag up and threw it out her side onto the sidewalk.

"Asshat," Sam said.

"Bitch," John asked.

"Jerk," Sam said.

Kimberly A. Biggerstaff © 2024

"Idiot," John said.

Suddenly, Sam crawled over Nick, grabbed John's shirt, pulled him towards her, and kissed John through the window.

"What the—OW! Get off me," Nick said.

Sam let go of John and he smiled at her. "I'm still mad at you," he said. "Need a ride?"

"No. Here." She tore the bloody cuff of her shirt and gave it to him. "DNA, in case you want to check. But I believe them."

"Sam . . ."

"Family, John."

"You're my family. And Barb and all the kids and grandkids," he said, glancing at Nick. "I'll think about it."

"First Gia's father, now your . . . whatever. Katrina's sister. Family coming out of the woodwork," Nick mumbled.

"Gia's father?" Sam said.

"It's a long story. Are you ready?" Nick said.

"Yeah," she told Nick. "Have a vodka with them, John," she called as they drove off. "Just take me home."

"But your hand. It looks bad."

"Yeah. I know. I'll go see Jason tomorrow morning. He's going to be pissed at me," she said. "You don't have to take me home. I'll call for a ride."

"No, if you promise you're going to see Jason in the morning, I'll take you home," Nick said.

"I promise. Thanks for sticking around, Nick."

"So, those guys didn't hurt you?"

"No. They were looking for their cousin."

"Why can't anyone just come right out and say what they want instead of playing games?"

"John's early life was complicated."

"A long story?" Nick asked.

"Yeah. Why don't you bring Sofia and come with me to New York? You can visit your sister," Sam suggested.

"Oh, I don't know about that. Gia's mad . . . I think she's mad. I don't know."

"Think about it. You're welcome to come. I'll let you know what time I'm leaving."

"Well, they haven't seen Sofia." Nick began to change his mind.

"Let me know."

Nick drove her home. She had already called Michael and told him she was okay. "Thanks for bringing her home, Nick," Michael said.

"She needs to go see Jason in the morning or some doctor."

"Did you hit someone?"

"Yes. Got any gummies or brownies? It's really hurting."

"How are gummies or brownies going to help with the pain?"

"None of your business. I have a card. Maybe I'll just take a pill." Sam leaned over and kissed Nick on the cheek. "Thanks again, friend."

"Get out!" Nick said. He called Gia and told her he was on his way home.

Chapter 24

When Nick got home, Gia's father was there.

"Hi, Nick!" Kevin said. "Did you save Sam?"

"Hello, Marine. Yes. She's fine. Turns out she really didn't need rescuing."

"Aww, man." Kevin was disappointed.

"But John and Andrew went charging in there and snuck around corners and saw Sam sitting with the two men and—"

"You're home," Gia said, walking in with Brian.

"Yeah. Piece of cake. No one got hurt, and Sam is fine. They were looking for John."

"All that drama to find John?" Gia asked.

"I know, right?"

"There's some food left on the table, if you're hungry," she told him.

"Thank you. And I'm sorry about what happened."

"It's okay. I forgive you this time."

"Nick, what happened?" Kevin asked.

"Oh, uh, John and Andrew asked the men to let Sam go, and they did."

Kevin pouted. "That was a bad story. You could have made it better," he said.

"Kevin, go get ready for bed. Bath time," Gia told him.

"I want to take a shower now," Kevin announced.

"I'll take care of him," Nick said.

"Hi, Nick," Brian said.

"Hello, Brian. Did you guys have a good visit?"

"Yes, thank you. I better get going."

"Bye Brian. Come on, Nick," Kevin said.

"Bye," Nick said, going upstairs to help Kevin with his shower.

"Dinner was great. Thank you. And thanks for letting me spend this time with you."

"I'll talk to you later?" Gia asked.

"Yeah. Goodnight," he said, leaving.

Upstairs, Nick was setting the water temperature in the shower for Kevin. "All right, Kevin. I'm going to show you, but I don't want you doing this by yourself, okay?" Nick told him.

"Okay."

"Like a bath, we get the water temperature right and then we pull this up, and that makes the water come out from up there."

"Neat."

"Just be careful since you'll be standing."

"That's why we have the ducks on the tub floor."

Kimberly A. Biggerstaff © 2024

"Yep."

Kevin washed his hair and body. "Okay, I'm done, Daddy—I mean, Nick," Kevin said quietly.

Nick heard him but didn't say anything about him calling him Daddy. "I think you can finish up yourself, right, Marine?"

"Yes, sir," Kevin said softly.

Nick could tell it bothered him. But he waited for him to get dressed and brush his teeth before he was going to say anything.

Kevin went downstairs and stood in front of Gia. "Mommy, will you tuck me in?"

"Sure. Is something wrong?"

"Just tuck me in, please," he said.

Gia smiled and went upstairs with him. Kevin crawled into bed, and Gia pulled the covers up over him. Then she sat down beside him. "What's going on, Kevin?"

"I made a mistake."

"What kind of mistake?"

"I called Nick . . . Daddy." He wiped his eyes as tears started to form.

"Oh, baby, come here." Gia pulled him up and hugged him. "It's okay. Your daddy knows you love him. And he will always be your daddy, no matter what. Nick is your stepfather, and he loves you too. You can call him whatever

Kimberly A. Biggerstaff © 2024

makes you happy. He thinks of you as his son, Kevin. I'll bet he'd be proud if you called him Daddy. And you wouldn't be hurting your daddy in heaven. I think he'd be glad you found someone who loves you as much as he did." She held him for a while until he stopped crying. He told her he missed his father and was forgetting what he looked like.

"Wait here. I'll be right back." Gia left and came back a few minutes later. "This is your baby book. See, here's one of you and your daddy. There's more." She looked around the room. "You used to have a photo of you and him in your old bedroom. What happened to it?"

Kevin shrugged his shoulders.

"Well, we'll find it or if you want a different one just let me know and we'll frame it."

"Can I keep looking at this?" Kevin asked.

"Yes, but you have school tomorrow, so don't be long. Good night, sweetie."

"Night, Mommy." Gia left the light on and pulled the door halfway closed.

Nick was standing nearby and startled her.

"Sorry," he whispered. "Is he okay?"

Gia motioned for them to go downstairs. They checked on Sofia first and then went down.

"He said he called you Daddy," Gia said.

"He did and then he said Nick."

Kimberly A. Biggerstaff © 2024

"I talked to him and told him he could call you whatever he wanted."

"That might not be good when he gets older." Nick smiled.

"He knows his father loves him and that you do too. Just let him decide what he wants."

"All right," Nick said. "So, your visit went well?"

"Yes. Does it bother you?"

"No. You have every right to get to know your father. Uh, when is he leaving?"

"Why?" Gia asked him.

"Because Sam asked me to go with her to New York tomorrow."

"Are you cheating on me with Sam?" Gia teased him.

"Yeah, right. She has to see Jason about her hand. I could take Sofia and see my sister."

"Oh. Tomorrow?"

"Yeah. Maybe you and Kevin could come up Friday afternoon and we could stay the weekend," he said.

"All right," Gia said.

"All right what?"

"You can go and we'll come up on Friday afternoon."

"Great. I'll let Sam and Deb know. We'll have to get you and Kevin tickets."

"No private plane for us?" Gia said.

Kimberly A. Biggerstaff © 2024

"I wouldn't want to assume anything," he said. Nick got on the phone and called Sam. But Michael answered Sam's phone.

"Hello?" Michael said.

"Michael? Is Sam okay?"

"Yes, she's a bit out of it. She took something for the pain. She said you might call or text."

"She asked me to go to New York tomorrow. I'm bringing Sofia and seeing my sister and Jason. If that's okay."

"Yeah, that's fine. She said be at the airport at eight. She also wanted to know if Gia and Kevin were coming."

"On Friday afternoon," Nick said.

"Good. You didn't buy tickets, did you?" Michael asked.

"Not yet."

"Frank will come back for them, okay," Michael said.

"Sam doesn't have to do that."

"It's no big deal. But you may have company. Some disabled veterans. It's part of her foundation."

"What foundation?"

"She has a foundation. We have a homeless shelter near my shop, and we fly disabled veterans to different places so they don't have to deal with other passengers or airline stuff," Michael told him.

"That's great. I didn't know any of that," Nick said.

Kimberly A. Biggerstaff © 2024

"I realized her plane was in the hanger a lot, and why not put it to use?"

"Well done."

"Is . . . that . . . Nicky?" Sam said, slurring her words. "He . . . saved . . . me."

"I did not save her. Tell her Sofia and I will see her at eight."

"Bye, Nicky!" Sam yelled. "Come . . . here . . . Mouse (Michael's nickname)."

* * * *

Nick and Sofia arrived five minutes early.

"Good morning, Sam. Thank you for letting us come along."

Sam growled. "No problem." She was drinking a large coffee.

"Hangover?"

"Tired. My hand was hurting, and I . . ." She stopped.

"Um, Colonel Barrett?" A man came on with a service dog. Grace looked at the other dog.

"Yes, I'm Colonel Barrett."

"Michael Kincaid said to get in touch with you when we arrived. I'm Roger Fixx."

"Yes. We're expecting you. Welcome. Just have a seat wherever you like. We're waiting on one more passenger."

"Hello? I'm Miles St. Clair," another young man said. He was in a wheelchair, and a woman was assisting him. "This is my wife, Kate," he said about the other woman behind him.

"Welcome. Have a seat. I'm Colonel Samantha Barrett. Just let me know if you need anything. This is General Nick Foster. We're both retired." Miles placed himself in a seat as the first woman took the airport wheelchair away.

"Colonel Barrett, is everyone aboard?" Frank, her pilot, asked her.

"Yes, that's everyone."

"We'll be leaving in a few," Frank said.

"Thank you, ma'am, for doing this," Kate said.

"No problem," Sam said, smiling at them.

* * * *

Sam reminded everyone they would be leaving Sunday and to be at the airport by 1 p.m. She had a car waiting for herself and Nick. She dropped Nick and Sofia off at Deborah and Jason's house, and she went to his clinic. Jason was expecting her.

* * * *

"Nick, it's been too long. Oh my, she is beautiful," Deb said, looking at Sofia.

"Sofia, this is your Aunt Deb," Nick said.

Kimberly A. Biggerstaff © 2024

Sofia made some noises but clung to Nick.

"So, it took Sam breaking her hand again to get you up here for a visit?"

"I'm married now. We have kids," he said.

"Yes, you are. I'm so happy for you."

* * * *

Jason brought Sam back with him that evening. He had done the surgery, and her hand was wrapped. He told her he may have to do some more things in the morning.

They had eaten dinner and were cleaning up when Deb began talking to Sam. She spoke quietly but with conviction.

"Jason told me about the kiss," she said, referring to a previous time Sam had come up.

Sam was sitting in a chair drinking some water. "I was . . . I wasn't myself. I apologized to him for that."

"Yes, he told me," Deb said. "I want you to sleep with him."

Sam spit out the water and began coughing. "I'm sorry, I must have misheard you."

"No, you didn't."

Sam got up and began to walk away.

"Wait, please," Deb said. "At least hear me out," she said.

Kimberly A. Biggerstaff © 2024

"I am not a prostitute. Go find him one, if that's what he needs," Sam said angrily.

"No. Just listen. If it's not you, it'll be his nurse. I'd rather it be you. He's been thinking about you since that kiss. I know he has."

"I was in a dark place then. I was on painkillers and was . . . ," Sam tried to explain.

"I don't care. I mean, he told me. I want him to get you out of his system. A one-time thing."

"No. Does he even know you're asking me this?" Sam asked.

"Yes. This was my idea," she said.

Sam looked at her. She could see something in her face and eyes. Was it pain? Doubt? "No. Tell Nick I'll see him Sunday."

"Where are you going?"

"To my hotel," she said, leaving.

* * * *

Later, Nick asked Deb where Sam was.

"She went to her hotel."

"Oh. Is everything okay?" he asked.

"Nothing for you to worry about." She smiled at him.

* * * *

Sam had a small drink of scotch. She shouldn't, but after what happened, she needed it. She took a soak in the tub to protect her hand and keep the bandages from getting wet. She had gotten out and put a robe on when there was a knock at the door.

She looked through the peephole. "You've got to be kidding me." She opened the door. "What are you doing here, Jason?"

"Checking your bandages."

"Bullshit. Go home or go to your nurse or find a hooker," she said.

"Sam, I'm sorry for what she asked. She shouldn't have done that. You shouldn't be drinking," he said, looking at the glass.

"I had a small one when I got back. That's all."

He came in as she stepped back. "Let me see your hand. I do need to check it."

She gave him the benefit of the doubt and turned and held out her hand.

"I need my light," he told her, reaching into his backpack and getting a head lamp. He put it on and slowly undid the bandage. "It looks good. Don't move it." He cleaned it up a little and put a fresh bandage on it. "Thank you," he said, smiling at her.

"Don't smile at me," she said.

"May I have a drink?" he asked.

"No. You need to leave," she said quietly.

Kimberly A. Biggerstaff © 2024

He could tell she was softening. He leaned in and kissed her. She didn't push him away.

"Don't do this," she said.

"Why not? I can't stop thinking about you." He gently kissed her again.

"You don't know . . . please, Jason . . . you're . . ."

"I'm a man. And right now, I want you." He touched her cheek with his fingers.

"I hope you brought something," she said as she went to the bedroom.

He stood there for a moment and then followed her.

* * * *

"Where's Jason?" Nick asked.

"He went to work early."

"Don't lie to me, Deb. He didn't come home last night, did he?"

"It's none of your business, Jason."

"You're right. Your marriage isn't any of my business," Nick said.

* * * *

"Good morning," Jason said, smiling at Sam.

"Oh my god. Get out, now," Sam said. "I'm such an idiot." She pushed him off the bed.

"Ow. Do you always do that?"

"No. Now get out. I can't believe I slept with my girlfriend's father. Go home."

"I'm going. It was a one-time thing anyway. I was curious," he said, standing up.

"Screw you."

"You already did and it was great," he said.

"Get out!" She threw a pillow at him.

"Can I grab a shower?"

"No."

"Fine, I'll grab one at the clinic. You need to come in today. I need to finish some things up on your hand."

"Get out!"

"Thank you, Sam. You may have saved my marriage," he said, walking out.

"Men are idiots," Sam said to herself.

* * * *

Gia and Kevin came in that evening. Nick and Deb picked them up.

"Can we see that tall building?"

"Which one?" Nick asked him.

"Um . . . both," Kevin said.

"I was telling him about the Empire State Building and the Freedom Tower," Gia said.

"Two good choices. Nick, you can use my SUV to take them," Deb said.

Kimberly A. Biggerstaff © 2024

"Mommy says you're my Aunt Deborah," Kevin said.

"Yes. Call me Aunt Deb."

"And Uncle . . ."

"Jason. He'll be home after work," Deb told him.

Nick looked at her. "Are you sure?" he thought silently.

They drove back to New Rochelle, and Kevin asked, "Where do I get to sleep?"

"I'll show you, Marine," Nick told him. "Grab your suitcase."

It wasn't long before Jason came home.

"Sam didn't come with you?" Nick asked.

"No," Jason said.

Nick expected more of an answer. He thought she'd come back for dinner. He decided to give Sam a call.

"I thought you'd come over for dinner," Nick said.

"No. Spend time with your family."

"Is everything okay?"

"Yeah, just another day in the life of Samantha Barrett," she said.

"Do you need to talk?" Nick asked.

"No. I'll see you Sunday."

"Sam, what are you doing? You don't have to be alone."

"I'm fine, Nick. I like to be alone sometimes," Sam said.

She hung up and pushed the man off her. "You can go," she said to him.

He sat up and got dressed. "Call if you need another massage. Your muscles were really tight."

"Just go," she said, taking a sip from the glass on the nightstand.

She had set up a massage, and before she knew it, she was in bed with him. When she heard the door close, she finished the glass and got up to get more.

She walked naked to the dining room table and poured more scotch into her glass. "Don't look at me like that, Grace." Her phone rang again.

"What is it?" she asked angrily.

"At ease, Colonel. Kevin would like to know if you want to go to the Empire State Building with us tomorrow."

"No. I've been there. And I don't like heights," she said, hanging up on him.

"I need to check on her. Something is wrong," Nick told Gia.

"Okay. Be careful," Gia said.

Nick asked Deb to borrow the vehicle. He drove to Sam's hotel and knocked on the door.

"Go away!" she yelled.

"Sam, it's Nick."

"Fuck," she said to herself. She went to the door and opened it.

"Oh my god, put a robe on," Nick said, turning his head.

"Fuck you. I didn't invite you here," she said. But she went and got a robe and put it on. She was almost drunk.

"What's going on? I know something is wrong," he said.

"Just leave me alone," Sam said.

"No," Nick told her. "Talk to me."

"I'm not telling you shit. Now get out." She threw her phone at him. It wasn't a good throw for a few reasons. She had to use her right hand, and her vision wasn't good. Her glasses were in the other room. She grabbed the bottle and her glass and sat on the couch in front of the fireplace. Nick followed her.

"Sam, don't do this. Talk to me."

"No. Go away." Then she stood, walked over to him, took her robe off and kissed him. "Unless you want me."

Nick pushed her away and walked out of her suite.

"Yeah. You're one of the few good guys left, Nick Foster." She raised her glass to him and finished it.

* * * *

Nick found Jason and asked to talk to him privately.

"What did you do?" Nick asked.

"What are you talking about?" Jason asked.

"Sam. Did you make a pass at her?"

"No," Jason lied.

Nick could see it in his face. He got angry.

"Damn you. You slept with her last night." He punched him in the mouth.

"Aww! You jackass!" Jason said.

"You don't know what you did."

"It was mutual, and your sister gave me the go-ahead," Jason said.

"She's involved with your daughter. Stay away from her."

"It was a one-time thing," he said.

"That doesn't make it right," Nick said.

"Jealous, Nick? She was great. Want details?" He smiled.

Nick was furious and tackled him. He hit him once more and then stopped. He got up and left him there.

"You're an asshole," Nick said.

He went upstairs and began packing. Gia came out of the bathroom and watched him. "Nick, what's wrong?"

"Let's go. We'll go to a hotel. We can still take Kevin to the buildings, and we'll leave on Sunday as planned. We can't stay here."

Kimberly A. Biggerstaff © 2024

"Why? What happened? Is Sam okay?"

"No, she's not. I mean, physically, she's okay," he clarified. "I can't talk about it now."

"Nick, it's late. The kids are asleep. Can't this wait until morning?" She touched him on the arm, and he stopped packing.

"Okay. We'll leave in the morning."

* * * *

Nick reserved a suite in the same hotel as Sam. He wanted to be near her and check on her. The suite wouldn't be ready until that afternoon, so he had them hold their luggage.

"I need to check on her."

"Do you want us to come? Maybe she'll go with us if she sees Kevin."

"Okay but be prepared to take the kids and leave."

"Nick, you're worrying me," Gia said.

"She's spiraling, Gia. I saw it in a friend years ago. The drinking and self-loathing behavior."

"Let's go," Gia said.

They went up to Sam's suite, and Nick knocked on the door.

Sam opened the door without checking. "What the f—" She stopped when Kevin ran in past her.

"Wow, this is big," he said.

"Get dressed and come with us," Nick told her.

"No."

"Please Sam. Come with us to the Empire Building," Kevin asked and ran off.

"That's a low blow, Nick. Using your kids." Sam looked at Nick.

"AHHH!" Kevin yelled, running from her room. "Naked man!"

"Fudge nuggets," Sam said.

"What's the matter, Kevin?" Gia asked.

"I am sorry . . . the boy is okay?" A very handsome young man came out with a towel wrapped around his waist and glistening from the water. He was Hispanic and Sam spoke to him in Spanish.

"He's fine. Get dressed and leave," Sam said.

"I didn't know you . . . ," the man began.

"It's fine. Just . . . go, please," she told him.

Nick cleared his throat and then saw Gia smiling and watching as he went back into the bedroom. "Stop that," he told her.

"Kevin, sit down," Gia said, putting Sofia down. "I'll make some coffee."

The man came out and left. He smiled at Gia as he walked through the room. She smiled back.

"Hey!" Nick called. "Don't look at her and don't look at him!"

Sam told them she needed a bath.

"Showers are faster," Kevin told her.

"I can't get my cast wet," Sam explained. "I'll try and be fast."

"We have time. Did you eat?"

"No, you can order room service, or we can go downstairs."

"I like that other place we stayed. We had our own pool," Kevin said.

"You're getting spoiled," Gia told him as she made coffee.

When Sam came out, Nick watched her. "Stop staring at me, Nick. Oh, sorry about . . . what I did."

"You knew that would get me to leave," he said.

"Do I want to know what she did?" Gia asked.

"NO!" they said in unison.

* * * *

After dinner, Sam yawned. "I'm going to bed. Alone," she added.

"Goodnight, Sam. Thanks for the model," Kevin said.

"You're welcome. Thanks for coming and getting me," she said, looking at Kevin. But it was really meant for Nick, and he knew that.

"Goodnight, Sofia." Sam tickled her and she giggled.

Kimberly A. Biggerstaff © 2024

After she left, Gia looked at him and said, "You are a good man, Nicholas." She leaned over and kissed him.

"Yuck," Kevin said, making a face.

Gia and Nick laughed.

Chapter 25

Sam was quiet on the plane ride back and Nick noticed. When they landed, the veterans thanked her.

"Did you have fun or get done what you needed?" Sam asked.

"Yes, ma'am. Thank you again," one said.

"Thank you, we appreciate the opportunity," the other told her.

"You're welcome," Sam told them. She sat back down and waited. She stared out the window. Nick asked Gia to wait for him in the hanger. He wanted to talk to Sam alone.

He sat in the seat across from her.

"Jason is an ass. And I don't know what my sister was thinking."

"Forget it, Nick. Go home," she said.

"No, I won't forget it," Nick told her.

"Look at you. Would you have had that guy if Jason hadn't sent you down the rabbit hole?"

"That was the second guy," Sam admitted to him.

"The second . . . ?"

"Jason and two others."

"I don't care how many. Jason started it, right?" Nick said.

"Nick . . . I'm . . . a . . ."

Kimberly A. Biggerstaff © 2024

"Don't do that. You're a good person. I didn't know you had a foundation and gave flights to disabled vets. Michael said you have a shelter too. You may slip every once in a while, but you have a good heart. You love your family, and I know you'd do anything for them. So, stop this self-deprecating behavior and go kiss your kids and . . . men." He stood. "I'm going to call Michael, and if you aren't there, I'm going to call Andrew. Don't go to your house to be alone and wallow in self-pity. That's an order, Colonel."

"Fine," she said, standing.

"Colonel? Unless there's anything else?" Frank said.

"No, Frank. Thanks for a great flight," Sam told him.

"Yes, ma'am."

Kevin was running around the hanger with his arms out like a plane.

"Kevin! You want to ride with me?" Nick asked.

"Yeah!" he said, running over.

"What do you say?"

"Thanks for the ride, Sam, and for going with us to the buildings."

"You're welcome," she said, rubbing his head. "See you later."

"Sam, I'm going to keep what happened to myself. But Gia knows something happened."

"Thanks for everything, Nick."

Kimberly A. Biggerstaff © 2024

He smiled and began to walk to get their luggage.

Gia came over to Sam and hugged her. "Thanks for the ride. And by the way, I don't know the details, but I do know that Nick hit him." She smiled and left.

Sam smiled a little. "Nick stood up for me," she thought to herself.

"Ma'am, I've got your bags. Ready when you are."

"I'm ready," Sam said.

Chapter 26

The following Saturday, Nick was helping Kevin with the model of the Empire State Building. Gia walked in and saw the model.

"That looks great," she said. "I'm going to the store. Do you guys need anything?"

"Pudding cups," Kevin said. "And grapes."

"Those little cheese wheels. The tiny ones," Nick said.

"Anything else?"

"Just the usual. Diapers, wipes, and stuff," Nick told her. "I thought I got everything during the week."

"You did, but there's some personal things I need."

"Oh, okay."

"Sofia, you want to come with Mommy?"

"Mama." She clapped.

"I'll take her with me."

"Okay." Nick was engrossed with the model.

"Bye."

Gia took Sofia and they went to the SUV. They went to the grocery store and got everything they needed. Gia had finished placing the groceries in the back and went to put Sofia in. She strapped her in, and when she was about to sit in the driver's seat, she was yanked back and pushed down.

"Wait! You can have it. Just let me get my baby!"

The window was down as she was letting the heat out. She reached inside and grabbed the steering wheel. He put it in reverse and backed up. "You're not taking my baby!" She punched the man in the face with her left hand as he drove backwards, dragging her, and then he put the SUV in forward and pressed the accelerator. She reached in her belly band and pulled out her gun and shot him. He yelled and went faster. He drove close to a parked car, which knocked Gia off. She yelled as her right arm broke and let go of the steering wheel. Her face and body smacked into the car, and she fell to the ground, hitting her head. Everything went dark as she was knocked out. The SUV eventually slowed and hit a truck. The driver slumped over the steering wheel, bleeding. Sofia was in the back, crying.

* * * *

"Yes, this is Nick Foster." Nick listened and then yelled for Kevin. "Kevin! We have to go, now!"

"We're not done."

"Listen. I don't want you to be scared. We have to go to the hospital. Your mom and Sofia were in an accident."

Kevin ran to the garage and waited for Nick.

* * * *

Nick was waiting for someone to give him more information. He sat in the chair and pulled out the photo of Gia and Sofia.

He had one other photo in his wallet of all of them. But this was after Sofia was born. A tear fell from his eye.

"Daddy, I'm scared," Kevin said.

"I am too, son. The doctor or someone will tell us something when they know." Nick stood and called Barb. She said they'd be right there.

"Mr. Foster?"

"Yes. Come with me." He followed the nurse to a room, holding Kevin's hand. "We checked the baby out and she's fine," he said, smiling at Sofia.

"Dada." She hugged him.

"What about Mommy?" Kevin asked.

"She's still in surgery," the nurse said. "We'll let you know as soon as we can."

"Kevin, let's go back out and wait for Barb."

* * * *

Half an hour later, Barb and John found him. John was pushing the stroller with the boys. Barb ran to Nick and hugged him.

"Sofia's okay?" Barb asked him.

"Yeah. She's fine," he said, handing her to Barb.

"What happened?" John asked.

"A carjacking. She probably would have let him go, but Sofia was already in the car." He looked at Kevin.

Kimberly A. Biggerstaff © 2024

"Kevin, let's take a walk," Barb said. She handed Sofia back and took Kevin down the hall.

Nick told John what he knew. "He drugged her and she shot him. He hit a car, which knocked her off. He was going fast when that happened. She hit her head."

"Nick!" Sam ran up to him.

"What . . . how . . . ?"

"John called me. Luke had a swim meet not far from here."

Nick told her what happened.

"You don't mess with a mama bear," Sam said.

"Sam!" Kevin yelled and ran to her. He hugged her tightly. He was crying. "Mommy's hurt."

"I know. But we have to believe she'll be okay. I know a place we can go," she told him. "We'll be back." She carried Kevin down the hall.

"Where are they going?" Nick asked John.

"The Chapel."

"She is? I didn't think she was . . . religious."

"We've spent a lot of time in hospitals. I think she first went when Lex was hit by a car. Laura was there and Sam was still upset about the two of them. It was before they got married. But Sam went and the two of them made up. Sort of.", "Nothing like a tragedy to bring people together," Nick said. He sighed and went to sit back down.

Kimberly A. Biggerstaff © 2024

Barb sat down next to him and put her arm around him. Nick set Sofia down. She stood holding onto his leg.

"You know you'll have to beat the boys away with a stick," Barb told him, looking at Sofia.

"I can't lose her, Barb. I just found her," Nick said.

"Mr. Foster?" a nurse said.

"Yes?" Nick stood up.

"Ms. Lorenzo is out of surgery and in recovery. Give us some time, and then you can see her. The doctor will be with you in a moment."

"Thank you." He hugged Barb. They waited and eventually a doctor came over to them.

"Mr. Foster?"

"That's me. How's my wife?" Nick asked.

"Ms. Lorenzo is resting. She suffered a concussion and a broken arm and collarbone, scrapes and bruises."

"But she'll be okay?"

"She should make a full recovery. You can go in."

"Thank you, doctor," Nick said, shaking his hand. "Thank you."

Barb and John let out a sigh of relief and smiled. "I got Sofia," Barb said.

Nick went to the room and went inside. A nurse was checking the monitors. Gia's eyes were closed, and it looked like she was sleeping.

Kimberly A. Biggerstaff © 2024

"She's still a little out of it from the sedative," the nurse said.

"Thank you," he said, looking at her. The left side of Gia's face was swollen from the impact of the car the man drove her into. Her right arm was in a cast and sling.

Nick sat in a nearby chair and waited. When Gia began to stir, he went to her. He looked at her and gently brushed the hair from her forehead.

"You're going to be okay, honey," Nick told her.

She focused on him and then said, "Sofia?"

"She's fine. Safe and sound."

"She . . . was in . . ."

"Shh. I know. She was in the car when he tried to take it. It's okay. You don't know what might have happened."

She tried to move some and made a face.

"Easy. You broke your arm and collarbone. And smacked your head on the pavement. You have a concussion."

"My face hurts."

"He drove you into a car, and your face hit it. Do you remember that?"

"Yes. Nick . . . I . . . I shot him."

"Yeah, and then he crashed into a truck. That's why he stopped. He passed out."

"Is he . . . ?"

"I don't know and don't care. I care about you, Sofia, and Kevin."

"The kids?" she asked.

"Out there with John, Barb, and Sam. I love you," he said, kissing her on the forehead.

"Love you." She closed her eyes and drifted back to sleep.

Sam and Kevin had come back, and Nick went out and told them all that Gia was doing well.

"Can I see Mommy now?" Kevin asked.

"She fell asleep, but we can go in."

"We can take the kids tonight if you want," Barb offered.

"Or I can. Whatever makes it easiest for you," Sam told him.

"Uh, I'm not sure. Kevin will probably want to stay, but we'll ask him. Thanks for coming." He looked at Kevin and then took Sofia. "Oh, Kevin. Your mom hurt her face and arm. Her arm is in a cast, and her face is swollen. She's going to be sore, so you have to be gentle, okay?"

"Okay."

"We'll be back," Nick said as he took Sofia and Kevin inside.

"Mama," Sofia said.

"Yes, that's Mommy."

"Is she okay?" Kevin asked Nick.

"I'll be fine," Gia said, trying to smile, but it hurt too much. "I feel better seeing you and your sister."

"Ms. Lorenzo. The police would like to talk to you."

"Yes, of course," Gia said.

"Maybe I should take the kids out while you give your statement," Nick said.

"Yes."

"I want to stay," Kevin said.

"We'll come back," Nick said. "Mom has to talk to the police."

"Nick, I want you to stay," Gia said.

"Okay," he said, taking the kids out. "Barb, would you watch the kids? She wants me in there. Sam, would you come in and listen?"

"She shouldn't . . ."

"Please. You know how they ask questions. I just want to be sure."

"Yeah," Sam said, going in with him.

The police sergeant taking notes looked at Nick and then Sam. She whispered to the other officer, "Just tell us what you remember, ma'am."

Gia told them what she could. She remembered almost everything.

"Why did you have a weapon, ma'am?"

Kimberly A. Biggerstaff © 2024

"Self-defense. To protect myself and my children."

They continued asking questions and Sam listened. She didn't see any problems with the questions or Gia's answers.

"We'll be in touch if we have any more questions."

"Sergeant? Is he—what happened to him?" Gia wanted to know.

"He died on the operating table, ma'am."

"I . . . ," Gia started, but Sam interrupted her.

"Gia . . . I think that's enough," Sam told her. Sam didn't want her commenting on the assailant. "You should rest."

The sergeant gave a slight smile and put her notebook away. "Thank you, ma'am. Get well." She nodded to her partner, and they began to walk out.

"May I talk to you . . . Colonel?" the sergeant asked Sam.

Sam didn't realize the sergeant knew who she was. She went into the hall with her. "You don't remember me, Colonel? That's okay. It was a while ago. You had shot a man and were upset about it. You gave me advice and tips about investigating."

"Brennan. Yes, I remember now. You're a sergeant. Congratulations."

Kimberly A. Biggerstaff © 2024

"I just passed the Lieutenant's exam. Just waiting for a slot. You really inspired me that day. I just wanted to tell you that. It's good to see you again," she said.

They shook hands and the police left. John came over and asked, "Do we know her?"

"She was one of the responding officers when I shot Brennan."

"Oh, yeah," John said. "How's Gia?"

"Seems okay. I think she remembers most of what happened."

"They said the guy died," John told her.

"Yeah. She asked about him."

"I have a feeling she may take that hard," John said.

"John, I'm hungry," Kevin told him.

"I guess we should go find something to eat, then," John told him. "How about it, Eric? Eddy, are you guys hungry?

"Fries," one said.

"Za, Daddy," the other said.

"Pizza? Where did you . . . never mind. Sam is a bad influence on you," John said.

"Colonel! We got this cool diaper bag from the vehicle." The Sergeant came back and handed her the bag. "Sorry, we almost forgot."

"Perfect timing. Thanks.

Kimberly A. Biggerstaff © 2024

"I can't believe you didn't get me one of those," John said to Barb.

* * * *

When Gia came home, Nick drove her crazy. He was trying hard to take care of her. Maybe too hard. He wouldn't let her do anything. After a week, Gia had enough.

"Nick! Stop babying me! I'm not an invalid!" she yelled at him.

Nick stared at her. "I'm sorry. I just—"

"Look, I didn't mean to yell at you. I appreciate everything you've done and are doing. I love you with all my heart, but you are driving me crazy. I can do some things now. Please let me help. I'll let you know if I can't."

"Okay. I'm sorry," Nick said.

"Please take the kids out. Better yet, why don't we go out to eat?"

"Kevin wants to go to Chuck E. Cheese's. The one in Fredericksburg."

"Why that one?" Gia asked.

"Sam owns it. Maybe we can call and have Finn and the kids come."

"That would be great. Thank you," Gia said. But it wasn't only Nick helping her that got on her nerves. She was having nightmares about what happened. She was waking up sweaty and ended up crying in Nick's arms more than once.

Kimberly A. Biggerstaff © 2024

He told her she should talk to someone, but Gia said they would go away. So when Nick called Sam, he asked her to come even if the kids couldn't.

"What's going on?" she asked.

"She's having nightmares. She's tired and snappy."

"Yeah, been there, done that, have more than one T-shirt. I'll be there."

* * * *

Nick drove them to Chuck E. Cheese's. Sam and Michael were there with the kids and Andrew and Luke.

"What's Jess doing today?" Gia asked.

"She's spending the night with a friend," Andrew said.

"Dad, come on," Luke said.

"You won't beat me," Andrew said, going with him to a game.

Michael and Nick took the boys and Sky off to play leaving Sam to talk to Gia. "Sofia, I'm going to get you," Sam teased her and tickled her.

Sofia giggled.

"So, how are you doing?" Sam asked her.

"Nick told you about the nightmares, didn't he?"

"Yes. As someone who has dealt with PTS for years, I have experience. You should talk to someone. If you want, I'll go with you. Or take Nick. But don't think they'll just one day go away. The next time you get in a car to drive or put Sofia in the car seat, you might have a panic attack. You should deal with it now."

"I'm fine."

"Everyone says that. Lex said that and when he finally yelled at his little brother, I had to say something. After my injury in the sandbox, I thought I was fine. There was so much I didn't remember. My marriage started to suffer. Therapy saved my life more than once. I still have issues. All that crap will stay with you. You just need to learn to manage it."

Gia took a deep breath. "I'm a marine. I've trained for war. Why does it bother me that I killed someone who was trying to steal my car with my baby in it?"

"I don't know. Maybe because you were at your local store just shopping and going home. War is different. In uniform, on your ship, in the sandbox, in the mountains, it's different. I killed people in war, and I killed people in self-defense or the defense of others. All legal. I didn't like it, but I had to do it. You had to do what you did. Who knows what he would have done with Sofia."

"Excuse me," Gia said, getting up and going to the lady's room. She would have moved faster if her body still didn't hurt. Sam gave her a few minutes and then took Sofia with her to find Gia.

"I didn't mean to upset you. I just thought you needed to hear the truth based on my experience," Sam said after she came into the lady's room.

"You're right and I know that," Gia finally said. "I'll think about what you said."

"Good. You're face looks a little better."

"A lot of makeup helps," Gia said. "Lucky, I didn't lose any teeth."

"Hey, let me sign your cast, and you can sign mine," Sam said. "Oh wait, are the stalls clean? I always do a check of the cleanliness when I'm here. I own the place, you know."

"Yeah. Nick told me when I asked why we had to come to this location."

"It was a good investment. And I love pizza," she said after checking the stalls. "Are you ready?"

"Yes," Gia said. They left the ladies room and went to the office. Sam found a Sharpie and signed Gia's cast. Then Gia signed Sam's. They did their best since each one's dominant hand was in a cast.

"Colonel Barrett, is everything okay?" the manager asked.

"You tell me," Sam said.

"No problems on my end. Just the usual minor stuff. May need to replace some games."

"I'm sure my kids or the guys will tell me if any of their favorites are broken."

"Is that one yours too?" he asked of Sofia.

"No this is hers. This is Gia, and this cutie pie is Sofia. Say hello, Sofia."

"She's cute. Well, let me know if you need anything or see anything," the manager said.

"I will," Sam said. She and Gia went back to the booth and ate more pizza.

"I needed this day out. Nick was driving me batty. Doing everything."

"Been there. I think it's natural to act that way," Sam said.

"Mommy, will you play a game with me?" Sky asked.

"You bet." Sam looked at Gia. "Want me to take Sofia?"

"No, she's fine. Go on," Gia said. "Put her in the high chair, please." Her collarbone was still healing, and she couldn't carry Sofia. She looked at Sofia as Sam left with Sky. She suddenly went back to that day. Gia tried not to think about it, but the images wouldn't go away. She closed her eyes, trying to shake the images.

Nick came back. "Everything okay?" he asked.

Gia was startled and became angry. "Don't sneak up on me like that."

Kimberly A. Biggerstaff © 2024

"I didn't. Are you all right?"

Gia sat there silently.

"Gia, if you—"

"Just go play with the kids," she snapped.

Nick looked at her with surprise. Then he sighed. He picked Sofia up and walked off. Michael came by and sat down. He ate a piece of pizza.

"You're quiet. Need anything?" Michael asked.

"No," Gia said.

"Is this your first time here?"

"Yes." Gia was still angry.

Michael could tell she wasn't in the mood to talk now, so he stopped speaking. Gia's mood had changed. She looked in the bag for her pain pills. Her body was hurting. Some of the kids came by for more pizza and drinks. When Andrew came by, Gia asked him if he could take her home.

"Um, yeah. Are you sure? Are you feeling okay?" Andrew asked her.

"I'm tired and sore."

"I can get Nick. Kevin can stay with—"

"I asked you. If I wanted Nick—" she snapped at him. "Forget it. I can call a cab."

Andrew was used to this type of behavior from Sam. "No, I can take you. Are you ready?"

"Yes," she told him, slowly sliding out of the booth.

Kimberly A. Biggerstaff © 2024

"Let me tell Sam so she can watch Luke," Andrew told her.

Gia didn't say anything and waited.

Andrew came back with Nick. "What's wrong?" Nick asked.

"I'm tired and sore."

"I thought you wanted to get out of the house," Nick said.

"Well, now I'm ready to go home," Gia said angrily.

"I'll drive you. Kevin can stay with—"

"Dammit, I asked Andrew," she said.

He stepped closer to her and said in a low voice, "I'm tired of you snapping at me. You need to talk to someone. Figure it out," he told her and walked away.

Gia looked at Andrew and they left. Andrew didn't talk to her. Finally, Gia spoke.

"I'm sorry for the way I spoke to you," she said on the way home.

"It's okay."

"No, it's not," she said.

"I understand. You've been through a traumatic experience, physically and emotionally, and you're still healing. Michael, John, and I have all seen Sam when she . . . well, we get it."

"That's no excuse. This isn't me." She then said to herself, "Sam was right. And so was Nick."

Andrew walked her inside the house and Gia said, "Thank you. I'm sorry I took you away."

"That's what friends are for. Will you be okay by yourself?"

"Yes, thanks. I'm just going to go lay down and rest," she said.

"Okay, if you need anything, you can always call. Michael, John, and I have dealt with Sam's . . . issues for years. We really do understand." He smiled and walked to the door and left.

Gia locked the door. She went upstairs, laid down on the bed, and fell asleep.

"No! You're not taking my baby!" she yelled and sat up. She groaned at the pain in her collarbone and laid back down and cried. A couple of hours later, she went downstairs and got a glass of water.

That evening, she called Sam. "Can you recommend someone?"

"My guy retired, but I can ask him if he knows someone," Sam told her. "I think you're doing the right thing. Can I get back to you?"

"Yes. Thank you," Gia told her. "Did everyone leave?"

"Yes. We're keeping Kevin, and Nick is on his way home." She hung up and decided to try to make it up to Nick. But she wasn't sure what to do. Then she decided to keep it simple.

* * * *

Nick came inside through the side door. He set Sofia down, and she stumbled off to the family room and sat with a book.

Nick saw something on the dining room table. He set the diaper bag down and picked up the note. "I'm sorry. Bring the bottle and two glasses upstairs. (Put Sofia in her crib.)"

Nick grabbed the bottle of wine and two glasses. Then he looked at the bottle and got a corkscrew. He put the corkscrew, bottle and two glasses in a tote bag and grabbed Sofia and took her to her room. He changed her diaper and put her jammies on her. "Be a good girl. I think Mommy wants to make up."

Nick took the bag into the bedroom but didn't see Gia. He took the wine out and opened it and then poured two glasses. Nick waited, thinking she was in the bathroom. He waited but was growing impatient. He went to the bathroom door and knocked. "Gia?"

"Come in."

"Are you . . .?" There were lit candles around, and Gia was in the tub with bubbles. "Are you okay? Do you need help getting out?"

"No, I was hoping you'd get in. Bring the wine."

"I can't fit in there with you," he said.

"Nick, I'm sorry. Sam's going to give me the name of someone I can talk to."

"Good. That's good." Nick stood there.

"The wine?" Gia asked.

Nick brought her a glass and tapped it with his. "You didn't take medication, did you?"

"At the restaurant. Get in. Please."

"You shouldn't—"

"Nick, please. It's one glass of wine."

Nick got undressed.

"Get in behind me," Gia told him. "Easy."

Nick slipped in behind her. He settled in and kissed her on the neck. He looked at the bruises on her back. They were fading but still there. Her right arm was resting on the tub as she tried to keep the cast from getting wet.

"I'm sorry, Nick," she said.

"I love you, Gia. I only want the best for you."

"I know."

"This water is getting cold," Nick said.

Kimberly A. Biggerstaff © 2024

"We can warm it," Gia said, trying to move forward. She groaned.

"Easy does it. Let's just get out," he said, running his hand on her back. Nick stood and got out. He wrapped a towel around his waist and went to help Gia. She tried to get up, but Nick told her to stop. "I'll help you. I don't want you slipping."

"It was easier getting in," she said. Nick helped her stand and she stepped out. He had his hands on her waist, and he looked into her eyes.

"I thought I was going to lose you. I don't know what I'd have done." He leaned down and gently kissed her. They sat on the bed, but Nick hesitated. He knew she was still hurting.

"It's okay. Just . . . go slow and easy," she told him. "I love you, Nick."

"I love you, too."

Kimberly A. Biggerstaff © 2024

Chapter 27

On Monday, Sam called Gia and gave her the name of a psychiatrist. She was a doctor at the hospital in the Pentagon. That would be convenient since Gia could go during work or after, if necessary. She still had the week off and was due to go back to work the following Monday.

"Did Sam give you the name of a doctor?" Nick asked on Wednesday.

"Yes. I made an appointment," Gia told him.

"Do you need a ride?"

"No, it's next Tuesday. I'll go during work."

"Oh, okay. He couldn't see you sooner?"

"It's a female and it's not an emergency. It's fine," she said.

On Thursday, Gia asked Nick about a vehicle. "I thought I'd drive you for a couple of days."

"No, we need a second vehicle," she told him.

"I just don't want to . . ."

"Never mind, I'll go myself."

"Hey, I'll get a vehicle," he said. Gia still had nightmares and was snapping at him. He tried to be patient, but it was getting more difficult. She hadn't yelled at Kevin . . . yet. But he was afraid it might not be long before she did snap or lose her temper with him.

Kimberly A. Biggerstaff © 2024

On Friday morning, Nick told her he was going out to run some errands. When he came back, he asked Gia to come outside. She went out and saw the brand-new SUV.

"I don't need a Cadillac."

Nick sighed. "Well, then take mine and I'll drive this one. You wanted a vehicle. I got you one. Sorry if it's not what you wanted. Guess I can't do anything right," he said, going back inside the house. He was tired of her attitude, and his patience was wearing thin.

Gia took the time to look at the SUV. It was very nice and had everything she'd want. It had a little refrigerator in the console for drinks and a rear entertainment system for the kids. She felt bad and went back inside to find Nick.

"Nick, I'm—"

"I have to go get Kevin," he said.

"We'll all go. Take the new car," she said. "I looked at it and I like it. Thank you."

Nick didn't say anything. He started to think he had overreacted. He had already bought a new car seat and went to install it. He came back in, picked Sofia up and took her to strap her in the seat. He opened the door and told Gia he was ready to go.

"What are you doing? Don't leave Sofia alone in the car!" she yelled at him. She raced past him and went to Sofia, looking all around.

Kimberly A. Biggerstaff © 2024

"I'm right here and can see her. Jesus. Are you coming?" he said, walking down the steps and over to the SUV.

"No. Just go," Gia said, going back into the house.

Nick picked Kevin up and hoped he'd run into Michael, Sam, or Andrew. He saw Michael first. He had parked instead of getting in the car line.

"Michael, can I talk to you?" Nick asked.

"Hi, General," Alan said.

"Hi, Nick," Finn said.

"Hey, General," Sky said.

"Hello, everyone," Nick said.

"Nick!" Kevin ran to him. "Why didn't you wait for me, Finn?"

"Sorry. I didn't know where you went," Finn said.

"Why don't we take the kids to that park just down the street? Then we can talk." Michael told Nick. After the kids were buckled up, Michael drove down to the park. Nick drove down and told Kevin to hold Sofia's hand. Then Nick put Sofia in a swing.

"So, what's up?" Michael asked.

"Gia. She's still having nightmares. Only now she gets up and goes into the other room and sleeps the rest of the night. She snaps at me."

"Didn't Sam give her the name of a doctor?"

"Yes. She made an appointment for Tuesday. I just don't know how much more I can take. She hasn't snapped at the kids yet, but I'm afraid it won't be long."

"What do you do when Sam gets in her . . . moods?"

Michael smiled. "Avoid her." Then he added, "I don't know. It can be tough. Sam does her own thing. When she's upset, she goes to her house to be alone." He paused and took a deep breath. "I have to thank you, Nick."

"Me? Why?" Nick was confused.

"She was different when she came back from New York. She told me what happened. Thank you for being there for her. I don't think she would have told me if you hadn't been there. She probably wouldn't have come back so soon. She might have stayed up there and continued her . . . well . . . thank you."

"She's a friend. She's done a lot for us."

"I know it's difficult, but you need to be patient with Gia. Talk to her when you can. Tell her how you're feeling. Support her."

"I guess I knew that," Nick said.

"If you ever need a break or want to go out for a beer, we're here," Michael said. "Sometimes we play poker."

"That would be great. She goes back to work Monday, so maybe things will get better. Thanks for listening."

"Is that a new SUV?" Michael had noticed.

"Yeah, I bought it for her."

"Nice."

* * * *

On Monday, Nick gave Gia a Marine Corps keychain for the SUV. "Um, thank you. You know, my neck is a little sore. Would you drop me off?"

"Yeah, no problem. You're wearing slacks," he commented.

Gia didn't say anything. In fact, she hadn't been talking much to him at all.

"Bye, Mommy," Kevin said. "Have fun."

Gia gave a half smile. "Have a good day at school." She looked at Nick. "Thanks for the ride."

"Sure," he said. He would have kissed her, but the way things were . . . he left it to her. But she got out and went on her way.

"Mama," Sofia said.

Nick shook his head and drove off.

* * * *

Gia kept coming up with reasons not to drive herself to work. Nick saw her once try to sit in the driver's seat of her SUV, but she couldn't do it. She came back and asked him to drive her.

"Gia, how's work? Everything okay?" he asked at dinner one night.

"Fine."

"Do you like the doctor?" he asked.

"Um, I've had to . . . reschedule. Too much . . . work," she told him.

Nick sighed and left the table.

"Mommy? Is Nick okay?" Kevin asked.

"Yes. Finish your meal," Gia told him.

* * * *

"Ma'am, I thought you'd want to know that Gunnery Sergeant Lorenzo has rescheduled her appointment three times."

"She's the referral, right?" the Major said.

"Yes, ma'am."

"Give me her information," Major Donner said. She took the folder and thumbed through it. Not much was there because the Gunny hadn't come in yet. She had been expecting her because her old friend and mentor called and told her to.

"When's my next appointment?" the Major asked.

"Thirty minutes."

"I'll be back," she said. Abby Donner walked to Gia's office. Jim stood up.

"May I help you, Major?"

"I'm looking for Gunnery Sergeant Lorenzo."

"She had to go to Fort Mead, ma'am. But she should be back anytime."

As if on cue, Gia walked in. "Major."

"Gunny, I'm Major Donner. Would you walk with me, please?"

"Yes, ma'am," Gia said. They walked out of the office and down the hall.

"You've rescheduled three appointments with me, Gunny."

"I've been trying to catch up. I was out for two weeks, ma'am."

"Whose idea was it to see me?"

"A friend, Colonel Samantha Barrett, got your name from her psychiatrist."

"Colonel Barrett."

"You know her?"

"No. Not personally. But I'd be interested in meeting her. Do you have any intention of keeping our appointment, Gunny?"

"I . . . don't know, ma'am."

"That sounds like an honest answer."

Gia stopped walking. When Abby realized this, she stopped and turned around.

"Do you always chase down your patients, Doctor?" Gia asked. She was getting angry.

Kimberly A. Biggerstaff © 2024

Abby saw her clench her left hand. "No. But I don't often get referrals from retired doctors." Abby walked closer to her.

"If you've gotten what you need from me, I'd like to go back to work," Gia told her.

"Gunny!" Sam said, walking towards Gia. "I was on my way to see you."

"Colonel Samantha Barrett, this is Major Donner."

"Nice to meet you, Major." Sam smiled. "You're the doctor . . ."

"Yes. It's a pleasure to meet you. I've been reading a lot about you."

"My book or the one he's working on?"

"Both. His book is very interesting. From a clinical point of view."

"Well, maybe we can have lunch sometime and discuss it." Sam was definitely flirting with her.

"I'd like that," Abby said.

"If you two are done flirting . . . I'm going back to work," Gia said walking away.

"Gunny," Abby called to her, but Gia kept walking.

"How's she doing?" Sam asked.

"I can't discuss . . . she's rescheduled her appointments. I went to see her."

Kimberly A. Biggerstaff © 2024

"So that's the first time you've spoken to her?" Sam asked.

"Yes."

"Would you like to . . . go somewhere and talk?" Sam asked her.

Abby smiled. "Talk?"

"I can tell you about Gia, if you have questions," Sam said, stepping closer to her. "Or you can ask about me."

"Are you flirting, Sam?" John asked.

"Maybe I am," Sam said, looking at John. "This is Major Donner. I didn't get your first name."

"No, you didn't." Abby smiled.

"General John Burke." John introduced himself. "Nice to meet you, Major."

"And you, General," Abby said.

"Sam, don't you have something to do?" John asked.

"No," Sam said, keeping her eyes on Abby.

"Sam."

Sam sighed. "She needs help, Doc." She said to John, "You're no fun, John." Without warning, Sam kissed him and left.

"She's . . ."

"Barrett the Beast?" Abby said.

John smiled. "Yeah. Nice meeting you, Major."

"General," Abby said, walking down the hall.

Kimberly A. Biggerstaff © 2024

* * * *

Gia was taking the dishes out of the dishwasher when Kevin ran in and accidentally bumped her arm, and she dropped a plate.

"KEVIN! Stop running in the house! Go to your room, right now!" Gia yelled at him. Kevin stared at her and began to cry. He ran out and found Nick.

"Mommy yelled at me," he said, hugging him.

That was the last straw.

Chapter 28

A few days later, Barb came to Gia's office. "Nick asked me to give you a ride home. So, whenever you're ready."

"Okay." Gia didn't think anything of it.

When she got home, she thanked Barb and went inside. No one was home. She went straight upstairs and changed into jeans and a Marine T-shirt. She went to the kitchen and found the note.

"Gia, I've tried to be patient and understanding. We tried to help you, but it seems you don't want help. I love you with all my heart, but you need help and won't get it. We can't go on like this. The kids and I are at a hotel. You can see them whenever you want.
—Nick"

Gia was shocked. She crumpled up the paper and threw it on the floor. She phoned Nick.

"How dare you take my children and leave! You bring them back right now!" Gia screamed at him.

"We'll come home when you go to therapy."

Gia hung up and threw the phone.

"Nick, where's Mommy?" Kevin asked.

"She's at home. She's not feeling good, so we're going to stay here for a while."

"Oh, she's sick. Okay," Kevin said.

* * * *

After two days, Gia couldn't take not seeing the kids. She strode into Barb's office like she owned the place. "Tell me where they are, right now!"

"Gunny?"

"Tell me where Nick took my children," Gia said through gritted teeth. Her left fist was clenched at her side. She clenched the right one as best she could with the cast.

"I don't know what you're talking about," Barb told her.

"He took my kids! Tell me where they are!"

"Gunnery Sergeant! You need to calm down." Barb was only going to take so much from her. She sympathized with what Gia had been through, but at work she needed to maintain a certain amount of discipline.

"I'm just an enlisted jarhead to you, aren't I? You never liked me. Not good enough for him, am I, MA'AM?" Gia emphasized the ma'am part.

"You need to leave. You're dismissed, Gunnery Sergeant Lorenzo," Barb ordered her.

"He won't get away with this." She walked out and slammed the door.

Jackson and Archer stared at each other in silence.

Barb immediately called Nick.

"Hello."

Kimberly A. Biggerstaff © 2024

"Did you take the kids and leave?" she asked.

"Yes."

"Oh Nick." Barb sighed.

"I told her she could see them whenever she wanted. And we'll go home when she goes to therapy," he said.

"She's pissed. If anyone else had come in and spoken to me like that, I'd have their stripes."

"I'm sorry. She needs to get help, Barb," Nick said.

"Where are you?"

"A hotel," Nick answered.

"Nick. What hotel?"

"You don't need to know."

"Are you sure you're doing the right thing?" Barb asked him.

"No, I don't know anything. She yelled at Kevin. That was it, Barb. I'm not letting her do that."

"I understand. Let me know if you need anything."

* * * *

"Where are you, Foster?" John yelled.

"Get a visit from a pissed-off Gunnery Sergeant?" Nick asked him.

"Yes, and I don't appreciate her attitude. I'm a general, for god's sake."

"Then write her up. Maybe it'll knock some sense into her."

Kimberly A. Biggerstaff © 2024

"Just figure it out, Nick!" John hung up. John wouldn't write her up. He couldn't do that to her, so he called Sam. Her phone went to voicemail, so she was probably at the Pentagon or Langley. "I wonder . . . ," he said to himself. He found the number and called.

"Is Colonel Barrett there?" John asked.

"She's in with Major Donner, sir."

John sighed. "This is General Burke. It's important I speak to her."

"Yes, sir," The woman said putting the call through.

"Okay, I'll try and talk to her again," Sam said.

"Stop it," a voice in the background said softly.

"Dammit, Sam! Can't you keep it in your pants?" John yelled at her.

"Don't yell at me. I said I'll talk to her," Sam said, hanging up. She kissed Abby's neck and moved her hand up her skirt. "What was that question you asked?"

* * * *

Sam walked out smiling. "Well, just the person I was on my way to see," Sam said to Gia.

"Screwing another marine?" Gia said.

Sam smirked at her. "Wow, I heard you were on a rampage. I don't know where Nick is. Now why don't you talk to her so you can get your life back," Sam said, referring to Major Donner.

Kimberly A. Biggerstaff © 2024

"I was going to . . . but forget it. You're all traitors, and I don't want anything to do with you," Gia said, leaving.

Sam sighed and went after her. "Hey! Gunny, stop." Gia kept walking. "Gia, stop. You need to—"

"I don't need help from a slut who goes around screwing everyone in a uniform or their girlfriend's father!" Gia yelled. The people in the hall stopped and watched them.

Sam got in her face. "I don't care what you've been through. No one talks to me like that. Nick was right to take the kids and leave you."

Gia pushed her and Sam dropped Grace's leash and pushed her back. Gia pushed her again, a little harder.

Sam sighed. "You need to dial it back. The last woman I fought with ended up with a broken body part. I wouldn't want to break your other arm."

"You talk too much, Colonel," Gia said, pushing her again. She pushed her hard enough that Sam stumbled back a few steps.

"You are asking for it." Sam started to walk away. She didn't want to fight with Gia. She understood Gia was still hurt and needed help.

"You are a one-eyed whore who doesn't deserve your kids. Why don't you give them to their real mother?"

Sam stopped and turned around.

"Uh oh," an onlooker mumbled.

"Shouldn't someone stop them?" someone said.

"You try to stop Barrett the Beast."

Sam wasn't far and turned quickly and tackled Gia.

"Argh." It had been a month since the incident, but Gia was still sore and the tackle hurt. Her collarbone wasn't completely healed, and she grimaced in pain.

Sam went to punch her but stopped. Her right hand cocked back, hovering.

"What are you waiting for?" Gia said. "Do it."

Sam looked at Gia, who was lying on the ground. "It's not worth it." She got up off of Gia. "All right. The show's over. Move along," Sam told everyone who had stopped to watch. "Get up," Sam told Gia. She held her hand out.

But Gia sat there and began to cry.

"No, don't. Not in uniform. Get up," Sam said.

"I've lost them. My son, daughter, my husband. I can't drive because I'm scared. I look at my daughter and blame her. What kind of mother am I?" Gia said through tears.

"Stand up, Marine. We can fix this. Go tell that to the doctor," Sam told her.

"What's the point?" Gia said, wiping her eyes.

"We've moved on to self-pity now. Are you going to sit there all day?" Sam just looked at her.

"What's going on?" Abby said, walking up on them. "Someone said there was a fight out here."

"Hardly a fight. I pushed her down."

"She tackled me," Gia said.

"You deserved it," Sam said.

Abby looked at Gia. "Are you all right? Are you hurt?"

"No, I'm not hurt. And no, I'm not all right." Abby and Sam helped Gia stand up slowly. "Major, I need to talk."

"Come with me," Abby said. They walked back down to her office.

"What about me?" Sam called. "You didn't ask if I was all right."

Abby turned her head and smiled at her.

"She owes me an apology," Sam said, watching them walk back. "Wow. I'd love to—"

"Love to what?" Barb asked.

"See her naked," Sam told her.

"Are you messing around with the Major?"

"Yes." Sam was honest. "Want to go fool around?"

"Thought you already did."

"Just some . . . Is that a no?" Sam asked.

Barb smiled and they walked off.

* * * *

Kimberly A. Biggerstaff © 2024

Gia spent an hour with Abby. She felt a little better afterwards and went back to her office. "Jim, I'm sorry for being a pain in the ass."

"Apology accepted. Your boss was looking for you. Word got around that you chewed out a major and a general."

"I need to make some more apologies," Gia said. She took a pain pill, and then she went to John's office and apologized to him. Then she went to Barb's. Captain Jackson told her that Colonel Barrett was in the office with her. Gia sat and waited. Finally, she couldn't wait any longer. She went to the door and knocked.

"Gunny . . . ," Jackson said.

"I'm sorry. I have to apologize," she said and walked in and closed the door behind her. Sam and Barb were on the couch.

"I need to apologize to both of you," Gia said.

"Now?" Sam said.

"Yes."

"That's twice you barged into my office, Gunny," Barb said, pushing Sam off her. She sat up and buttoned her shirt.

"Don't do that. I wasn't finished," Sam said to Barb.

"Ma'am, I apologize for barging into your office and speaking to you the way I did."

"Apology accepted," Barb said.

"Colonel, I'm sorry for what I said to you."

"No," Sam said. "Now get out." She pushed Barb back down.

"Sam." Barb looked at her.

"You didn't hear what she said to me. She got off lucky."

"I understand, Colonel," Gia said. She knew what she said was hurtful and wrong. She hoped Sam would forgive her someday. "I'll be going, ma'am."

"Thank you, Gunny," Barb said.

"Thank you, ma'am." Gia went to the door.

"Aunt Gia?" Barb said.

"Yes?" Gia gave a slight smile.

"Lock the door behind you," Barb said.

"Yes, ma'am," Gia said to her, leaving. She apologized to Captain Jackson and Lieutenant Archer as well. She started to go to her office but went to her boss's instead.

"Sir, Gunnery Sergeant Lorenzo reporting."

"Gunny. What the hell has happened to you?"

"No excuse, sir."

"I understand PTS. I'm not saying I know what you went through, but I do understand PTS. Are you seeking therapy?"

"Yes, sir. I had a session with Major Donner earlier."

He started to speak, but his phone rang. Answering it, he motioned to Gia to wait. "Yes?" He listened and then said, "Yes, sir. I understand." He hung up and looked at her. "Well, you have friends in high places, Gunny. That was General Burke."

"Sir, I'm willing to take my punishment. I lost control and yelled at two officers. There's no excuse for that behavior from an NCO (Non-Commissioned Officer)."

"You will continue counseling or therapy. Is that understood, Gunny?"

"Yes, sir."

"You miss one appointment or raise your voice to another officer, I will have your stripes. Is that clear?"

"Sir, yes, sir." She had been standing at attention, and she was feeling the pain in her back. She grimaced. The pain pill wasn't working.

He saw the pain on her face. "Are you all right, Gunny?"

"To be honest, no, sir."

"Go get checked out. Remember what I said. You're dismissed, Gunnery Sergeant."

* * * *

Sam's tackle set Gia's recovery back a little bit. She was lucky she didn't hit her head when she went to the ground. But her body was feeling the effects.

Kimberly A. Biggerstaff © 2024

A few days later, Gia called Nick. "I wanted to let you know that I'm seeing that doctor. Twice a week. I already had two sessions this week."

"I'm glad to hear that. Kevin wants to talk to you. I told him you weren't feeling well." He handed the phone to Kevin.

"Mommy, are you feeling better?"

"A little bit, yes. How's school?" Gia asked.

"Good," Kevin said. "We're learning about the ocean."

"That's great. Kevin, I'm really sorry I yelled at you," Gia told him.

"Were you sick when you yelled at me?"

"I guess so, but I still shouldn't have yelled at you," Gia said.

"I forgive you," Kevin said. "I miss you, Mommy."

"I miss you too, sweetheart."

"Here's Sofia," he said.

Gia talked to Sofia. Kevin was holding the phone near her. It was on the speaker function, and Sofia was babbling. Nick took the phone back after a minute.

"Nick, I need more time, please."

"Okay. Just let me know. Things are better then?"

"It's only been a few days," Gia said.

"Right. Well, give me a call."

"I will." She hung up.

* * * *

When Nick left that day, he had taken his SUV. He left the new one for Gia. She went to it and opened the door. "It's in the garage. No one else is here." She tried to get in and just sit in it. She touched the steering wheel. She jumped when she heard the doorbell. "Dammit." She closed the door and went to answer the door.

She looked out the peephole. "Sam. What are you doing here?" she said as she opened the door.

"I . . . I accept your apology. But don't ever talk to me like that again, or I will hurt you." She was serious.

"I believe you. I'm really sorry for what I said. You've done nothing but been a good friend and have helped us. You're a great mom to your kids, and I'm sorry I said otherwise."

"I brought a pizza. Are you hungry?" Sam said, holding the box.

"Come in. Maybe you could help me with something."

They ate pizza and talked.

"Nice vehicle," Sam said when they went to the garage.

"I can't get in. You were right. I start to get anxious and go back to that day."

Kimberly A. Biggerstaff © 2024

"What does the Doc say?"

Gia told her and they talked about it. Then Sam had an idea. "The first time I was at the Empire State Building, I wouldn't go near the window. They talked to me and had me take small steps backwards until I was at the window and then had me turn around. It was beautiful."

"You want to distract me. How?"

"I don't know. Maybe I'll do this," Sam said and kissed her. Gia was surprised and stepped back away from her.

"Don't do that," Gia said.

"Look where you are."

Gia was leaning against the driver's seat. She was facing out, but it was the furthest she had gotten.

"Do you always resort to kissing, sex, or violence to get your point across?" she asked Sam.

"No. Maybe. I guess. This isn't about me. How do you feel?"

"Not bad." But five seconds later, she got up. "Okay, that's all I can do." She got up.

"It's a start."

"Don't do that again," Gia said, referring to the kiss.

"You didn't like it?" Sam smiled.

"I didn't say that. I just . . ."

"So you did like it," Sam teased.

Kimberly A. Biggerstaff © 2024

"Don't do that. Did you make out with the Doctor?"

Sam smiled. "Yes. Do you want to make out?"

"What is wrong with you? No," Gia said.

Sam's phone buzzed. "Well, that is interesting. I have to go." She looked at Gia. "Unless you want me to stay?"

"No. Thanks for the pizza and for helping me," Gia said.

"Okay. I have to call for my ride. How about a glass of wine before I go?"

"Sure. Just don't try and seduce me," Gia told her.

"I thought you were immune to my advances," Sam teased her.

"I am. But you may not be immune to mine," Gia teased back.

* * * *

Gia was nervous as Barb drove her home. Since she had apologized and was seeking help, Barb had been giving her rides to work and home. Before that, she had been using a car service.

Gia wanted to wait until she had conquered the driving before Nick came home, but it was taking longer than she thought. She missed him and the kids, so she called him and asked him to come home. She even gave Abby's number to Nick so he could talk to her if he had questions.

"Are you okay?" Barb asked her.

Kimberly A. Biggerstaff © 2024

"Yeah, just nervous."

"You're doing good, Gia. You look better and sound better. I mean, you don't seem as tired."

"I'm not having nightmares as much. Last night, I slept through without one."

"That's great," Barb told her.

"Thanks for the ride," Gia said, getting out of the SUV.

"Anytime. Good luck."

Gia took a deep breath and unlocked the door.

"Surprise!" Kevin yelled.

"Mama, mama," Sofia said, toddling over to her.

Gia smiled, gently picked her up and hugged her. Kevin hugged her. Gia kissed Sofia and held her tight. "I missed you guys." Gia looked at Nick and smiled.

"Hi," Nick said.

"Hi," Gia said back to him.

Kevin let go of Gia, and she walked over and hugged Nick. She was still holding Sofia.

"I'm so sorry, honey. I didn't know what else to do," Nick told her.

"I know. It was the kick I needed," she told him. "I'm sorry, too."

* * * *

Kimberly A. Biggerstaff © 2024

"Dinner was fantastic. You didn't have to go to so much trouble," Gia told him as they cleared the table.

"It was fun. Kevin likes to help me," Nick said.

"I'm glad you're teaching him to cook. Every boy should learn to cook at least one really good meal."

"Wish I knew that back in college," Nick said, chuckling."

"Kevin?" Gia called. "Did you have homework or anything?"

"Nick checked me. I have a spelling test."

"Oh, ok."

"Kevin, let your mom test you."

"Okay." He got his list of words from his backpack and brought it to Gia. She quizzed him and he knew them all.

"Great job, Kevin. I'm proud of you." Gia hugged him.

"Thanks, Mommy. If I get a one hundred, Finn is going to give me a plane."

"What if he gets one and you don't?" Nick asked.

"I have to give him a ship."

"Serious bet. Sure you want to do that? Are you willing to give your ship away?"

"I'm getting a hundred. I won't lose," Kevin said.

"Nick, call Sam and—" Gia began.

"Wait. The boys made a bet. This is a teaching moment for one of them. Let's see what happens."

"We should at least let them know," Gia told him.

"I'll call." Nick went to Sofia and picked her up. He took her to his office with him. Sitting at his desk with Sofia on his lap, he said, "Here, let's get that game for you." He cued up a learning game on an iPad he took from his desk drawer.

He called Sam, but her phone went to voicemail. So, he called Michael. He told Michael about the bet.

"That's why he asked me to test him. He hardly ever asks me to quiz him. So, are we going to use this as a lesson about bets?"

"Yes, if you agree."

"Yes. Sounds good. Do you know where Sam is?"

"No. Not my turn to watch her. Are you worried?"

"No. I'm used to it," he said. "Talk to you later."

Nick said goodbye and hung up. Sometimes he felt bad for Michael, Andrew, and even John. Sam was going around from man to man to Barb. He didn't know how Katrina put up with her for all those years. He put Sofia down and gave her the iPad. "Come on. Out of Daddy's office."

"Daddy."

She followed him to the family room and went to a toybox. "Bear!"

"Where's your bear?" Nick asked. Sofia took all the toys out, but it wasn't there.

"Bear," Sofia said sadly.

"Gia! Have you seen her bear?"

"No."

"Oh, I know where it is. Your suitcase. Let's go look." They found her bear and sat back down in the living room. She had two bears. One had Marine dress blues, and one had MARPAT, Marine camouflage. She played mostly with the camo one. The other was sitting on a special shelf in her bedroom that Nick built.

"Gunny," she said.

Nick looked at her. "What? You did not say that. Say it again."

Sofia shook her head. She smiled at him. "Gunny."

"Gia! Come here, quick!" Nick yelled.

"What is it?" Gia asked him.

"Sofia, say it. Say it."

Gia waited.

"She said—" Nick started.

"Gunny!" Sofia said and ran to Gia.

"You called me Gunny. Aww. What about Mama?"

"Bear. Gunny."

"She named the bear Gunny," Gia told Nick.

Kimberly A. Biggerstaff © 2024

"Oh. Well. Still, she . . . said it." Nick smiled. "I was invited to a party a week from Saturday. Would you be my plus-one?"

A party? Yes, okay."

"Uh, we have to wear our uniforms."

"That's fine. Looking forward to it," Gia said. "I've been working on it, but I haven't been able to drive yet."

"I'll take you to work. How far have you gotten?"

"Sitting in the seat for a minute or so."

"You'll get there."

"You may have to help me sometimes."

"Whatever you need," Nick told her.

Gia played with Sofia while Nick helped Kevin with his shower. Then they switched. Gia placed Sofia in her crib after kissing her good night. "You have a birthday soon. We'll have to figure out what we want to do. It's a big one. Number one. Night, night, sweetie."

Gia turned out the light and closed the door halfway. Kevin was in his room, reading a book from one of his favorite shows.

"Thirty minutes, son," Gia told him.

"Yes, ma'am."

"I set the timer for you."

"Thanks, Mommy," Kevin said.

Gia went downstairs and sat on the opposite end of the couch from Nick. She grabbed a magazine and swung herself around and set her feet on Nick's lap. He was reading a book.

"How's your collarbone?"

"Fine. Sam didn't hurt me. I have a doctor's appointment next week."

"Okay, I'll take you." He lowered his book and looked at her. "What do you mean Sam didn't hurt you?"

"We got in a shoving match. I started it."

"And . . ."

"And . . . she tackled me."

"She tackled you?"

"Nick, calm down. I needed it to happen. It got me to go talk to the doctor."

"Still . . ." Nick wasn't happy about that.

Gia yawned after a while. "I'm going to bed."

"Hmm." Nick was engrossed in his book.

Gia went up and changed into a white silk nightie. She had bought it especially for that night. After an hour, she got up and went downstairs. Nick was asleep on the couch. She sighed.

"Nick, come upstairs. Nick."

He stirred and opened his eyes. "Oh, I guess I fell asleep."

"I was waiting for you," she said, standing in front of him.

"I wasn't sure you wanted to . . . Is that new?" He smiled and took her in with his eyes.

"Yes. I bought it for tonight."

"Oh, okay. Let's get you out of that," he said, getting up. He took her hand and led her upstairs.

"I have something for you, too," Gia told him.

"Uh, oh. I hope it's not too crazy," he told her.

She went to her closet and retrieved a box. She handed it to him. He slowly opened it.

"Silk boxers."

"Go put them on," she told him. He did and when he came back out, she ran her hands over his chest. "You're in really good shape for an old guy," she teased.

He picked her up and laid her gently on the bed.

He looked her in the eyes and asked, "Want to make a baby?"

THE END

www.ingramcontent.com/pod-product-compliance
Lightning Source LLC
Chambersburg PA
CBHW060808030726
47503CB00002B/402